A NEW KIND OF DESTROYER

Drake Mangan, the auto mogul, had had a long hard day at the office. Now he was ready for a long hard night at his penthouse. He found his gorgeous mistress Agatha exactly where he wanted her, lying on her back in bed.

"There you are," he said delightedly. "Come to papa."

But Agatha did not rise to the occasion, and only then did Mangan see the hole in Agatha's red silk pajama top and the deeper red of Agatha's blood.

Mangan turned when he heard the bedroom door slam. The man who had slammed the door was tall and lean. In his gloved hand, he held a black pistol, its long barrel pointed directly at Mangan's chest.

"Who the hell are you?" Mangan snapped.

The man smiled a cruel smile. "You can call me Remo. . . ."

_____ THE DESTROYER #69 _____

BLOOD TIES

#69

The Destroyer

BLOOD TIES

WARREN MURPHY & RICHARD SAPIR

A SIGNET BOOK

NEW AMERICAN LIBRARY

For Devin of Massachusetts,
who will have to grow up before
he understands what we all lost.

Copyright © 1987 by Richard Sapir and Warren Murphy

All rights reserved

SIGNET TRADEMARK REG. U.S. PAT. OFF. AND FOREIGN COUNTRIES
REGISTERED TRADEMARK—MARCA REGISTRADA
HECHO EN CHICAGO, U.S.A.

SIGNET, SIGNET CLASSIC, MENTOR, ONYX, PLUME, MERIDIAN
and NAL BOOKS are published by NAL PENGUIN INC.,
1633 Broadway, New York, New York 10019

First Printing, July, 1987

1 2 3 4 5 6 7 8 9

PRINTED IN THE UNITED STATES OF AMERICA

Prologue

Chiun, reigning Master of Sinanju, aged head of an ancient house of assassins that had served the world's rulers since before the time of Christ, said wearily, "I am confused."

"I knew if I waited long enough, you would come around to my way of thinking," said Remo Williams, his pupil.

"Silence, white thing. Why is it that everything must be a joke with you?"

"I wasn't joking," Remo said.

"I will speak to you at another time when you can manage to keep a civil tongue in your ugly head," Chiun said.

"Suit yourself," Remo wanted to say. But he knew that if he said that, his life would be made miserable and he would still wind up listening to what it was that had confused Chiun. So instead he said, "Forgive me, Little Father. What is it that has you confused?"

"Very well," Chiun said. "I do not understand about Aids."

"What don't you understand?" Remo said.

"If Aids is so terrible, why does everyone want to have Aids?" Chiun asked.

"I don't know of a single person who wants to have Aids," Remo said.

"Don't tell me that. You think I am a fool? People are always getting together to have Aids. I have seen it many times with my own eyes."

"Now, *I'm* confused," Remo said.

"With my own eyes," Chiun insisted. "On television, often interfering with regular programming. All these famous, fat, ugly people running around, singing and dancing for Aids."

Remo thought about this for a long time while Chiun drummed his long fingernails on the high-polished wood floor in the living room of their hotel suite.

Finally, Remo said, "You mean things like Live Aid and Farm Aid and Rock Aid?"

"Exactly. Aids," Chiun said.

"Chiun, those have nothing to do with Aids, the disease. Those are concerts to raise money for the poor and hungry."

It was Chiun's turn to ponder. Then he said, "Who are these poor and hungry?"

"Many people," Remo said. "In America and around the world, poor people without enough to eat. Poor people who don't even have clothes to wear."

"You say America. You have such poor in America?" Chiun said suspiciously.

"Yes. Some," Remo said.

"I don't believe it. Never have I seen a nation which wasted more on less. There are no poor in America."

"Yes, there are," Remo said.

Chiun shook his head. "I will never believe that," he said. He turned toward the window. "I could tell you about poor. In the olden days . . ." And because Remo knew he was now going to get for the thousandth time the story of how the village of Sinanju in North Korea was so poor its men were forced to hire themselves out as assassins, Remo sneaked out the hotel-room door.

*   *   *

When he came back, he paused in the hotel hallway outside the door to their suite. From inside, he heard a sobbing sound. Even softer than that, he heard singing.

He opened the unlocked door. Chiun sat on a tatami mat in front of the television set. He looked up at Remo, tears glistening in his hazel eyes.

"I finally understand, Remo," he said.

"Understand what, Little Father?"

"What you were talking about. What a terrible problem poverty and hunger are in the United States."

He pointed to the television set where a man was singing.

"Look at that poor man," Chiun said. "He cannot even afford trousers which are not torn. He must wear rags around his head. He probably cannot afford a haircut or even soap, and yet he keeps trying to sing through the pain of it all. Oh, the terrible pervasiveness of poverty in this evil, uncaring land. Oh, the majesty of that poor man trying to bear up under it."

Thus Chiun lamented.

Remo said, "Little Father, that's Willie Nelson."

"Hail, Nelson," Chiun said, brushing away a tear. "Hail, the brave and indomitable poor man."

"Willie Nelson, for your information, is rich enough to buy most of America," Remo said.

Chiun's head snapped toward Remo.

"What?"

"He's a singer. He's very rich."

"Why is he dressed in rags?"

Remo shrugged. "This is Farm Aid. It's a concert to raise money for farmers," he said.

Chiun examined the singer on television again. "Perhaps he would be delighted to have a concert for something that will ensure this dirty thing"—he waved at the television set—"a place of honor in the history of the world."

"I'm waiting," Remo said.

"Assassin Aid," Chiun said. "This creature can present a concert with the proceeds to go to me."

"Good plan," Remo said.

"I am glad you think so," Chiun said. "I will leave it to you to make all the arrangements."

"Gee, Little Father," Remo said. "I would love to." Chiun looked at him suspiciously. "But unfortunately I called Smith while I was out and he has an assignment for me."

Chiun dismissed it with a wave of his hand. "A mere trifle," he said. "Assassin Aid. Now this is a major thing."

"We'll talk about it when I get back," Remo said.

When he left the suite, he heard Chiun yelling to him. "A concert. And I will recite a poem, an Ung poem, written especially for the occasion. 'Hail, Nellie Wilson, Savior of the Poor.' He will love it."

"Why me, God?" Remo mumbled.

1

Maria had a gift. Others might have called it a talent or a power, but Maria was a religious woman, a devout Catholic who took Communion every day at St. Devin's Church and she believed that all good things came from God. To Maria, her ability to see into the future was just simply a gift from the Almighty.

The gift had saved her life once before. And as she pulled away from the florist's shop with a bouquet of spring flowers on the seat beside her, it was about to save her life again.

But not for long.

Maria drove with a string of black rosary beads clutched between her right hand and the steering wheel. She kept looking into the rearview mirror for the silver sedan she half-expected to be following her and when it was not there, she exhaled a sigh, whispered a quick "Hail Mary" and counted off another bead on the rosary that had belonged to her mother, and to her mother before her, back in Palermo, back in the old country.

I never should have confronted him, she thought. *I should have gone straight to the police*.

Maria was almost out of Newark when she had the vision. There was a quiet intersection ahead and suddenly

Maria felt light-headed. Her field of vision turned a flat gray and then there were the familiar thin black crisscrossing lines she had seen so many times before and never understood. She braked to a stop. When her vision cleared an instant later, she saw the intersection again—but not as it was. She saw it as it would be.

There was the little Honda she was driving. Maria could see it as it approached the intersection, paused, and started through. It never reached the other side. The car was obliterated by a monster of a tractor trailer which rolled right through the car before skidding to a stop. Maria saw a hand sticking out of the shattered windshield of the small car and with a sick shock she recognized the black rosary entwined in the lifeless fingers. Her lifeless fingers.

As the vision faded, Maria pulled over to the side of the road and parked. A metallic-gold van passed her, heading toward the intersection. She had only seconds to bury her head in the steering wheel before the chilling squeal of brakes forced her head up.

Ahead, the van slewed to a ragged stop, then spun around. There came a dull crump as the trailer, the same one she had seen in her vision, sideswiped the van's front end and roared on.

"Oh, God."

Maria jumped from her car and ran to the damaged gold van. A young man in jeans climbed out on wobbly legs.

"Are you all right?" Maria asked.

"Yeah . . . yeah, I think so," the man said. He looked at the crumpled front of his van. "Wow. I guess I was lucky."

"We were both lucky," Maria said and went back to her own car, leaving the young man standing in the middle of the road with a puzzled expression on his face.

It was the second time the gift had saved Maria. She had been driving the first time it happened too, on her way to Newark Airport to catch a flight. But there was traffic on Belmont Avenue and while she fretted and waited, the same black crisscrossing lines swept her vision and suddenly she saw a jetliner lift into the sky, then drop like a brick across the bay to crash and burn in Bayonne Park. Maria knew that it was her flight. She didn't know how she knew; she just knew. She also knew that the flight had not actually taken off yet and there was still time.

Maria had leapt from her car, ignoring the honking horns and the cursing of motorists, and frantically called the airline terminal from a pay phone. But no one at the airport wanted to believe that a jetliner was about to burn on takeoff. Was there a bomb on the plane? they asked her. No.

Was she reporting an attempted hijacking? No.

Then how did she know the plane was going to crash when it took off?

"I saw it in a vision," she blurted, knowing that it was the wrong thing to say.

Oh, the people at the airport said. Thank you very much for calling. And the line went dead.

Maria walked back to her car, tears streaming from her eyes, knowing it would have been better to have lied, to have said anything else, just so they delayed the flight. She should have told them that she was a hijacker and demanded a ransom.

She eased her car out of traffic and turned around to return home. She had gone only a few blocks when the plane appeared in the sky. It looked like any other jet but Maria knew it wasn't just any other jet. The plane climbed laboriously, hesitated, the sun flashing on its tipping wings. For a moment, she thought everything would be all right. Then it fell. Maria squeezed her eyes tightly, twisting the steering wheel in her hands, trying to block out the sound. But she couldn't. It was a dull faraway explosion that might have been distant thunder.

All 128 passengers died that day, but Maria was not one of them.

For Maria, the gift had begun in childhood with the

ability to know who was on the other end of a ringing telephone. As she grew, the gift got stronger, but she did not take it seriously until her senior year in high school.

Then, in art class, Mr. Zankovitch had assigned everyone to work in clay. Maria found a soothing pleasure in kneading the moist gray material in her hands and out of her imagination fashioned the bust of a young man with deep-set eyes, high cheekbones, and strong handsome features. Everyone was amazed at the realistic quality of the face, including Maria, who had never worked with clay before.

Maria took the fired-clay head home and set it on a bookshelf and did not give it another thought until the day she brought her fiancé home to meet her family. Her mother had remarked at the close resemblance the young man bore to that familiar bust. Before the young man became her husband, Maria destroyed the small statue, lest the young man ask embarrassing questions to which, truthfully, Maria had no answers.

She misjudged her husband. He would have asked no questions, just as he answered none about his "business" that kept him away more than he was home. They were intimate strangers and when Maria could bear it no longer, she shocked and humiliated her family by getting a divorce. There had been a baby but he went with the father and Maria never saw her son after that. And now he lay buried in a small New Jersey cemetery, with only Maria to bring flowers to his grave.

She was fifty-six, black-haired, with the full figure of a thirty-five-year-old. Her eyes were the color of Vermont maple syrup and there was pain and wisdom in them in equal measure. She wore a pale lavender coat as she stepped from her car at the entrance to Wildwood Cemetery, slipped past the wrought-iron gates and down the grass-lined path she had walked so many times before. She clutched the flowers tightly in her arm. The air was sweet with the scent of fresh pines. And as she walked, she thought about death.

Much of her life, she realized, had involved death, because of the gift. It had been a mixed blessing, her ability to see into the future. Sometimes it had been useful, but when she began to foresee the deaths of friends and relatives—often years before the fact—it could be depressing. Maria had known the exact hour of her mother's death three years before the cancer claimed her. Three long years of holding that terrible secret in her heart while she pleaded with her mother to go for that long-deferred physical examination. By the time Maria had gotten her mother to the doctor, it was already too late.

So Maria had learned to keep her visions to herself, learned that some things were just meant to be. But she had seen her own death twice and had avoided it both times. Yet one day, Maria knew, death would not be denied.

Maria passed behind a man standing with his head bowed before a grave, but she scarcely noticed him. She was thinking of another death—her son's. The gift had not been with her then and she had not foreseen it, never imagined that her son would be arrested and die in prison for a crime he never committed.

There was nothing she could have done. She had let her husband have the boy when they were divorced, thinking he would be better able to give his son the advantages he needed to succeed. At that time she told herself it was for the best. Who could have foreseen that it would turn out like this?

I should have, Maria said to herself.

One final visit to the grave and she would go to the police. After that, it wouldn't matter. Nothing would.

Maria's heels clicked on the black asphalt as she came to the fork in the cemetery path. She knew it well. There was the desiccated old oak tree and beyond it, the marble shaft with the name DeFuria cut on its face. The sight of it meant she should leave the path.

She picked her way to the grave of her son.

As she walked toward the familiar stone, measured footsteps sounded behind her and Maria, stirred by an impulse that was at first surprise and then intuition, turned on her heel and saw death walking toward her.

Death was a tall man in a gabardine topcoat, a man with deep-set eyes and a hard face, made harder by a scar that ran along his right jawline. She had never seen his face look so uncaring before.

"You followed me," she said. Now there was no surprise in her voice, only resignation.

"Yes, Maria. I knew you would be here. You always are at this time. You never could let go of the past."

"It's my past to do with as I will," she said.

"Our past," the man with the scar said. "Our past, Maria. And we're stuck with it. I can't let you go to the police."

"You killed our . . . my son."

"You know better than that."

"You could have saved him," Maria said. "You knew the truth. He was innocent. And you stood by. You let him die."

"I'm sorry I ever told you about it. I wanted you back. I thought you'd understand."

"Understand?" The tears were flowing now. "Understand? I understand I let you have the boy and you let him be slaughtered."

The tall man held his gloved hands out, palms up. "All I wanted was a second chance, Maria." He smiled at her. "We're not young anymore, Maria. It makes me sad to see you like this." His smile was wistful and sad. "I thought we could be together again."

Maria held the flowers to her chest as the man casually drew a long-barreled pistol from under his coat.

"If I didn't know you so well, my Maria, I would trade you your life for a promise of silence. I know your word would be good. But you would not give me your promise, would you?"

The smooth fleshy pouch under Maria's chin trembled, but her voice was clear, firm, unafraid.

"No," she said.

"Of course not," the tall man said.

At that moment, the black lines crisscrossed in her sight and Maria saw the vision. She saw the gun flash, witnessed the bullets thudding into her body, and saw herself fall. And she knew that this time, the premonition had come too late. This time there could be no escape. But instead of fear, Maria felt a calm suffuse her body. For she saw beyond her death, beyond this cool fall afternoon with the sun dying behind the pines. She saw the fate of the man, her ex-husband, her murderer, with a clarity of vision she had never before experienced and she intoned her last words:

"A man will come to you. Dead, yet beyond death, he will carry death in his empty hands. He will know your name and you will know his. And that will be your death warrant."

The smile left the tall man's face like an exorcised ghost.

"Thanks for the prediction," he said. "I know you too well to ignore it, but I'll worry about that when I come to it. Meanwhile, there's now. I'm sorry it had to be like this." He raised the black pistol to his eye. "Good-bye, Maria."

He fired twice. Two coughing reports, like mushy firecrackers, slipped from the silenced weapon. Maria skipped back under the impact and lost one open-toed shoe. Her body twisted as she fell and the bosom of her lavender coat darkened with blood. She was already dead when her head struck the gravestone.

Death wasn't what Maria had expected. She did not feel herself slip from her body. Instead, she felt her mind contract within her head; contract and shrink, tighter and tighter, until her head felt as small as a pea, then as small as the head of a pin, then smaller still until her entire consciousness was reduced to a point as infinitesimally tiny as an atom. And when it seemed that it could compress no tighter, her consciousness exploded in a burst of white-gold light, showering the universe with radiance.

Maria found herself floating in a pool of warm golden light and it was like being back in the womb, which for some reason she could suddenly recall with perfect clarity. She could see in all directions at once and it was wonderful. It was not like seeing with eyes but more like seeing in the visions she had experienced while she lived. Maria could not understand how she could see without eyes, without a body, but she could. And in every direction, the golden light stretched forever and ever. Far away, tiny specks shone. Somewhere, far beyond the golden light, she knew there were stars.

But Maria did not care about the stars. She just floated at peace in the warm amniotic light, waiting. Waiting to be born again. . . .

At Wildwood Cemetery, the man in the gabardine coat knelt and watched the light go out of Maria's syrup-brown eyes. Stripping off a glove, he closed her eyes with gentle fingers. A tear fell from his face to her forehead as a parting benediction.

He stood up. And then he noticed the bouquet of flowers—peonies mixed with the white pips of baby's breath—that Maria as her last act in life had dropped at the foot of the grave where she fell. It was a simple grave, a small stone of granite incised with a plain cross.

And two words. The name of a dead man.

REMO WILLIAMS.

The scar-faced man left the flowers where they lay.

2

His name was Remo and he was patiently explaining to his fellow passenger that he actually wasn't dead at all.

"Oh, really?" the other man said in an exaggeratedly bored voice while he stared out the jetliner window and wondered how long they'd be stacked up over Los Angeles International Airport.

"Really," Remo said earnestly. "Everybody thinks I'm dead. I've even got a grave. Legally dead, yes. But actually dead, no."

"Is that so?" the other man said absently.

"But sometimes people ignore me as if I were actually dead. Like right now. And it bothers me. It really does. It's a form of discrimination. I mean, if I weren't legally dead, would people like you stare off into space when I'm taking to them?"

"I'm sure I don't know or care."

"Deathism. That's what it is. Some people are sexist and some people are racist. But you, you're a deathist. You figure that just because there's a headstone back in New Jersey with my name on it, you don't have to talk to me. Well, you're wrong. Dead people have rights too."

"Absolutely," said the other man, whose name was Leon Hyskos Junior. He was a casual young man in a

Versace linen jacket and no tie, with mild blue eyes and
blown-dry sandy hair. He had been sitting in the smoking
section in the rear of the 727 by himself, minding his own
business, when this skinny guy with thick wrists suddenly
plopped into the empty seat beside him. The skinny guy
had said his name was Remo Williams but not to repeat it
to anybody because he was legally dead. Hyskos had given
this Remo, who was dressed like a bum in a black T-shirt
and chinos, a single appraising glance and decided he was
squirrel food. He had turned away but the man had not
stopped talking since then. He was still talking.

"You're just humoring me," Remo said. "Admit it."

"Get lost."

"See? Just what I said. You know, I don't tell this story
to just anybody. You ought to be flattered. It all started
back when I was a beat cop in New Jersey. . . ."

"You're a cop?" Leon Hyskos Junior asked suddenly, his head snapping around. He noticed Remo's eyes
for the first time. They were dark, deep-set, and flat. They
looked dead.

"I *was* a cop," Remo said. "Until they executed me."

"Oh," Hyskos said vaguely. He looked relieved.

"They found a drug pusher beaten to death in an alley
and my badge was lying next to him. But I didn't touch
him. I was framed. Before I figured out that it wasn't a
show trial put on for the benefit of community relations or
something, they were strapping me in the electric chair.
But the chair was rigged. When I woke up, they told me
that from now on, I didn't exist."

Maybe talking to him would make him go away, Hyskos
thought. He said, "That must have been hard on your
family."

"Not really. I was an orphan. That was one reason they
picked me for the job," Remo said.

"Job?" said Hyskos. He had to admit, it was an interesting story. Maybe it was those dead dark eyes.

"Yeah, job. This is where it gets complicated. See,

back awhile one of the Presidents decided that the country was going down the tubes. The government was losing the war on crime. Too many crooks were twisting the Constitution to get away with raping the nation. It was only a matter of time before organized crime put one of their own into the White House and then, good-bye America. Well, what could this President do? He couldn't repeal the Constitution. So instead, he created this supersecret agency called CURE and hired a guy named Smith to run it."

"Smith? Nice name," Hyskos said with a smirk.

"Nice fella too," Remo said. "Dr. Harold W. Smith. It was his job to fight crime outside the Constitution. Violate the laws in order to protect the rule of law. That was the theory. Anyway, Smith tried it but after a few years he realized that CURE would have to do some of its own enforcement. You couldn't count on the courts to send anybody to jail. That's where I came in."

"You do enforcement?" Hyskos said.

Remo nodded. "That's right. One man. You don't think they run my tail off?"

"Too big a job for one man," Hyskos said.

"One ordinary man anyway," Remo said. "But see, I'm not ordinary."

"Not normal either," Hyskos said.

"There you go again. More deathism," Remo said. "See, CURE hired the head of a Korean house of assassins to train me. His name is Chiun and he's the last Master of Sinanju."

"What's Sinanju?"

"Sinanju is the name of the fishing village in North Korea where this house of assassins began thousands of years ago. The land there is so poor that a lot of times they didn't even have food for their babies and they used to have to throw them in the West Korea Bay. They called it 'sending the babies home to the sea.' So they started hiring themselves out to emperors as assassins. They've been doing that for centuries. They even worked for Alexander

the Great. As time went on, they developed the techniques
of what they called the art of Sinanju.''

"I thought you said the village was Sinanju," Hyskos
said. The story was getting boring again.

"It is. But it's also the name of the killing art they
originated."

"I guess those Koreans don't like to waste a good word,
do they?" Hyskos said.

Remo shrugged. "Guess not. But let me finish. We'll
be landing soon. You've heard of karate and kung-fu and
ninja stuff. Well, they're all stolen from Sinanju. Sinanju
is the original, the sun source, the real thing, and if you
survive the training, a person can realize his full physical
and mental potential. His senses are heightened. His strength
is increased. With Sinanju, you can do things that seem
impossible to normal people. It's sort of like being Super-
man, except you don't have to dress up. That's what
happened to me because of Sinanju."

"Aren't you the lucky one? To be so perfect and all,"
Hyskos said.

"Yeah, well, don't think it's all peaches and cream. I
can't eat processed food. I eat rice. I can't have a drink.
Do you know what I'd give to be able to have a beer? And
all the time, yap, yap, yap, Chiun's complaining that I'm
an incompetent white who can't do anything right."

"He doesn't like you?" Hyskos said.

"No, it's not that. He just expects perfection all the
time. Chiun thinks I'm the fulfillment of some freaking
Sinanju legend about some dead white man who's really
the incarnation of Shiva, some kind of silly-ass Hindu god,
and after Chiun dies, I'm going to be the next Master of
Sinanju. Dealing with him's not easy. Do you know he
wants me to get Willie Nelson to run a benefit concert for
him? And Chiun's already one of the richest men in the
world. Can you believe that?"

"Not that, I'm afraid, or anything else," Leon Hyskos
Junior said.

"Too bad, because it's all true."

"Why tell me?" Hyskos said.

"Well, Chiun couldn't come on this mission with me because he's getting ready to renegotiate his contract, so I had to do this job alone and I guess I just felt like talking to someone. And you seemed like the logical person, Leon."

Hyskos noticed that his arms had started trembling when Remo unexpectedly called him by name. He hadn't mentioned his name. He was sure of it. He took hold of both armrests to steady them. It helped. Now only his biceps shook.

"You're on a mission now?" Hyskos asked in a thin voice.

"That's right. And for once, it's an assignment that's close to my heart. I'm representing dead people. I think that's appropriate, a dead man representing other dead people. Would you like to see pictures of my constituents?"

"No thanks," Hyskos said, tightening his seat belt. "I think we're about to land."

"Here. Let me help you with that," Remo said, taking the short end of the seat belt and pulling it tight with such force that the fabric smoked and Leon Hyskos Junior felt the contents of his bowels back up into his esophagus.

"Uuuuuurrrppp," Hyskos said, his face turning guppy-gray.

"That's better," Remo said. "We wouldn't want you to faw down, go boom." He pulled out his wallet, and a chain of photos in clear plastic holders tumbled out. Remo held the chain up to Hyskos' sweating face and began counting them off like a proud parent.

"This is Jacqui Sanders when she was sixteen. Pretty, huh? Unfortunately, she never reached seventeen. They found her body in a ravine outside of Quincy, Illinois. She'd been raped and strangled."

Leon Hyskos Junior tried to say something but only a series of foul-smelling burps came out.

"And this girl used to be Kathy Walters. I say used to be because she was dead when this picture was taken. She was found in a ravine too. Same deal, but a different ravine. The same thing happened to this next young lady too. Beth Andrews. Her body turned up in a Little Rock sand pit. I guess they don't have ravines in Little Rock."

Remo tapped two more pictures in quick succession. "And these were the Tilley twins. You can see the resemblance. But there wasn't much of a resemblance when their bodies were found in an Arkansas ravine. The guy who did a job on them smashed in their heads with a flat rock. But maybe you recognize the faces. They were in all the papers last week. Or maybe you recognize them for a different reason."

Remo looked away from the pictures and his eyes met those of Leon Hyskos Junior. And there was death in Remo's eyes.

Hyskos slipped a hand into his coat pocket and pulled out a small automatic. He pointed it at Remo's stomach.

"Hey, you're not supposed to have those on airplanes," Remo said. "Put it away before the stewardess catches you."

Hyskos let out a loud belch and some of the color returned to his face. "How did you know?" he asked.

"That you're the Ravine Rapist?" Remo said. "Well, remember I told you about CURE? All these killings you did made you a priority item. So the computers were fed all the facts about the killings and worked out your trail path and then, don't you know, your name kept turning up on a gas credit card all along that path. Then you did a really dumb thing. You booked this flight out of New Orleans and Smith sent me to intercept you and—ta-dah—here I am."

Remo smiled.

"You're supposed to kill me. Is that what you're saying?" Hyskos said.

"Exactly. So what do you say? Should I strangle you or

what? Normally, I don't do strangulations but this is a special case.''

"You're not going to do anything except what I tell you. Don't forget, I'm holding the gun."

"Oh, the gun. I meant to ask. How'd you get it past the metal detector?"

"New kind of gun. Plastic alloy."

"No fooling? Let me see," Remo said. He dropped the wallet, and before Hyskos could react, Remo's right hand snapped out and Hyskos felt his gun hand go numb. There was no pain, just a sensation as if the tissues of his hand were filling with novocaine. And suddenly, Remo had the flat pistol in his hands. He examined it closely. Remo jacked back the slide, but it caught. Remo pulled it anyway and the safety catch snapped. Then the ejector mechanism came off in his hands.

"Shoddy workmanship," he muttered.

"It's supposed to be stronger than steel," Hyskos said.

Remo grunted. He tried cocking the weapon with his thumb but managed to break off the hammer. "I'm not so good with guns," he said, handing it back. "I think I broke it. Sorry."

The Ravine Rapist took the pistol and pulled the trigger three times. It didn't even click. He dropped it.

"I surrender," he said, throwing up his hands.

"I don't take prisoners," Remo said.

Hyskos looked around wildly for a stewardess. He opened his mouth to call for help but found he could make no sound because his mouth was suddenly filled with the pieces of the new non-metallic-alloy pistol that was stronger than steel.

"You look kind of faint," Remo said. "I know just what to do for that. Just stick your head between your knees until your head clears. Like this."

And Remo took Leon Hyskos Junior by the back of the neck and slowly pushed his head downward, slowly, inexorably, and Hyskos felt his spinal column slowly, gradually begin to separate. He heard a pop. Then another. Then a third. It felt as if his head was exploding.

"If we weren't landing," Remo whispered, "I could make the pain last longer. And in your case I'd like to. But we're all slaves of the clock."

Hyskos felt his teeth break as, in his pain, he bit down hard on the gun in his mouth. And then he heard another pop, this one louder than the rest, and then he heard or felt nothing more.

Remo put the wallet of photos into the man's jacket pocket, and fastened his own seat belt as the airliner's tires barked as they touched the runway.

"My goodness, what's wrong with him?" a stewardess asked Remo when she saw Hyskos hunched over in his seat.

Remo gave her a reassuring smile. "That's just one of my constituents. Don't worry about him. He's just decomposing after his long flight."

The stewardess smiled back. "You mean decompressing, sir."

"If you say so," Remo said and left the aircraft. He went into the terminal and grabbed the handiest flight, not caring where it was going so long as it was in the air within five minutes.

No, Remo didn't want a drink. He still wasn't hungry either. He thought he had made that clear the last three times the stewardess had come to his seat to ask.

"Yes, sir," the stewardess said. "I just like to make sure. My job is to look after the needs of my passengers." She was a willowy blonde in a tight blue uniform set off by a bright yellow scarf. Her eyes were such an intense blue that it almost hurt to look at them. Under other circumstances, Remo thought he might have become interested in her—other circumstances being when she wasn't practically shoving her perfumed breasts in his face every five minutes to ask the same question.

"Why don't you check the other passengers?" Remo suggested.

"They're fine," she said, batting her sparkling blue eyes.

"No, we're not," several people chorused at once.

"What?" the stewardess asked. Her nametag said Lorna.

"We're thirsty. Some of us are hungry. When are you going to stop messing around with that guy and take care of us?" This from a matronly woman in the third row.

Lorna looked up. Most of the forward rows of the aircraft were filled with unhappy faces. They were all pointed in her direction. The drink-serving cart was blocking the aisle, preventing anyone from getting to the rest room.

"Oh," she said. Her pouting face flushed with color. "I'm sorry. Please be patient."

She looked back down at Remo and immediately forgot her embarrassment. A pleasured smile swept her face. "Where were we?" she asked Remo.

"I was telling you that I was fine and you were having trouble with your ears," said Remo, who didn't like all the attention coming his way. It wasn't the stewardess's fault. All women reacted to him like that. It was one of the side effects of Sinanju training. Chiun had once explained that when a pupil reached a certain level in the art of Sinanju, all aspects of his being began to harmonize with themselves and others could sense it. Men reacted with fear; women with sexual appetite.

But as women's appetite for him increased, Remo found he was less and less interested in them. Part of it was the Sinanju sexual techniques Chiun had taught him. They reduced sex to a rigid but monotonous series of steps that sent women into frenzies but sent Remo reaching for a book. The other part was psychology: when you could have any woman you wanted, anytime, anywhere, you didn't want any woman.

That had always bothered Remo. When he had reached that level, he had asked Chiun, "What good is being so desirable if you lose interest in sex?"

Chiun had sat him down. "A master of Sinanju has two purposes: to support his village and to train the next Master."

"Yeah?"

"It is obvious, Remo."

"Not to me, Chiun. What does that have to do with sex?"

Chiun had thrown up his hands. "To train a new Master, you must have the raw material. A pupil. In your case, that is the rawest material of all, but I hope when it is time for you to train a new master, you have better material. A member of my village, preferably one belonging to the bloodline of my family."

"I still don't get it."

"You are very dense, Remo," Chiun had said. "When it is time for you to train your successor, you must take a Sinanju maiden for your wife. You will have a son and you will train him."

"What has that got to do with anything?"

Chiun sighed and folded his hands in his lap. Finally, he said, "I will try to make this simple enough for even you to follow. When it is time for you to select a maiden from my village to produce your successor, nothing must stand in the way of that selection. Therefore you have learned the ways to make a woman want to breed with you. Do you understand now?"

"Oh, I get it. The all-important next Master comes first. It doesn't matter what the girl thinks about it, does it?"

Chiun raised a long-nailed finger. "The secrets Sinanju has taught you will conveniently sweep aside all obstacles to your happiness."

"I think that sucks," Remo said. "I don't want some woman to breed with me because some trick of mine makes her think I'm irresistible. I want it to be a woman who loves me for myself.''

"There are no blind maidens in my village," Chiun said. "Heh-heh. There are no blind maidens in Sinanju." And pleased with his little joke, Chiun had left Remo alone with his disappointment over his new sexual powers.

Over the years, it had only gotten worse. So when Remo had found an attractive stewardess practically crawling into his lap, his interest totally vanished.

"Are you sure there's nothing?" Lorna asked again.

"Well, there's one thing," Remo said.

"Anything. Just name it."

"Would you buy a ticket for a concert to aid assassins?" Remo asked.

"Will you be there?"

"Sure. Me and Willie Nelson."

"I'll go. So will my friends. Put me down for a hundred tickets."

"Thank you," Remo said. "That's very encouraging."

"Anytime. Anything else?"

"Yes. Where's this flight going?"

"You bought the ticket. Don't you know?"

"I was in a hurry. Where?"

"Salt Lake City. Have you been there before?"

"I'll let you know when I get there," said Remo, who had traveled so much over the last decade that all cities kind of blurred together.

"Do that," Lorna said. "And if you need a place to stay, just let me know."

But they never got to Salt Lake City. Over Utah, a man went into the washroom and came out with a machine pistol.

"This is a hijacking," the man said. And to show he was serious, he fired a short burst through the cabin ceiling.

The jet instantly began losing pressure. The seat-belt sign came on and the overhead panels popped open to disgorge the yellow plastic oxygen masks. The pilot threw the plane into a steep dive, leveling off at fourteen thousand feet, where the air was still thin but breathable. Dust and grit flew into the cabin. The cold air misted and turned white.

"Please stay calm," Lorna said over the sound system. "Slip the mask firmly over your mouth and pull on the plastic tube. Breathe normally." She demonstrated the proper method even as the jetliner lost altitude at an alarming rate.

There was no panic. Except for the hijacker. He was panicking.

"What is happening? What is happening?" he repeated, waving his machine pistol.

"We're about to crash," said Remo, who appeared suddenly beside him.

"I won't allow it," said the skyjacker. "Tell the pilot not to crash. My death will not aid the cause."

"What is your cause anyway?" Remo asked.

"Serbo-Croatian genocide," said the frightened man.

"Causing or avenging?" Remo said.

"Avenging."

"How does hijacking an American jet solve a European problem?"

"Because it is wonderful public relations. American press gets me coverage all over the world and most of the reporters find some way to blame it all on America. It is the new way," the skyjacker said.

"This is an even newer way," Remo said, and with a blurring motion, he took the hijacker's weapon and blended it into a new shape, a sort of fuzzy metallic ball with the man's two hands firmly encased inside.

"Please. Everyone, sit down. We are about to land."

It was Lorna's voice and she was standing in the aisle as if they were about to land at an airport and not in the open spaces of Utah. Remo felt a wave of admiration for her courage. He slapped the hijacker into a seat.

"I'll settle with you later," Remo said and plopped into a seat on the other side of the aisle.

For a long time, there was no sound. But the ground got closer. Then there was a grinding noise as the jetliner hit. It seemed to go on forever.

And then there was silence.

3

Chiun, reigning Master of Sinanju, last of an unbroken line that dated from before the days of the Great Wang, first of the major Sinanju assassins, sat unmoving on his woven mat. His hazel eyes were closed. His impassive countenance, the exact color and texture of Egyptian papyrus, might have been molded from clay by delicate fingers. Even his wispy beard moved not, so deep was his meditation.

For three hours he had sat thus, serene and unmoving. For three hours, he had searched his thoughts, prayed his prayers, and silently asked the counsel of his ancestors, the great line of Sinanju. Three hours, and Chiun—hopefully to be known to future generations as Chiun the Great Teacher—found that the decision still eluded him like a spring butterfly eluded the net.

At length, the tufts of hair over his ears trembled. The eyes of the Master of Sinanju opened like uncovered agate stones, clear and bright and ageless. He floated to his feet in a smooth motion. The decision had been made.

He would wear the gray silk kimono and not the blue one with the orange tigers worked on the breast.

Chiun padded silently to the fourteen steamer trunks resting in a far corner of the apartment. The trunks were

never unpacked because of the dismal—no, the odious—
work to which the Master had committed himself in this
barbarian land of America. Odious. Yes. That would be
the word he would use. Emperor Smith would understand
Chiun's displeasure if he used that word. After all, Smith
was white, and in Korean, in the old language of Chiun's
ancestors, "odious" was a synonym for "whiteness." He
would not mention that to Smith, however. He would only
tell him that it was odious that Chiun must move from
hotel room to hotel room like a vagrant, never having a
place to rest his head, never having a home in which to
unpack his fourteen steamer trunks. It was no way for a
Master of Sinanju to live.

Chiun found the gray silk kimono and even though he
was alone in the hotel suite, he went into the bedroom to
change, taking care to close the door tightly and to pull the
shades. He emerged moments later and left the hotel,
which was near Central Park.

On the street, he hailed a cab. The first three drove past
without stopping.

Chiun responded by calmly walking into the path of
the fourth cab to approach. The taxi screeched to a halt,
the bumper coming to within a millimeter of Chiun's
knees.

The driver stuck his head out the window and yelled,
"Hey! What's with you?"

"Nothing is with me. I am alone. I would hire this
conveyance."

"This is a cab, dummy, not a conveyance," said the
driver. He pointed to his roof light. "See that. It's turned
off. That means I'm already hired."

Chiun looked at the light, sniffed, and said, "I will pay
you more."

"Huh?"

"I said I will pay you more than your present passenger.
What price?"

"Buddy, I don't know what boat you fell off, but that

ain't the way it's done in America. First come, first served.
Now get out of my way.''

''I see,'' said Chiun, seeming to drop the golden coin he
had plucked from his kimono as an inducement for the
driver. The coin bounced, rolled, and came to a stop
beside the cab's front tire. Chiun swept out a long-nailed
finger and retrieved the coin. The taxicab suddenly listed
to port, air escaping from the settling left-front tire with a
lazy hissing.

''What gives?'' said the driver.

''Your tire,'' said Chiun. ''It gives up its life. Too bad.
Your fault for buying American.''

The driver climbed out and looked at the flat tire.

''Dammit,'' he said. ''I musta run over a nail back
there. Hey, lady, come on out of there. I'm gonna have to
change this.''

A middle-aged woman with oversize glasses and an
undersize dress draping her big body stepped out of the
cab.

''I'm late already,'' she said. ''I can't wait.''

''Suit yourself,'' said the driver, yanking a tire jack and
lug wrench from his trunk. Muttering to himself, he
scrunched down beside the offending wheel and began
working to loosen the lug nuts. He looked up when he
heard the passenger door slamming shut.

''Hey? What do you think you're doing?''

From the back of the cab came a squeaky voice. ''I am
in no rush,'' said the Master of Sinanju pleasantly. ''I will
wait for you to finish.''

''My lucky day,'' grumbled the driver.

''It is fate,'' said Chiun, delicately flicking a shred of
vulcanized rubber from his fingernail, where it had caught
after he had withdrawn it from the unfortunate tire.

Three hours later, the cab dropped Chiun off at the stone
entrance to Folcroft Sanitarium in Rye, New York, north
of Manhattan. At first the driver had not wanted to take

Chiun that far, but after some haggling and an examination of the old Oriental's gold coins, the driver had agreed.

"This is a different route," said Chiun as they passed the city limits of Asbury Park. "I have never come this way before."

"New road," said the driver, who was sure that the old gook did not know that Asbury Park was due south of New York while Rye was due north. He was getting double the fare shown on his meter and had visions of taking the rest of the week off after this one fare. "We're almost there."

"You have said that before," Chiun said.

"It was true before. It's true now. Just hang on."

After touring Hoboken, Newark, and the shopping malls of Paramus, New Jersey, the driver finally wended his way toward Rye. He was very courteous when he let Chiun off at his destination.

"That'll be $1,356. Not counting tip, of course."

"That is more than I paid the last time," Chiun said.

"Rates've gone up."

"Have they tripled?"

"Could be," said the driver. He smiled politely. He was thinking of the rest of the week off. Maybe going to a ball game.

"I will make you a deal," said Chiun, counting the coins in his change purse.

"No deals," protested the driver. "You agreed to double the meter."

"True," said Chiun. "But I did not agree to a tour of the provinces south and west of New York."

The driver shrugged. "I got a little lost. It happens."

"And I did not agree not to destroy your wheels."

"Destroy my . . . You've gotta be kidding."

Chiun stepped from the cab and kicked the right-rear tire. "What will you give me in return for this wheel?" he asked. "It is a good wheel, firm and sturdy. It will carry you far along your difficult return journey."

"I won't give you squat. That's my tire."

Chiun reached over and drove an index finger into the tire. When he removed his finger, the tire let go with a bang. The car settled suddenly.

"Hey! What'd you do to my tire?"

"No matter. You can change it. A man who charges $1,356 for a simple ride must have many extra wheels."

The driver watched as the little Oriental—he had to be nearly eighty, the driver thought—walked to the front of the cab and thoughtfully surveyed both front tires.

"Will you take $947 for the pair?" asked Chiun.

"That's robbery."

Chiun shook a long-nailed finger in the air.

"No," he said. "It is haggling. You haggled with me. Now I haggle with you. Quickly. Do you accept?"

"All right. Yes. Don't blow the tires. I gotta drive all the way back to the city."

"Through Asbury Park," said Chiun, walking to the left-rear wheel. "Good. Now I still owe you $409 for your services. Will you give $500 for this remaining wheel?"

"But then I'd owe you ninety-one dollars," the driver protested.

"No checks," said Chiun.

Dr. Harold W. Smith did not like to be interrupted but when his secretary described his visitor, he pressed the concealed button that dropped the desktop computer monitor into a well in his Spartan oak desk.

It was just force of habit because while the secret computer system accessed every other major computer and information-retrieval system in the world and therefore knew all the world's secrets, Chiun would have had no idea what it all meant. Only Smith as head of the secret agency CURE understood it. Chiun couldn't, and Remo was hopeless with machinery. He had trouble dialing a telephone; a computer was beyond his reach.

"Hail, Emperor Smith," said Chiun.

"That will be all, Mrs. Mikulka," Smith said to his secretary.

"Hadn't I better call an orderly?" the gray-haired woman asked, with a sidelong glance at the old Oriental.

"Not necessary," said Smith. "And please. I'll take no calls."

Mrs. Mikulka looked doubtful but she closed the door quietly after her.

"I didn't summon you, Chiun," said Smith.

"Yet your pleasure at my arrival is returned threefold," Chiun said.

"Remo isn't with you?" asked Smith, sitting down. He had thin white hair and the expression of a man who'd just discovered half a worm in his apple. He had been young when he had set up CURE, but now he had grown old in its service. He adjusted his Dartmouth tie.

"Remo has not yet returned from his latest mission," Chiun said. "But it is of no moment."

"Odd," said Smith. "I had a report that his target had been . . . terminated."

Chiun smiled. Smith was always uncomfortable with the language of death. "Another jewel in your crown," he said and wondered why Smith always greeted success with the same sour expression as bitter defeat.

"I wish you wouldn't call me that," said Smith. "Emperor. You know very well that I am not the emperor."

"You could be," said Chiun. "Your President has lived a full life. Perhaps it is time for younger blood."

"Thank you, no," said Smith, who had long ago grown weary of trying to explain to Chiun that he served the President and was not a pretender to the Oval Office. "Now what can I do for you, Master of Sinanju?"

Chiun looked shocked. "Have you forgotten? It is time to renegotiate the contract between the House of Sinanju and the House of Smith."

"The United States," said Smith. "Your contract is

with the United States. But it's not due to expire for another six months."

"When entering into protracted and difficult dealings," said Chiun solemnly, "it is best to begin early."

"Oh. I rather thought we could simply renew the old contract. It's quite generous, as you know."

"It was magnanimously generous," agreed Chiun. "Considering the false understanding on which it was based."

"False understanding?"

Smith watched as Chiun unrolled his straw mat and placed it on the floor, carefully arranging an array of scrolls beside the mat before settling into place. Smith had to stand in order to see Chiun over his desktop.

Smith sighed. He had been through these negotiations before. Chiun would not speak another word until Smith was seated at eye level. Smith pulled a pencil and a yellow legal pad from a drawer and stiffly found a place on the floor, facing the old Korean. He balanced the pad on a knee. After so many years of writing on a computer keypad, the pencil felt like a banana in his fingers.

"I am ready," said Smith.

As Chiun opened a scroll, Smith recognized it as a copy of the last contract he had signed. It was on special rice paper edged in gold and had itself cost hundreds of dollars. Another unnecessary expense.

"Ah, here it is," Chiun said, looking up from the scroll. "The poophole."

"I beg your pardon."

"It is a legal term. Poophole. Have you never heard of it? Most contracts have them."

"You mean loophole. And our contract is ironclad. There are no loopholes."

"There is a saying in my village," said Chiun. " 'Never correct an emperor. Except when he is wrong.' And you are wrong, great leader. The poophole is in the paragraph about training a white in the art of Sinanju."

"As I recall, you charged extra for that," Smith said.

"A mere pittance to wipe out what I thought was a great shame. An odious shame. But as it turns out, I made a mistake."

"What kind of mistake?" asked Smith, who knew that Chiun's mistakes invariably wound up costing him money.

"I was not training a white at all," Chiun said, beaming at the happy thought.

Smith frowned. "What do you mean? Of course Remo's white. True, we don't know who his parents were, but all you have to do is look to see that he's white."

Patiently, Chiun shook his head. "No Chinese, no Japanese, no non-Korean ever before has been able to absorb Sinanju training. Yet this supposed white has taken to Sinanju like no other in the history of my humble village."

"That's good, isn't it?" asked Smith, who could not figure out what Chiun was driving at.

"Of course," said Chiun. "It means that Remo is really Korean." He mumbled some words in the Korean language.

"What did you say?"

"Just his name. Remo the Fair. He is part Korean. There can be no other explanation."

"Perhaps Americans just naturally take to Sinanju," Smith said. "You've never had to train an American before Remo."

Chiun made a face. "You are being ridiculous. But enough. Remo is learning Sinanju faster than any Korean. Therefore Remo is not white."

"And therefore," said Smith, "your earlier demands for extra payment for training a white are no longer valid."

"Exactly," Chiun said.

Smith hesitated while he searched Chiun's face, but the expression was bland. Smith had never been able to read his face.

"Are you saying that you're willing to take less money because of that?" he asked.

"Of course not. I contracted to train a white for you, and knowing whites, you would have gotten somebody who jumped around, grunting, breaking boards with much noise. Instead, you have gotten a true Master of Sinanju. You have been getting a bargain for all these years and this will require an adjustment, not only on our next contract, but radioactive payments on all preceding contracts.''

"Retroactive," Smith said. "You mean retroactive payments.''

"Good. Then we are in agreement. I knew you would understand, wise Emperor.''

"I do *not* understand," Smith snapped. "but I don't want to argue the point. Just tell me. What are your demands this time?''

Calmly, slowly, Chiun picked up another scroll and unrolled it.

"We do not have demands," he said haughtily. "We have requirements and they are these.'' He began to read from the scroll.

"Two jars of emeralds. Uncut.

"Twenty jars of diamonds of different cuts. No flaws.

"Eight bolts of Tang-dynasty silk. Assorted colors.

"One Persian statue of Darius. Of shittimwood.

"Rupees. Twelve bushels.''

He stopped as Smith held up a hand.

"Master of Sinanju. Many of those items are priceless museum pieces.''

"Yes?" said Chiun.

"Tang-dynasty silk, for example, is not easily come by.''

"Of course," said Chiun. "We would not ask for it otherwise.''

"I don't think any Tang-dynasty silk exists in the modern world," Smith said.

"I have Tang-dynasty silk," said Chiun. "Back in the treasure house of my ancestors. In Sinanju.''

"When why do you want more?''

"You never asked that question during previous negotiations when I asked for more gold. You never said to me,

'Master of Sinanju, why do you want more gold? You already have gold.' "

"True," said Smith. "But this is different."

"Yes," said Chiun, beaming now. "It is different. This time I am not asking for more gold. I have enough of gold, thanks to your generosity. But in times past my ancestors were paid in tribute, not always gold. Now I wish to be paid in tribute as befits my heritage."

"My government pays enough yearly tribute to feed all North Korea," Smith said evenly. "You have brought to Sinanju more wealth than it has seen in all the thousands of years of Sinanju history before you."

"No Master before me ever was forced to dwell in a foreign land—an odious land—for so long," said Chiun. "I am the first to be treated thusly."

"I am sorry," said Smith, who despite being the only person in charge of an unlimited secret operating fund kept track of his secretary's consumption of paper clips. "I think your requests are unreasonable."

"I must restore the glory of Sinanju," said Chiun. "Did you know that just yesterday Remo told me that he was planning to run a benefit concert for me. He said that he was tired of seeing me poor, hungry, and destitute and that he was going to ask Nellie Wilson to run an aid program for me. Did you know this?"

"No. Who's Nellie Wilson?"

"He is a noble singer who stands on the side of the poor in this oppressive land. Remo said he would gladly sing for me, but I told him that it would not be necessary, that Emperor Smith would not fail the House of Sinanju." His eyes looked down at the floor. "But I was wrong, I see. Still I will take no charity from anyone, even so great a man as Nellie Wilson. If America cannot help me, I will simply seek outside employment."

"The terms of our contract expressly forbid it," Smith said.

"The terms of our *old* contract," Chiun said with a

small smile. "And it appears there may be no new contract."

Smith cleared his throat. "Don't be hasty," he said. "Of course, we want a new contract with you, but we cannot provide you with things that no longer exist in the world. Nor, I must point out, could any other prospective employer."

"We are not intransigent, O great Emperor. While our heart aches at your inability to provide us with the few meager items we requested, perhaps something else could be worked out."

"I will double the amount of gold we now ship to your village."

"Triple," said Chiun.

"Double is a gift. Triple is impossible," Smith said.

"Whites are impossible," said Chiun. "Beyond that, the word does not exist in Sinanju."

"I will triple the gold," Smith said wearily. "But that's it. That's final. Nothing more."

"Done," Chiun said quickly.

Smith relaxed.

"That takes care of the gold," Chiun said pleasantly. "Now on to other items. . . ."

Smith tensed. "We agreed. No other items. No other items."

"No," Chiun said. "You agreed no other items. I agreed to the gold."

"What other item?" Smith said.

"Only one. Land. Remo and I have no permanent home in this odious land of yours."

"We've been through this before, Master of Sinanju," said Smith tightly. His legs were tingling from sitting on the floor. "It's too dangerous for you and Remo to stay in one place for long."

"The land I have in mind is in a far place," said Chiun, who noticed from Smith's fidgeting that his legs were falling asleep. In negotiating, he always waited for that to happen before asking Smith for the really difficult items. "The place I have in mind is large, with many fortifications, and therefore easily defended. Remo and I would be safe there."

"Where?" asked Smith.

"Yet it is a small parcel, compared to the lands the Egyptians once bestowed upon Sinanju."

"Can you point it out on a map?"

"And it is near no dwellings," continued Chiun. "Oh, there are some minor structures existing on the land but no one lives in them. I would not even ask that they be razed. It may be that Remo and I could make do with them, although they are not really houses."

"Can you be more specific?"

Chiun made a show of searching his scroll.

"I do not know its exact location," he said. "It is . . . yes, here it is. It is in the province of California. But it is not even on the ocean. And I understand it is overrun with mice and other vermin."

"California is a big place," said Smith.

"It has a name," said Chiun.

"Yes?"

"Ah. Here it is. It is a funny name, but I do not mind. Remo and I will learn to live with it. And the mice."

"What is the name?"

Chiun looked up from his scroll hopefully.

"Disneyland it is called."

Lloyd Darton paid his $49 and accepted the room key from the desk clerk. On the seedier side of Detroit, he could have rented a room for just an hour, but that was the kind of hotel where a man could get killed just standing at the registration desk and Darton wasn't the sort to take chances. Better to waste a few dollars, especially since he was here on business. He waved off the bellhop and took the stairs to his room rather than wait for the elevator.

He carefully double-locked the door of the room, placed

his single suitcase on the bed, and unlocked it with a key.

It held an assortment of weapons, locked in place by straps and plastic blocks. Satisfied that nothing had been damaged, he closed the lid and sat on the bed. It was 8:46 P.M. His customer should be along soon and Lloyd Darton hoped to be out of the room by 9:30 at the latest.

There was a knock on the door at 8:56. The man who stood there was tall, fiftyish, with the kind of eyes Lloyd Darton had seen many times before. All his customers had them. A scar was faintly visible along the right side of the man's jaw.

"Hello," Darton said.

The man just nodded as he entered the room. He waited until the door was locked again before he spoke.

"You made the changes I asked for?"

"Sure did. Over here." Darton flipped open the suitcase lid. "I fixed the sight for you too. It was a little off. Of course, that won't matter with these new add-ons."

"Skip the sales pitch," said the man with the scar, whose name Darton did not know. All his customers were nameless. They knew him, knew where to find him, but he never asked their names. It was a one-sided business relationship, but so was the money. That was one-sided too and it all fell on Darton's side of the ledger.

"Here it is," said Darton, hefting a shiny black handgun. He took an assortment of devices from the case and in a few quick motions, he attached a folding stock, a telescopic sight and barrel extension, converting the pistol to a takedown sniper's rifle. He inserted a clip, snapped back the slide to show the action at work, and presented it to the other man.

"Don't get much call for this kind of custom work," Darton said. "While you're here, why don't you look at some of the others? You might see something you like better than—"

"There's nothing better than my old Beretta Olympic,"

the other man interrupted, sighting down the pistol's long barrel.

"If you say so. It's just . . . it's not considered, well, a professional weapon, if you know what I mean."

"It's a target pistol. I'm going to use it on targets. What could be more professional?"

Darton nodded wordlessly. The man had a point and he certainly had the professional look to him. Except that he was sighting down the barrel with Darton at the other end. That was not professional at all. It was not even good gun safety. Or good manners for that matter.

"I can understand your affection for the Olympic," Darton said quickly. "But I find that most people in your business like to change their tools. It reduces complications."

"Don't you think I know that?" asked the man with the scar. "This piece has sentimental value for me. It reminds me of my ex-wife." He lined up on Darton's sweat-shiny forehead. Darton winced. He loved guns. He bought them, he sold them, he repaired them, he remodeled them, and he hunted with them. They were both his hobby and his business and he loved them. But he didn't like to have them pointed at him.

"Do you mind?" Darton asked, looking at the gun barrel.

The man with the scar ignored him. "You test-fire this?" he asked.

"Of course. It fires true. No bias. It's perfect for the kind of work you do."

"Oh? What kind is that?"

"You know," Darton said.

"I want to hear you say it."

"My guess is that you kill people with it."

"You keep trying to tell me my business," said the man with the scar.

"I didn't mean anything by it, Mr.—"

"Call me Remo."

"Mr. Remo. I just want you to have the best your money can buy, Mr. Remo."

"Good. I'm glad to hear that. Because I want this weapon and I want something else from you."

"What's that."

"I want to check the action myself. I have some serious work ahead of me and I don't like to work with a cold piece just out of the shop."

"How can I help?" asked Lloyd Darton.

"Just stand still," said the other man and split Darton's sweat-shiny forehead with a single shot. The floral bed-spread behind him suddenly developed an extra pattern. In red.

"I don't like people telling me my business," said the man to himself. He disassembled the Beretta, slipped the pistol into a spring-clip holster, helped himself to extra clips, and quietly left the room with the attachments nes-tled in a briefcase Lloyd Darton had thoughtfully planned to throw into the bargain.

Walking down the steps, he thought of the work ahead. Detroit was a new city for him. A new start and maybe a new life. It all felt strange to him.

But he had work to do and that was the most important thing. In his pocket was a list. Four people. And the contractor wanted them hit in public places. Imagine that. Wanted the whole thing done out in the open. It was crazy, but the money was even crazier and that made it worthwhile. Even if he didn't know the name of his employer.

As he walked through the lobby, he thought of Maria. Lately, she had been on his mind a lot.

He hadn't wanted to kill her. But he was a soldier, a soldier in an army that wore no uniforms, belonged to no country, and yet had invaded almost every civilized na-tion. There were those who referred to the Mafia as a family but that was a myth, like claiming the Holocaust had never happened. The Mafia was no family; it was like an enormous occupying army.

As his capo, Don Pietro Scubisci, had once told him:

"We own the banks. We own the courts and the lawyers. We own pieces of the government. And because we don't dress like soldiers," he had said, tapping his chest with palsied fingers, "because we deny everything, people don't know. Our hands are at their throats and because we smile and talk of 'business interests' and donate to the Church, the fools pretend we're not there. Their foolishness is our greatest strength. Remember that. And remember, we always come first."

"Always," he had agreed.

"Your mother, your father, your wife, your children," Don Pietro had said, ticking them off on his fingers, one by one. "They come second. If we ask, you will deny them. If we tell you, you will leave them. If we order it, you will kill them."

It was true. He believed it so deeply that when it came down to his honor as a soldier and the woman he had loved, he made the right choice. The only choice. He had acted instantly, ruthlessly. Like a soldier. Maria had planned to talk, and to protect the Invisible Army of the Mafia, she had had to die. And he had come here, to Detroit, to begin a new life.

As he got behind the wheel of his rented car, he could not stop thinking of Maria and the last words she had spoken to him.

"He will know your name and you will know his. And that will be your death warrant."

"This time, Maria," he said half-aloud, "you're wrong." But he thought he heard her tinkling laugh somewhere in the night.

Remo Williams smelled the fumes even before the jet skidded to a stop. He glanced up and saw the trickle of smoke insinuating itself between two of the wall panels. It was all unnaturally quiet. People were still in their seats, hunched over, stunned from the carnival-ride impact of the plane's crash landing.

Remo heard something sparking. It was an electrical fire and he knew it would start small but could spread through the cabin as if it were lined with flashpaper.

And even before that, the deadly acrid fumes of burning plastic would kill everyone aboard.

All six emergency exits were blocked by the bodies of unconscious passengers and Remo found the place in the ceiling where the hijacker had fired the warning burst that had depressurized the cabin and tossed the giant craft out of control. He could see sky through the pattern of bullet holes. Remo balanced on the top edge of a seat, inserted his fingers into as many of the holes as he could, and made two fists. The aluminum outer skin gave under the pressure of his hands, hands that instantly sensed weak points, flaws in the alloy, and exploited them. The ceiling tore with a harsh metallic shriek.

Remo ran with the tear, racing the length of the cabin

from tail to cockpit, peeling the metal as if it were the lid of a sardine can.

Now the hot Utah sun filled the cabin. People were beginning to stir, coughing into their oxygen masks. He started to free the people from their seat belts in the fastest way possible, grabbing a handful of seat belt and ripping it free from its moorings.

"Okay," Remo called as he moved along the rows. "Everybody up for volleyball."

He had to get them moving. But some of them, he saw, would never move again. Their heads hung at impossible angles, their necks snapped on impact.

Behind him, the sparking of the electric fire turned into a hissing sputter. Remo turned and saw Lorna, the stewardess, turning a red fire extinguisher on the galley. The chemical foam beat down the licking flames but also sucked away the breathable air.

The young blond woman fell to her knees, her face purpling.

Remo hauled her back and boosted her up to the roof.

"Catch your breath," he called up. "I'm going to start passing people up to you."

She tried to speak but could manage only a cough. With red eyes, she made an Okay sign with her fingers.

Remo hoisted a man up out of his seat and over his head in a smooth, impossible motion. He felt Lorna take the man from his grasp.

Other passengers began to revive. They pulled off their oxygen masks and with a few quick words, Remo organized them. The strong lifting the weak. The first ones to reach the top of the fuselage pulled those who came after. In a few minutes, only Remo remained in the cabin. Even the dead had been removed.

"That's everyone," said Remo. "I think."

Lorna called down, "Make sure. Look for children on the floor."

"Right." Remo checked every seat. At the very rear of the plane, he found the hijacker, huddled under his seat.

"Oh, yes. You," Remo said. "Almost forgot about you." He grabbed the man by his collar, took hold of his belt, and swung him like a bag of manure. The hijacker screamed as Remo let go, and the man sailed up and out the hole in the roof.

Remo started to reach for the ceiling but a faint sound made him stop. He opened the rest-room door. There was a little girl inside, perhaps five years old, crouched down under the tiny sink, her thumb in her mouth and her eyes squinted shut. She was moaning softly; that was the sound Remo had heard.

"It's all right, honey. You can come out now."

The little girl shut her eyes more tightly.

"Don't be afraid." Remo reached in and pulled her to him and carried her from the plane just before the flames exploded into the cabin.

An hour later, the aircraft fire had burned itself out, leaving a smoking, gutted hulk lying in the coral-pink sandstone desert. The sun was starting to go down in the sky.

Lorna finished splinting a woman's broken arm. She stood up and brushed dust from what was left of her uniform. She had been using scraps of the skirt and sleeves as makeshift bandages.

"That's the last of them," she told Remo. "Have you seen anything?"

"Just flat desert in all directions," Remo said. "But there should be rescue here soon. Radar should have picked us up, right?"

Lorna shook her head. "Not necessarily," she said. "Sometimes you get in between the two radar coverages and you're in a dead spot. But when we don't show up on time, they'll start tracing us backward. They should get here."

"You did good work, Lorna," Remo said.

"You did too. The others think the cabin split open on impact, you know."

"And you?" Remo said.

"I saw you tear it open."

"You better take something for that concussion," Remo said. "You're imagining things."

"Have it your own way," she said. "Anything you want done?"

"Why me?"

"The cockpit crew died on impact. I guess you're in charge."

Remo nodded. He was watching the little girl he had pulled out at the last minute. She was kneeling in the sand beside two still figures, a man and a woman. Someone had placed a handkerchief over each of their faces.

Remo walked over and knelt alongside the girl.

"Are these your parents?" he asked.

"They're in heaven," the little girl said. There were tears in her eyes.

Remo hoisted her in his arms and brought her back to Lorna.

"Take care of her," he said.

"What are you going to do?" the stewardess asked.

"What I've been trained to do," Remo said, and he walked out into the desert alone.

The wind had shifted the sands, covering the tracks, but it made no difference to Remo. The wind followed its path and the sand moved according to subtle laws that in some way were clear to him.

There had been footprints, he knew. The way the sand had fallen in told him that, and now Remo was not tracking the footprints, but tracking the afterimages made by the footprints. Here the sand was piled too high. There it rilled and scalloped unnaturally.

He was close. Very close.

Remo Williams had killed more men in his past than he could count. Some were just targets, names punched up out of Smith's computers. Others he dispatched in self-defense or in defense of the nation. There were times he killed as casually as a surgeon scrubbed his hands and there were times Remo had been so sick of the killing that he wanted to quit CURE.

But tonight, with the dying red sun in his eyes, Remo wanted to kill for an unprofessional reason. For vengeance.

He found the hijacker standing on a low spur of rock. The man looked down when he saw Remo approach. He had worked his hands out of the mangled remains of his machine pistol.

"I do not see anything," the skyjacker said, indicating the horizon with a sweep of his arm.

"I do," said Remo through his teeth.

"Yes? What?"

Remo came up to the man with a slow purposeful gait. The sand under his shoes made no sound.

"I see an animal who places a cause over human life. I see someone less than human who, for stupidity, deprives a little girl of her parents."

"Hey. Do not shout at me. I am also a victim. I too could have been killed."

"You're about to be," said Remo.

The hijacker backed away, wide-eyed.

"I surrender."

"So did everyone on that flight," Remo said.

He had been taught to kill three times in his life—in Vietnam, as a policeman, and as an assassin. Each approach was different, with only one rule in common: strike as quickly as possible.

Remo ignored the rule. He killed the hijacker carefully, silently, an inch at a time. The man died slowly and not easily. And when his final shriek had stopped reverberating, what remained of him did not look even remotely human.

When it was over, Remo dry-washed his hands with the fine red sand that rolled as far as the eye could see, like an ocean of blood.

5

If success could be measured in newspaper headlines, Lyle Lavallette was the greatest automotive genius since Henry Ford.

The press loved him and his roomful of scrapbooks, which had become so voluminous that he had had all his clippings transferred to microfiche, were filled with references to "The Boy Genius of Detroit" or "Peck's Bad Boy of the Automotive Industry" or "Maverick Car Builder." That was his favorite.

He came by the headline coverage the old-fashioned way: he earned it. In one of the most conservative low-key industries in America, Lyle Lavallette was a breath of fresh air. He raced speedboats; he danced the night away at one fancy disco after another; his best friends were rock stars; he squired, then married, then divorced models and actresses, each successive one more beautiful and empty-headed than the one before. He was always good for a quote on any topic and three times a year, without fail, he invited all the working press he could get an invitation to, to large lavish parties at his Grosse Pointe estate.

Unfortunately for Lavallette, his bosses in Detroit were more interested in the bottom line than in the headline. So

Lavallette had lasted no more than five years with each of the Big Three.

His first top-level job was as design head for General Motors. He advised them to make the Cadillac smaller. Forget the fins, he said. Nobody'll ever buy a car with fins. Fortunately, Cadillac ignored him and then fired him.

Later he showed up in Chrysler's long-range planning division. He told them to keep making big cars; people want to ride in plush-buckets, he said. When Chrysler almost went belly-up, Lavallette was fired. Some felt that it was one of the secret prices Chrysler had to pay to get a federal loan.

Lavallette worked for Ford Motors too, as head of marketing. He told the brass to forget building four-cylinder cars. They would never sell. Ford, he said, should forget about trying to compete with Japanese imports. The Japanese make nothing that doesn't fall apart. Eventually, he was fired.

It was in the nature of Detroit that none of these firings was ever called a firing. Lavallette was always permitted to resign; each resignation was an excuse for a press party at which Lavallette dropped hints of some new enterprise he was getting himself involved in and, their bellies filled with expensive food and expensive wine, the newsmen went back to their offices to write more stories about "What's Ahead for the Maverick Genius?"

What was ahead was his own car. Lavallette went to Nicaragua and convinced the government there to put up the money to open a car plant. His new car would be called, naturally, the Lavallette. Five years after he started gearing up, the first car rolled off the assembly line. Its transmission fell out before it got out of the company parking lot.

In the first year, seventy-one Lavallettes were sold. The transmissions fell out of all of them. On those sturdy enough to be driven for two months without breaking down, the bodies rusted. Fenders and bumpers fell off.

Lavallette sneaked out of Nicaragua late one night and in New York announced the closing of the Lavallette factory. He called the Lavallette "one of the great cars of all time" but said that Sandinista sabotage was behind its failure. "They didn't want us to succeed," he said. "They blocked us every step of the way," he said.

The press never noticed that he didn't really explain who "they" were. His wild accusations were enough to ensure him a spate of stories about the Maverick Genius that the Communists Tried to Crush. No one mentioned that the Nicaraguan government had lent Lavallette ninety million dollars and stood to lose its entire investment.

And now it was time to meet the press again.

In his penthouse atop the luxurious Detroit Plaza Hotel, Lyle Lavallette, president of the newly formed Dynacar Industries, primped before a full-length dress mirror.

He was admiring the crease in his two-hundred-dollar trousers. It was just the way he liked it, straight-razor sharp. His Italian-made jacket showed off his wasp-thin waist and his broad shoulders. After a moment's reflection, he decided his shoulders did not look quite broad enough and made a mental note to order more padding with his next suit. The white silk handkerchief in his breast pocket formed two peaks, one slightly higher than the other. Just right. It matched his tie and his tie matched his white hair. For years, he had told the press that his hair had turned white when he was fifteen years old. The fact was that as a teenager he was called "Red" and he now had his hair stripped and bleached every week by a hairstylist, that being the only way he could guarantee that he would not appear as a headline in the *Enquirer*: "MAV-ERICK CAR GENIUS SECRETLY A REDHEAD."

Just the thought of such a headline made Lavallette wince. He picked up a hand mirror just as his personal secretary stepped into the suite.

"The press is here, Mr. Lavallette," the secretary cooed. He had hired her out of nearly sixty applicants, all of whom he subjected to what he called "the elbow test."

The elbow test was simple. Each applicant was taken aside and asked to clasp her hands behind her head until her elbows projected straight ahead, like a prisoner of war in an old movie.

"Now walk toward the wall," Lavallette told them.

"That's all?"

"Until your elbows touch the wall."

The applicants whose elbows touched the wall before their chests did were disqualified. Out of the seven passing applicants, the only one who hadn't tried to slap him or bring a sexual-harassment suit was Miss Melanie Blaze and he had hired her instantly. She was nothing as a secretary but she was good for his image, especially now that he was between wives. And he liked her for the way her cleavage entered a room a full half-beat before the rest of her.

"You look fine," she said. "Are you ready for the press conference?"

"It's not a press conference," Lavallette said. "That comes tomorrow."

"Yes, sir," said Miss Blaze, who could have sworn that when a businessman called in the media for the express purpose of making a formal announcement, it constituted a press conference.

"Would you please hold this mirror for me, Miss Blaze?"

The young redhead sauntered on high heels to take the mirror and was immediately sorry she had.

"Aaargghh!" howled Lavallette.

"What is it? What's wrong?" she squealed. She thought he must have seen a precancerous mole on his face.

"A hair," Lavallette shrieked. "Look at it."

"I'm looking, I'm looking. If we get you to a doctor, maybe it can be cut out," she said, remembering that hair growing out of a mole was a bad sign. But she still couldn't see the mole.

"What are you yammering about, you idiot? There's a hair out of place."

"Where?"

"Back of my head. It's as plain as day."

Miss Blaze looked and looked some more. Finally, Lyle Lavallette pointed it out.

Yes, there was a hair out of place, Miss Blaze agreed. But it would take an electron microscope for anyone to see it.

"Are you making fun of me, Miss Blaze?"

"No, sir. I just don't think anyone will notice. Besides, it's at the back of your head. The cameras will just be shooting front views, won't they?"

"And what if an *Enquirer* photographer is in the pack? What if he sneaks around to the side? You know how they latch on to these things. I can see the headline now: 'LYLE LAVALLETTE, HEAD OF DYNACAR INDUSTRIES, LOSING HAIR. Shocking Details Inside.' They'll have my face in between the Abominable Snowman and the woman in Malaysia who gave birth to a goat. I can't have it."

"I'll get a comb."

"No, no, no. Take a comb to this hair and we'll have to start all over again. It'll take hours. Get a tweezers. And some hair spray. Hurry."

When she returned, he said, "Good. Now carefully, really carefully, use the tweezers and put the hair back in its proper groove."

"I'm doing it. Just stop shaking, huh."

"I can't help it. This is serious. Is it in place?"

"I think so. Yeah. It is."

"Okay. Now, quickly . . . use the spray."

Miss Blaze shook the can and applied a quick jet.

"More. More than that. Lard it on. I don't want that sucker popping up at a crucial moment."

"It's your hair," said his secretary, who noticed that the ingredients on the can included liquefied Krazy Glue. She emptied half the can on the back of Lavallette's snow-white hair. He looked it over and permitted himself one of his dazzlingly perfect smiles. It could not have been more perfect if he still had his natural teeth.

"Okay, we're all set. Let's go get 'em," Lavallette said.

"You sure go to a lot of trouble over the way you look, Mr. Lavallette," she said.

"Image, Miss Blaze," Lavallette said. He gave his shirt cuffs a final shoot so they projected a precise half-inch beyond the jacket sleeves. "Image is everything."

"Substance too," she said lightly.

"Substance sucks. Image," Lavallette insisted.

"Who are we waiting for anyway?" a photographer asked a newsman inside the hotel's grand ballroom.

"Lyle Lavallette."

"Who's he?" the photographer asked.

"The Maverick Genius of the Car Industry," the reporter said.

"I never heard of him. What's he done?"

"Back in the old days, when there was a General Motors and a Ford and a Chrysler company, back before all the buyouts and mergers, Lavallette was the guiding genius who led them to new heights."

"I still never heard of him," the photographer said.

"Then you're a clod," the reporter said.

"I got no problem with that," the photographer said. He looked up as he heard a smattering of applause, and saw Lavallette walking to the podium behind which was mounted the ten-foot-square logo of the new Dynacar Industries.

"Is that him?" the photographer said.

"Yes. That is Lyle Lavallette, Maverick Genius."

"He bleaches his hair," the photographer said.

"Take his picture anyway," the reporter said disgustedly. Some people, he thought, had no sense of history.

Lavallette was bathed in electronic light from all the

photographers' strobe units flashing. He could never understand it. Why didn't the print media just hire a handful of photographers to take a few pictures and then divvy them up? Instead, they hired a zillion photographers to take a zillion pictures and only a fraction of them ever made it into print. What happened to the rest? Lavallette imagined a big file somewhere holding enough photos of himself to have a different one printed beside every definition in the dictionary.

Well, today he was glad to see all the photographers. It showed that Lyle Lavallette hadn't lost his touch with the press and he was going to give them enough to keep them interested.

He let the picture-taking go on for a full three minutes, then stepped behind the podium and raised a quieting hand.

"Ladies and gentlemen of the press," he began in a sonorous voice. "I'm happy to see you and happy to see so many old friends. In case you were wondering what happened to me, let me just tell you that Maverick Car Builders don't die and they don't fade away either. We just keep coming back."

There was a warm-spirited chuckle through the audience.

"As some of you know, I've spent the last few years working in Nicaragua, fighting my lonely fight against totalitarian oppression. There are some, I know, who think I failed because the car I built there did not establish itself among the major car lines of the world." He paused and looked around the room dramatically. The errant hair, he knew, was still in place and he was pleased with the way things were going. If only they kept going just as well.

"I don't think I failed. I helped to bring some good old car-making know-how to Nicaragua and I'm sure the lives of the people will never be the same because of our efforts there. That alone would have been enough of a success for me because spreading freedom is what the auto industry is all about. But I had an even greater success while I was there." He paused again to look around.

"While I was fighting my lonely battle against oppression, I spent all my free time in my research-and-development laboratory and I'm proud to tell you today that this effort paid off. We are preparing to announce a car design so revolutionary, so important that from this time on the automobile industry as we have known and loved it will be forever changed."

A gasp rose from the crowd. The television people jostled closer, bringing their videocams in to Lavallette's tanned face. He wondered if they were trying to get prints of the retinas of his eyes. He'd read somewhere that retina prints were like fingerprints, no two being alike.

"This discovery is so world-shaking that two days ago, industry thieves broke into the new Dynacar Industries building here in Detroit and made off with what they believed was the only existing prototype of this new car," Lavallette said. He smiled broadly. "They were wrong."

He lifted his hands to still the shouted barrage of questions.

"Tomorrow in the new Dynacar building, I will unveil this great discovery. I am herewith extending an invitation to the heads of General Autos, American Autos, and National Autos—the Big Three—to attend so they can personally see what the future will be like. I will take no questions now; I will see you all tomorrow. Thank you for coming."

He turned and stepped down from the podium.

"What did he say?" asked a reporter from *GQ* who had been busy taking notes on what Lavallette was wearing and had not listened to what he said.

"He said the press conference is tomorrow," said another reporter.

"Tomorrow? Then what was this?"

"Search me."

"Hey. What was this if it wasn't the press conference?"

the *GQ* reporter called out to Miss Blaze as she walked away behind Lavallette.

She started to shrug. But instead she screamed. She screamed because, as the news people surged to record Lyle Lavallette leaving the room, two shots rang out and Lavallette was slammed against the wall.

"He's been shot. Someone shot Lavallette."

"What? Shot?"

"Someone call an ambulance," shrieked Miss Blaze.

"Where's the gunman? He must be in this room. Find him. Get his story."

A network newsman jumped up behind the podium and waved his arms frantically. "If the gunman is still in this room, I can offer an exclusive contract to appear on *Nightwatch*. We'll also pick up your legal fees."

"I'll double that offer," yelled someone from a cable news system.

"I didn't mention a price," said the network man. "How can you double it?"

"I'm offering a blank check," the cable man said loudly. He jumped up onto the small stage at the front of the room, yanked his checkbook from his pocket, and waved it around his head, hoping the gunman would see him. "Name your price," he shouted. "A blank check."

"A credit card," the network man shouted back. "I'm offering a network credit card. That's better than his blank check."

"Oooooh," groaned Lyle Lavallette on the floor.

"Can we quote you on that?" a woman with a microphone asked him.

The television news people had their cameras aimed in all directions. They filmed Lyle lavallette lying on the gold rug with a stupid expression on his face. They filmed Miss Blaze, his secretary, with her Grand Canyon cleavage and hot tears streaming down her cheeks. They filmed each other. They missed nothing.

Except the gunman.

After firing two shots point-blank at Lyle Lavallette's chest, the gunman had slipped his Beretta Olympic into the hollow compartment built into his video camera and pretended to shoot more footage. He did not try to run away because he knew he would not have to. In the entire history of the universe, no newsman confronted with disaster, whether natural or man-made, had ever offered assistance. They filmed people burning to death and never made an attempt to throw a blanket over the flames. They interviewed mass killers, on the run from the police, and never made any attempt to have the criminals arrested. They seemed to believe that the only people who should be apprehended and put in jail were Presidents of the United States and people who did not support school busing.

So the gunman waited until the ambulance came and took Lyle Lavallette away. He waited around while the police were there, and pretended to take film of them. When the police were done interviewing people and taking down everyone's name, he left with the other newsmen.

He heard one of them say, "It's awful. It would only happen in America. Who'd shoot a Maverick Car Genius?"

"They must have thought he was a politician. Probably the President shot him because he thought Lavallette was going to run for President."

"No," another one said. "It was big business. The capitalists. The Big Three had him shot because he was going to hurt their car sales."

The man with the scar who had shot Lyle Lavallette listened to all of them and he knew they were all wrong. Lyle Lavallette was shot simply because his was the first name on the list.

That afternoon, the Detroit *Free Press* received an anonymous letter. It said simply that Lavallette was only the first. One by one, the automakers of America would be killed before they had a chance to totally destroy the environment. "Enough innocent people have already died from air-polluting infernal machines," the letter said. "It is time some of the guilty died too. And they will."

Harold Smith took another swig of Maalox. Beyond the big picture windows of his office, looking out on Long Island Sound, a skiff tacked close to the wind. Strong gusts blew up and pushed against the sail and the skiff listed so sharply it looked ready to capsize. But Smith knew that sailcraft were balanced so that the sail above and the keel below formed a single vertical axis. The wind could push the sail over only so far, because of the counterpressure from the keel below the water. When the sail reached its maximum tilt, the wind glanced harmlessly off. Perfect equilibrium.

Sometimes Smith felt CURE was like that. A perfectly balanced keel for the sailboat that was the United States government. But sometimes—just as a really rough sea could capsize a sailboat if it was struck in just the wrong way at the wrong time—even CURE could not always hold America on an even keel.

It felt that way right now. Smith had just gotten off the telephone with the President.

"I know I can only suggest missions," the President had said. His voice was as cheerful as if he had just finished his favorite lunch.

"Yes, sir," Smith said.

"But you know about this Detroit thing."

"It looks as if it might be serious, Mr. President."

"Darned tootin' it's serious," said the President. "The car industry is just getting back on its feet. We can't have some environment cuckoo killing everybody in Detroit."

"Fortunately, Lavallette is still alive," Smith said. "He was wearing a bulletproof vest."

"I think all the rest of them need more than a bulletproof vest," the President said. "I think they need your two special men."

"I'll have to make that decision, Mr. President. This might just be the work of a vicious prankster."

"I don't think it is, though. Do you?"

"I'll let you know. Good-bye, Mr. President," Smith said and disconnected the telephone that connected directly with the White House.

Smith had disliked being abrupt but it was the tone he had taken with all the previous Presidents who had turned to CURE to solve a problem. It had been written into the initial plans for CURE: a President could only suggest assignments, not order them. This was to prevent CURE from ever becoming a controlled wing of the executive branch. There was only one presidential order that Smith would accept: disband CURE.

Smith had been abrupt for another reason too. Remo had not yet reported in after his last assignment against the Ravine Rapist on the airplane, but while checking the reports of the Lavallette assault, Smith had run across his name.

The police at the scene had dutifully taken down the name of everyone in the room where the automaker was shot.

And at the bottom of the list was printed the name of Remo Williams, photographer.

It was not the kind of name like Joe Smith or Bill Johnson that someone would just make up out of the air. Anyone who wrote down the name "Remo Williams" had to know Remo Williams . . . or be Remo Williams.

And no one knew Remo Williams.

Smith shook his head and drank some more Maalox. The conclusion was inescapable. For some reason, Remo was free-lancing and it was time for Smith to act.

6

"I say we leave," said Lawrence Templey Johnson.

He was a big, bluff man, the kind who ran wild in America's corporate boardrooms. Even with his suit reduced to cutoff pants and his white shirt a rag, his take-charge manner clung to him like a stale odor.

"I say we stay," said Remo quietly. "So we stay. End of discussion."

It was turning cold now on the desert. The sunbaked sand had given up the last of its stored heat, and now the chill was setting into everyone's bones.

"Why?" demanded Lawrence Templey Johnson. "I want to know why."

Remo was looking at a woman's broken arm. Lorna had put on a splint, but the woman was still in deep pain.

Remo took the woman's shattered arm in his fingers and gently kneaded the flesh from wrist to elbow, not sure of what to do, but growing more confident as he worked the arm.

He could sense the breaks. Three of them, all below the elbow, and the broken pieces of bone had not been aligned correctly.

"I want to know why," Johnson repeated. He was using a foot-high rock near the hull of the burned-out jetcraft as a soapbox and he sounded like a politician in training. He was starting to get on Remo's nerves.

"How does it feel now?" Remo asked the woman.

"A little better. I think."

Remo suddenly squeezed and the woman gasped, but when the first shock subsided, both she and Remo knew the bones had been properly aligned. Remo massaged a nerve in her neck to ease the dull healing pain that would come later.

"Thank you," the woman said.

"I'm talking to you," said Lawrence Templey Johnson. "How dare you ignore me? Who do you think you are?" He looked around at the survivors, who sat, dully, on the sand near the plane. "Look at him," he told them. "Look how he's dressed. He's a nobody. He probably fixes cars for a living. I'm taking charge here and I say we're leaving."

Remo stood and casually brushed sand off the legs of his chino pants.

"We're staying because it's just a matter of time before the rescue planes come," Remo said. "If we start wandering around this desert, we might never be found."

"We've been waiting hours for these so-called rescue planes," the other man snapped. "I say we leave."

"I say we stay," Remo said coldly.

"Who appointed you cock of the walk? Let's put it to a vote," said Johnson, who had visions of a Hollywood movie chronicling how he had led his stranded fellow passengers out of the desert. Starring Roger Moore as Lawrence Templey Johnson. He would have preferred David Niven but David Niven was dead. "We'll vote. This is a democracy."

"No," said Remo. "It's a desert. And anybody who wanders out into it is going to die."

"We'll see about that." Johnson raised his voice. "Everybody in favor of getting out of here, say 'Aye.' "

No one said "Aye." They voted with their rear ends, keeping them firmly planted in the sand.

"Fools," Johnson snapped. "Well, I'm going."

"I'm sorry. I can't let you do that," Remo said.

"Why not?"

"Because I promised myself we'd all get out of here alive. I'm not going to let you become buzzard bait."

Johnson jumped off the small rock and marched toward Remo. He poked him in the chest with his index finger. "You're going to have to get a lot bigger real quick if you think you're going to stop me."

"Say good night, Johnson," Remo mumbled. And mumbled an answer to himself: "Good night Johnson." And pressed his right hand into the bigger man's throat, squeezed for a moment, then caught him as he crumpled and laid him on the sand next to the plane.

"He's not hurt, is he?" Lorna asked.

Remo shook his head. "Just asleep." He looked around at the other crash survivors, who were watching him. "He'll be okay, folks. Meantime, I think all of you ought to move closer together to try to keep each other warm. Just until the rescuers get here."

"They're really coming?" the little girl asked.

"Yes," Remo said. "I promise."

"Good. Then I'm going to sleep."

Later, with the stars wheeling in the ebony sky above their heads, Remo and Lorna slipped away from the others.

"You've never told me your last name," she said, as she took his arm.

"I don't have one," Remo said. He sat on a slightly elevated dune and the young woman moved down lightly beside him.

"I thought you were a real wiseass back on the plane, even if I was attracted to you. But I was wrong. You're no wiscass."

"Don't get too close to me," he said.

"What?"

He took a long look at a big moon, perched atop a spire,

miles away. It looked like a futuristic desert lamp. The wind blew a fine sand spray off the tops of the small dunes. The sand hissed.

"When the rescue planes come, I'm leaving. My own way. I'd appreciate it if you'd just not even mention me," he said.

"But you're the one who saved everybody. You got them out of the plane. You've taken care of them since then. That little girl . . . she adores you."

"Yeah. Swell. But I'm still vanishing when the planes come, so just forget about me."

"Why? Are you a criminal or something?"

"Not a criminal, but something," Remo said. "You know, I never had a family. This is the first time I ever felt I belonged with people." He laughed bitterly. "And it took a plane crash to make it happen."

"It happened though," she said.

"When do you think the planes will come for us?" he said.

"Soon," she answered. "I'm surprised they haven't arrived by now."

She put her hands to his face. "But we have a little while, don't we?" she asked quietly.

"We do," he said and brought Lorna down to the sand with him. Their lips met first, hungry and sad. Remo reached for her right wrist instinctively, ready to begin the slow finger massage that was the first of the thirty-seven steps of the Sinanju love technique.

Then he remembered how it had always been with Sinanju love techniques.

"Hell with it," he mumbled and he just took her. Their bodies joined pleasurably, unrhythmically. Each time one of them came to a peak, the other slid off it. It was long, elemental, sometimes frustrating, but natural, and when the peak did come, it came to both of them at once.

And that made it worth all the effort in the world, Remo thought.

She fell asleep in his arms and Remo looked at the sky, knowing their first time together was also their last.

The telephone had been ringing, on and off, for hours but Chiun had declined to answer it. It was probably Remo calling and if Chiun answered it and then asked him had Remo yet spoken to Nellie Wilson, Remo would have some lame excuse about how he had been too busy, and it would all just annoy Chiun, the way Remo always did. And it was also good to let Remo wait awhile, lest he develop the habit of telephoning and expecting Chiun to answer immediately, like a servant.

Three hours of intermittent telephone ringing seemed like enough punishment to Chiun so he went to the telephone in the corner of the hotel room, lifted the receiver, and said slowly, "Who is speaking?"

The receiver crackled and hissed in his ear.

"Who is there? Who is there?"

More crackling and hissing and Chiun said, "Fool device."

"Chiun, this is Smith," came the voice.

"Emperor Smith. I thought you were Remo."

"Why?" asked Smith sharply. "Have you heard from Remo?"

"No, but I expect him to call at any moment."

You don't know where he is either?" Smith asked.

"I have not heard from him," Chiun said.

"Chiun, I have a report that indicates Remo may be in Detroit. He is trying to kill America's top automobile executives."

"Good," Chiun said. "At least he is working."

"No. You don't understand. He's not on assignment."

"He is practicing then," Chiun said. "That is almost as good."

"Chiun, I think he's free-lancing for someone else."

"Strange," Chiun said under his breath. Louder, he said, "He is perhaps trying to earn extra money to donate to the impoverished of Sinanju. That would be nice.''

"We have to stop him,'' Smith said.

"What do you have against the poor of Sinanju?'' Chiun asked.

"Listen to me, Master of Sinanju. Remo is running amok in Detroit, I think. He may be on the other side.''

Chiun spat. "There is no other side. There is only Sinanju.''

"He shot a man today.''

"Shot?''

"With a gun,'' said Smith.

"Aiiiieeee,'' wailed Chiun.

"Now you understand the gravity of the situation,'' Smith said.

"A gun,'' said Chiun. "To profane Sinanju with a mechanical weapon. It is not possible. Remo would not dare.''

"Someone shot the president of Dynacar Industries earlier today. People took a list of names of everyone there, and Remo's name was on the list.''

"There is your proof that you are mistaken,'' Chiun said. "Remo cannot even write his own name.''

"Chiun, you have to go to Detroit. If Remo shows up and is free-lancing, you have to stop him.''

"This is outside our contracted agreements,'' Chiun said.

"We'll talk about that later. I'm sending a car for you and I've booked you on a flight in an hour.''

"Outside our contract,'' Chiun repeated.

"We'll worry about that later,'' Smith said.

"Earlier we had discussed some land,'' Chiun said.

"Forget Disneyland. If Remo's acting on his own, you have to stop him. That's in the contract. And then there won't be any more contracts.''

"Very well. I will go. But I tell you that Remo would never use a gun or any boom thing.''

"When you get there, you can see if that's right or not," Smith said. "This would-be killer has threatened the heads of all the major auto companies."

"Then who will I guard?" Chiun asked. "How do I choose?"

"Today, the gunman tried to get Lyle Lavallette. He's a very high-profile automaker. Always in the press. It may be logical that his next target will be Drake Mangan, the head of National Autos. He's just written a book and he's on a lot of television shows. If Remo or whoever it is is trying to make a publicity splash, Mangan might be next on the list."

"I will go see this Mangan and I will bring you this impostor's head, so you can apologize to both Remo and me for your error. Good-bye."

Chiun slammed down the telephone, cracking the receiver and sending internal parts flying like popping corn.

Working for a white was bad enough but working for a white lunatic was worse. Still, what if Smith were right? What if something had happened and Remo was working on his own?

Chin looked across the room at his thirteen steamer trunks. He decided he would pack light. He would not be in Detroit for long. Just six steamer trunks.

7

Drake Mangan had become the head of the huge National Auto Company the old-fashioned way: he had married into it.

Since the beginning of the auto industry, the Cranston family—beginning with Jethro Cranston, who hooked a steam engine onto a horseless carriage back in 1898—had spearheaded virtually every major development that ran on rubber tires. When old Jethro had died, his son Grant took over and Cranston went international. And when the next son, Brant, took over, everyone knew the future of Cranston Motors was assured for at least another generation. A drunk driver in a Ford pickup changed all that when he plowed into Brant Cranston's limousine at a stop sign in 1959.

Control of the company fell then into the somewhat shaky hands of the sole surviving Cranston, Myra. At the time, Myra was twenty-two, spoiled, and on her way to earning a black belt in social drinking. Drake Mangan was her boyfriend.

They had been in a restaurant overlooking the Detroit River when the bad news came. Drake Mangan had picked the restaurant, whose wines were the priciest in the city, to break the bad news that he was calling it quits after eight

months of dating Myra and not getting to first base. He
waited until Myra had gone through two bottles of Bor-
deaux before broaching the subject. He hoped she was
drunk enough not to throw a tantrum because her tantrums
were famous.

"Myra, I have something very important to tell you,"
Mangan began. He was an impressive man of thirty, although
his hooded dark eyes and aquiline nose made him look a
solid ten years older. He was chief comptroller at Cranston
Motors and had been attracted to Myra solely because she
was the boss's daughter. But even that enticement had
worn thin after eight months of dating the woman Detroit
society had nicknamed the Iron Virgin.

Myra giggled. Her eyes shone with giddy alcoholic
light.

"Yesh, Drake."

"We've been together for almost a year now—"

"Eight months, " Myra corrected, lifting her glass in a
toast. "Eight looooooong months."

"Yes. And there comes a time in every relationship
when it either grows or dies. And I think that in the case of
ours, it has—"

At that moment, a pair of uniformed police officers
came to their table, their faces so solemnly set that they
might have been a pair of walking bookends.

"Miss Cranston?" one of them said. "I regret to inform
you that there's been a terrible tragedy in your family.
Your brother is . . . gone."

Myra looked at the officer through an uncomprehending
alcoholic haze.

"Gone," she said. "Gone where?"

The officers looked even more uncomfortable. "What I
mean to say, Miss Cranston, is that he is deceased. I'm
sorry."

"I don't understand," said Myra Cranston truthfully.
She gave a little bubbly hiccup at that point.

Drake Mangan understood. He understood perfectly. He

handed each officer a twenty-dollar bill and said, "Thank you both very much. I think I should handle this."

The officers were happy to comply and walked quickly from the restaurant.

"What was that all about?" asked Myra, filling another pair of wineglasses. She had red wine on the right and white wine on the left. She liked to drink them alternately. Sometimes she mixed them. Once she had mixed them in a saucer and sipped from it.

"I'll explain later, darling," Mangan said.

"First time you ever called me darling," Myra said with a giggle.

"That's because I've made a discovery," Drake Mangan said, summoning up all the sincerity he could muster. "I love you, Myra."

"You do?" She hiccuped.

"Passionately. And I want to marry you." He took her clammy blotched-skin hand in his. "Will you marry me, dearest?" He felt like throwing up but business was business.

"This is so sudden."

"I can't wait. Let's get married tonight. We'll find a justice of the peace."

"Tonight? With my brother gone? He'd want to be there."

"He'll understand. Come on, let's get going."

The justice of the peace was reluctant.

"Are you sure you want to marry her?" he asked dubiously.

"Of course," said Mangan. "What's wrong with her?"

"Your intended can barely stand up."

"Then we'll have the ceremony sitting down. Here's the ring. Let's get on with it, man."

"Are you sure you wish to marry this man, miss?" the justice asked Myra.

Myra giggled. "My brother's gone but he won't mind."

The justice of the peace shrugged and performed the ceremony.

There was no honeymoon. Just a funeral for Brant Cranston. Even after the funeral, there had been no honeymoon, and now, almost thirty years later, Myra Cranston Mangan was still, as far as her husband knew, a virgin.

But Drake Mangan didn't care. He now had control of Cranston Motors and he kept control of it during all the buyouts and mergers and reorganizations that got rid of the classic old Big Three and created a new Big Three: General Autos, American Autos, and National Autos, which Mangan now headed.

President of National Autos. Drawing his million-dollar-a-year salary. It was all that mattered to Drake Mangan. Except, maybe someday, getting into his wife's pants. Just to see what it was like.

After the attempt on Lyle Lavallette's life, the police had offered him protection. He turned them down. He had declined to brief the FBI about his personal life and habits. "No one is going to try to kill me. Really," he said.

His wife in a sober moment suggested he hire extra bodyguards.

"I already have two bodyguards, which is two more than I need," he told her.

The two bodyguards were a pair of former Detroit Lions linebackers. Drake Mangan had hired them for two reasons: they were tax-deductible and he was a football fan and liked to hear their war stories over lunch. The rest of the time, he kept them cooling their heels in the first-floor lobby of the National Autos building while he held sway in his twelfth-floor office. They were nice guys but when they were bored, they had a tendency to play with their guns.

Which was why, when Drake Mangan heard gunshots drifting up from the lobby via the elevator shaft, he was only mildly interested. Certainly not surprised and definitely not afraid. Things like that happened, and sometimes several times in a slow week.

Nevertheless, Mangan ordered his executive secretary to call the lobby.

"Ask Security what's going on down there."

The secretary came back into his office almost immediately, looking worried.

"Mr. Mangan, there seems to be some trouble."

"What kind of trouble? Has one of those walking sides of beef shot himself in the foot again?"

"No, Mr. Mangan. One of them shot a security guard."

"Damn. Don't they know what that does to our insurance rates?"

The secretary shrugged and Mangan said, "Well, get them up here and let's see what's going on."

"I can't. They were shot too. By the other security guards."

"What the hell's going on down there?" he said. "How many people are shot? Who did you talk to?"

"I'm not sure. He had a funny little voice. Kind of squeaky, Oriental, maybe. He said he was the one they were shooting at."

"Anything else?"

"Yes, sir. He said he was on his way up."

"Up? Up here?"

"This is the only up I have any knowledge of, Mr. Mangan."

"Don't get smart. Get the police."

At that moment, the muted hum of the elevator rose to their floor.

"It's him," said Drake Mangan, looking for a place to hide.

The elevator doors purred open. A figure glided out and appeared in the office door.

Drake Mangan leveled an accusing finger at the figure.

"You! Assassin!" he shouted.

Chiun, Master of Sinanju, smiled at the rare display of recognition from a white man.

"I do not sign autographs," he said. He wore a peach

kimono tastefully trimmed in black. His hazel eyes were birdlike in their survey of the room. "I will need an office if I am to stay here," Chiun said. "This one will suffice."

"This is my office," Mangan said stonily.

"For a white, your taste is almost adequate," Chiun said.

"What did you do with my bodyguards?"

"Nothing," Chiun said, examining cut flowers on a long table. "They did it to themselves. I merely informed them that I was here as a personal emissary of their government and they refused to admit me. Then they began shooting one another. They were very excitable."

Mangan looked incredulous. "They shot one another trying to shoot you?"

Chiun shrugged expressively. "I would not call it real trying."

Mangan nodded to his secretary, who slipped back out into her reception area. A push-button telephone began beeping electronically.

"What did you say about the government?" Mangan asked in a loud voice, hoping it would drown out the sound of his secretary dialing for help.

Chiun looked up from the flowers and decided to ignore the telephoning.

"You are most fortunate," he said. "Ordinarily I am employed to protect the Constitution. Today, I am protecting you."

"Protecting me? From what?"

"From wrongful assassination, of course," Chiun said. "Is there any other kind?"

Chiun spat on the Oriental rug, which he recognized had been made in Iran. "Of course. Killing with guns is wrongful. Killing without payment is wrongful. Killing—"

"Who sent you?" interrupted Mangan when his secretary poked her head back into the office and gave him a thumbs-up sign. Good. Help was on the way. He just had to stall this old fool.

"I cannot say," whispered Chiun and pressed an index finger to his lips. "But he secretly rules this land on behalf of your President. Just do not tell anyone, or your government may fall."

"I see," said Mangan who did not see at all. Gingerly, he slipped into the padded leather chair behind his massive desk. It was a big substantial desk, excellent for ducking behind in the event of shooting, which Mangan expected momentarily.

"Perhaps then someday you may explain it to me," said Chiun. "Now. Down to business. Have you had any contact with anyone calling himself Remo Williams?"

"No. Who's Remo Williams?"

"Remo Williams is my pupil. He is Korean, like me. Possibly as much as one-sixteenth Korean. But there is another who is calling himself Remo Williams. This one means you harm and I am here to protect you from him."

"And you work for the President?"

"I work for no one," Chiun snapped. "I have a contract with the emperor. *He* works for the President." Chiun smiled. "But I'm sure the President knows I am here."

Just then, the elevator doors opened and four policemen ran into the office, guns drawn.

"Start shooting," Mangan yelled. "Everyone's expendable but me." As Chiun turned toward the door to the office, Mangan ran out, past his secretary's desk and into a small alcove, where he picked up a telephone.

Behind him, he heard one of the policemen say: "Now don't give us any trouble, old-timer, and you won't get hurt." He heard an answering chuckle.

"Let me talk to the President," Mangan said into the telephone.

The White House operator asked, "Is this an emergency, Mr. Mangan?"

"I'm a personal friend of the President's. I poured

seven figures' worth of corporate profits into his reelection. I don't need an excuse to talk to him."

"One moment, please, sir."

Mangan held the phone, expecting to hear shooting from inside his office. But there was nothing but silence.

In a few seconds, the President of the United States was on the line. "Good to hear from you, Drake. What's on your mind?"

"I have a situation here, Mr. President. I know this is going to sound wild but did you, by any remote chance, send some Chinaman here to protect my life?"

"Describe him."

"Maybe five feet tall, maybe eighty years old. Dressed in some kind of colored dress or something. He just trashed my entire security force."

"Good. Then he's on the job," the President said.

"Sir?"

"You can relax now, Drake. You're in good hands."

"Good hands? Mr. President, He's old and wrinkled."

"It hasn't stopped me," said the President. "I had him sent there to protect you."

"From what?"

"From the same nut who shot Lavallette," the President said. "We can't very well have all of Detroit's brains wiped out, can we?"

"We use a Chinaman for protection?"

"A Korean. Never call him Chinese," the President said. "I can't be responsible. Is the young fella there too?"

"The old man's alone," Mangan said.

"Well, one of them's enough," the President said. "Let me know how this all turns out. Regards to the wife. And by the way, I wouldn't mention any of this to anyone. I've already forgotten this conversation."

"I understand, Mr. President. I think."

Mangan dropped the receiver and ran back to his office. Christ, the old gook *was* from the President and Mangan had turned four Detroit cops loose on him. If he was dead already, how would Mangan explain it to the President?

Chiun was not dead. He was sitting calmly behind Mangan's desk. The four police officers lay in the center of the office carpet, all their wrists bound together with their own four sets of handcuffs.

They were writhing around on the floor, trying to get loose. Once of them saw him and yelled, "Mr. Mangan. Call for reinforcements."

Mangan shook his head. "That won't be necessary, men. Heh, heh. Just a case of mistaken identity. The old gentleman here is part of my security team."

"Then get us out of here," another policeman called.

Mangan dug into their pockets for the handcuff keys and freed them all, even though he did not like touching members of the proletariat.

"You sure this guy's all right?" one of the policemen asked Mangan. The officer was rubbing his wrists, trying to get circulation back into his fingers.

"Yes. He's okay. It was all my error," he said.

"You know we're going to have to file a report on this," the cop said.

Mangan smiled and said, "Maybe we can work something out."

In the hallway outside his office, he worked something out. The policemen would each be able to buy their next new cars at half-price. In return, they would just simply deal with the unfortunate shootings down in the lobby as accidental gunshots. And they would forget the old man.

He saw the policemen on to the elevator and then went back into his office.

"Err, Mr.—"

"Chiun. Master Chiun, not Mister."

"Master Chiun. I've checked you out. You are who you say you are."

"I could have told you that and saved us both a great deal of trouble," Chiun said petulantly.

"What's done is done. If you're here to protect me, what should I do?"

"Try not to get yourself killed," Chiun said.

The rescue helicopters came during the night. Remo was the first to hear them and he quietly woke Lorna from her sleep.

"The planes are on the way," he said.

"I don't hear them," she said.

"You will in a minute."

"Good. It'll be wonderful to get back to civilization," she said.

"Truth is, I'll sort of miss you all," Remo said.

"What do you mean?"

"This is where I get off," he said. "Last stop."

"You're not going back with us?" She paused; the first whirrings of the approaching helicopters were now faintly audible over the broad desert.

"No," Remo said. "People would ask too many questions."

"Where will you go?" she said. "This is the desert."

"I know, but trust me, I can find my way out. No problem at all."

"You can't do that."

"I have to. I just wanted to say good-bye to you. And ask a favor."

"Name it."

"Don't mention my name. You're the only one who knows it and if anybody mentions me, just don't mention my name. Let me just be a passenger who wandered off."

"You sure you want it this way?" she said.

"I do."

She threw herself into Remo's arms. "I won't ask you any questions," she said. "But you just be careful."

"I will. And take care of that little girl," Remo said. He squeezed the woman once, then turned and ran off across the sand, just as the rescue craft's light became visible a mile away across the desert.

Remo ran just until he was out of sight, then slowed down and began loping north at a casual pace. A few miles away, Remo climbed onto an outcropping of rock and looked back. Two giant helicopters were parked on the sand, next to the burned-out jetliner. He could see people being helped aboard the two craft. He nodded to himself, in satisfaction, and turned away again.

The sun was coming up off to his right, turning the dunes to rose color. Later, as the sun went higher, it bleached the sand white. It was late afternoon when the sand gave way to rock. Remo spent the time thinking. In a curious way, he already missed the scene of the aircraft wreck. He had been raised an orphan and had never had a family; they had looked up to him; they had relied on him. It was a strange, but a pleasant, feeling, and once again he pitied himself for all that he had missed, and would always miss, in his life.

"Ah, that's the biz, sweetheart," he growled to himself and started to run northward.

He found the town just after sunset and used a pay phone in the local tavern. No matter how small a town was, he thought, it had a tavern. Maybe that's what created towns; maybe somebody built a tavern and then a town grew up around it.

He dialed Chiun's hotel in New York but got no answer in the room. Then he dialed a special code. The call went through a number in East Moline, Illinois, was rerouted through a circuit in Iola, Wisconsin, and finally rang the telephone on the desk of Dr. Harold W. Smith.

"Yes?" Smith's lemony voice said.

"Smitty, it's me," Remo said. "I'm back."

There was a long silence.

"Smitty? What's the matter?" Remo said.

"Remo?" Smith said slowly. "Is Chiun with you?"

"No. I just called his number but he didn't answer. I thought you'd know where he is."

"I'm happy to hear from you, Remo," Smith said.

"Then why do you sound like you just got a call from your dead grandmother?"

"Are you still in Detroit?"

Remo looked at the receiver in his hand as if it were personally responsible for the stupid words coming through the earpiece.

"Detroit? What are you talking about? I'm in Utah."

"When did you arrive in Utah, Remo?"

"Yesterday, when my goddamn plane crashed in the desert. And stop talking to me like I'm Jack the Ripper, will you?"

At Folcroft Sanitarium, Smith keyed a one-word command into his terminal: TRACE.

The green letters blinked and a telephone number appeared almost instantly on the screen. Smith saw that it was a Utah area code. The computer also told him that Remo was calling from a pay phone.

"Hello. Smitty. Whistle if you hear me."

"I heard you, Remo," Smith said. "What was that about a plane crash?"

"My flight went down in some desert about eighty miles from here."

"Flight number?"

"Who cares about the freaking flight number? Listen, I just saved a planeload of people out in the desert. And I got out alive. Why are you being so annoying?"

Smith's computer, on command, began scrolling the facts of a Los Angeles–Salt Lake City flight that had disappeared the previous day.

"Did your flight originate in Los Angeles?"

"Of course. I did that guy, the way you wanted, and then I got out of there on another plane right away."

"And you haven't been in Detroit?"

"Why would I be in Detroit? I buy Japanese."

"Remo, I think it would be best if you returned to Folcroft right away."

"You sound like you want to stick me in a rubber room," Remo said.

"You should be debriefed on your experience."

"Debrief this. I was in the desert and it was hot and everybody's safe and I planted the skyjacker in the sand and that's that. End of debriefing."

"Don't get upset. It's just that I wanted to talk to you."

"Where's Chiun? Talk about that."

"He's away," Smith said.

"He didn't go back to Sinanju again, did he?"

"No."

"He's where, Smitty? Where is he?"

"He's on an errand," Smith said.

"An errand? Chiun wouldn't do an errand for the Shah of Iran if he came back to life. Is he on assignment?"

Smith hesitated a moment. "Something like that."

"Where is he?"

"I can't really tell you that. Now if you'll just—"

"Smitty," said Remo, "I'm going to hang up. But before I go I want you to listen carefully."

"Yes?" said Smith, leaning into the phone.

In Utah, Remo brought the palm of his hand to the telephone speaker with such force that the receiver snapped into pieces.

Smith howled in pain but he howled into a dead telephone. Remo was gone.

8

The black car pulled up so silently that he did not hear it coming.

The tinted window on the driver's side opened just a crack. He could not see the driver.

The gunman with the scar down the right side of his jaw stepped from his own car and walked over to the other vehicle. Every window, even the windshield, was tinted so dark that in the weak light of the underground garage on the Canadian side of the Detroit River, he could not see the driver, except as a deep shadow in the deeper darkness of the car's interior.

"Williams?" the invisible driver asked.

"Call me Remo," the gunman said. "Nice car. Never saw one like it."

"I'd be surprised if you had. It's Lavallette's big surprise, the Dynacar. I stole it."

An envelope was pushed out the crack of the car window.

"Here. I'm paying you for the Lavallette hit. I want Mangan taken out next. There's an address in the envelope. It's a woman Mangan visits every Thursday night. You can get him there."

"I haven't got Lavallette yet," the gunman said.

"You did fine. Follow the plan and take them in the

order I give you. There's plenty of time to get Lavallette at the end of this. I don't mind if he's sweating a little bit."

"I could have finished him at the news conference," the gunman said. "I had time."

"You did right. I told you no head shots and you followed instructions. I want them all looking good for their funerals. It's not anybody's fault that Lavallette was wearing a bulletproof vest."

"I've got a reputation to live up to," the gunman said. "When I clip a guy, I don't like him planning press conferences later."

"We follow the plan. Take them in order. And no head shots."

The gunman counted the money in the envelope, then shrugged. "It's your show," he said. "That letter to the paper. Was that your idea?"

The unseen driver said softly, "Yes. I thought we could raise a little smoke screen. It might make things a little tougher for you though."

"How's that?" the gunman said.

"They might be expecting you. Probably more security."

The gunman shook his head. "None of it matters to me."

"I love dealing with professionals," the driver said. "Now get Mangan."

The tinted window sealed automatically and without any engine sound at all, the sporty black car slid up the garage ramp and out toward the street, like a fleet ghost.

The gunman who called himself Remo Williams got into his car and waited as he had been instructed to do.

It was a flaky contract and he did not like flaky contracts. They were unprofessional. He would have preferred a clean hit on a boat somewhere or under an overpass at night. Strictly business. This deal smelled too much like a personal vendetta.

He checked his watch. Five minutes had passed and he started his car and drove from the garage. There was no

sense in spooking the client. By now he would be far
enough away. A good professional watched. out for the
details. The details were everything. It would just be bad
form to leave the garage right on his tail and two minutes
later find yourself stopped next to him at a traffic light.
Things like that made clients nervous.

The gunman had no curiosity at all to know the name of
the man who had hired him to flatten four of Detroit's
biggest wheels.

He did not, for a moment, believe that the client was
some environmentalist nut who wanted the automakers
dead because they were polluting the air. His bet would be
that it was some kind of business rivalry, but it didn't
matter. Not so long as he was being paid.

It was the business of not being able to shoot any of
them in the head that bothered him the most. The client
should have known that head shots were the most certain.
You could shoot a guy all afternoon in the chest and he
might not die.

The gunman had seen it himself, firsthand. It had been
his first contract. The target was named Anthony "Big
Nose" Senaro, a mastodon of a man who had cut into the
don's numbers business in Brooklyn. Senaro had gotten
word he was about to be hit and skipped to Chicago.

The gunman had found him there, working as a laborer
in the stockyards. He waited until Senaro was eating lunch
one day, walked up to him and fired three shots into Big
Nose's massive chest. Big Nose had let out a bull roar and
charged him.

He had fired his full clip at Senaro. There was blood
everywhere but the big guy kept on coming, like a refrigerator on casters.

The gunman ran and for an hour, Senaro had chased
him around the stockyard. Finally Senaro cornered him,
put his big fingers around the gunman's throat, and began
to squeeze. Just as the gunman was about to black out,
Senaro gave a mighty sigh and collapsed from loss of blood.

The gunman scrambled away, losing a shoe to Big Nose's clutching hands. He never finished the hit. And Senaro eventually recuperated and went on to make a name for himself in Chicago.

The don had been understanding of the gunman's failure.

"It is always difficult," Don Pietro had told him, "the first time, eh? The first time for everything is always an unhappy time."

"I will get him next time," the gunman had assured Don Pietro, even though his stomach quaked at the thought of facing the big man again.

"There will be no next time. Not for you and Big Nose. You are both lucky to live. Big Nose will not return to bother us but he has earned his life. And you, you have earned our respect. We will have much work for you."

The other hits had gone down better. The gunman had made a name for himself too. Using head shots. That one restriction still bothered him. It was unprofessional.

But the client was always right.

At least for the time being.

Drake Mangan was on a conference telephone call with James Revell, president of the General Auto Company, and Hubert Millis, head of American Autos.

"What are we going to do?" Revell said. "That lunatic Lavallette has rescheduled his press conference for tomorrow and we're all invited. Do we go?"

Millis said, "We've got to. We can't look like we're afraid of Lavallette and his damned mystery car. Freaking thing probably won't start anyway."

"I don't know," Mangan said. "I'm afraid someone will start pegging shots at us."

"The security people will take care of that," Millis said. "You know what sticks in my craw?"

"What's that?" said Mangan.

"At one time or another, Lavallette worked for all of us and every one of us fired him," Millis said.

"Damned right. The guy said to take the fins off the Cadillacs," Revell said. "A damned moron. He deserved firing."

"No," said Millis. "We shouldn't have fired him. We should have killed the son of a bitch. Then we wouldn't be having all this grief."

Mangan chuckled. "Maybe it's not too late," he said. "It's agreed then. Tomorrow, we'll all be at Lavallette's press conference."

The other two men agreed and Mangan disconnected his conference call.

He'd go, but he'd be damned if he'd go without the old Oriental. If the President of the United States said that the old gook could protect Mangan, well, that was good enough for Drake Mangan. What's-his-name . . . Chiun could accompany him anywhere.

Except where he was going tonight.

The old maniac had a way with labor relations, though. Drake Mangan had to admit that.

After Mangan had evacuated the office, Chiun had decided he wanted something painted on the door. He had the secretary send up the head of the auto-body-painting division.

The door was open and Mangan heard the conversation from outside, near his secretary's desk.

"You will paint a new sign on the door," Chiun had said.

"I don't paint doors," the division head had said.

"Hold. You are a painter, are you not?" Chiun had said.

"Yes. I'm in charge of body finish on cars."

"This will be much easier than painting a car," Chiun had said.

The division head snapped, "No. Never. I don't paint doors."

"And who has given you these instructions?" Chiun asked.

"The union. I don't paint doors."

"Those instructions are no longer operative," Chiun had said. "You are now in charge of painting doors for me. Starting with this one."

"Who says? Who the hell are you anyway?"

"I am Chiun."

"I am leaving," the division head said. "The union's going to hear about this."

From his spot outside, Mangan heard a muffled sound. He craned his neck and peered through the door. The old Oriental had the division chief by the earlobe.

"I would like gold paint," he had said.

"Yes, sir. Yes, sir," the man had said. "I'll be right back with the paint."

"Five minutes," Chiun had said. "If you do not return in five minutes, I will come looking for you. You will not like that."

The division head had scurried from the office. When the elevator did not answer immediately to the button, he went running down the stairs.

Drake Mangan was impressed. Twisting ears. He had never tried that in dealing with the auto union. It was never too late to learn new things in the complicated field of labor relations.

Now the door to the office that Chiun had commandeered was closed. The division head knelt on the floor in front of it, painting the last few letters of the legend Chiun had given him.

It read: "HIS AWESOME MAGNIFICENCE."

Mangan guessed Chiun would not come out until the painting was done, so he ran over and pressed the elevator button.

"Leaving, Mr. Mangan? I'll tell Master Chiun."

"No. Don't do that."

"But he's your bodyguard."

"Not tonight. I have a very important appointment tonight. Tell him I'll see him first thing in the morning."

The elevator door opened and as soon as Mangan stepped inside, his secretary hit the intercom button.

"Master Chiun, Mr. Mangan has just left. I thought you should know."

Chiun opened the door. He paused to read the almost-finished sign on the door, then patted the painter on the head.

"You do reasonably good work," he said. "For a white. I will keep you in mind if I have other tasks to perform."

"Okay, okay. Just no more ear-twisting, all right?"

"As long as you behave," Chiun said. "Don't forget to put stars under the words. I like stars."

"You've got stars. Count on it. You've got stars."

Drake Mangan parked in front of the high-rise apartment building near St. Clair Shores, as he had almost every Thursday night since he had been married.

He rode the elevator up to the penthouse apartment he rented for his mistress. Over the years, the mistresses had changed but Mangan had kept the same apartment. He chalked it up to tradition. In his heart, he told himself, he was just a traditional sort of man.

He shut the apartment door behind him with the heel of his shoe and called out, "Agatha?" The penthouse was decorated in the worst possible taste, down to zebra-striped furniture and black velvet paintings of clowns on the wall, but the softly lit atmosphere was redolent of Agatha's favorite perfume, a musky scent that even smelled lewd. Just sniffing it made the cares of the day fall away like dead skin and Mangan could feel the juices stirring deep inside his body.

"Agatha. Daddy's home."

There was no answer.

"Where are you, baby?"

He shucked off his topcoat and draped it over one of the offending black-and-white sofas. The door to the bedroom was open a crack and a warm light, softer than candlelight, seeped out.

She was in the bedroom. Great. No sense wasting half the evening in small talk. He could get small talk at home. It was the only thing he ever did get at home.

"Warming up the bed for me, Agatha?" He pushed the door open.

"There you are. Come to Papa."

But Agatha did not rise from the bed. She lay on her back, dressed in red silk pajamas, staring at the ceiling. One arm was casually tucked under her wealth of blond hair. A leg hung off over the edge of the bed.

She looked like she was watching the fly that buzzed her generous chest.

But she wasn't. Mangan knew that when he saw the fly alight on the tip of her long nose. She didn't twitch. She didn't even blink.

He stepped forward and said, softly, "Agatha?"

The door slammed shut behind him. Before he turned, Mangan finally saw the hole in the red silk of Agatha's pajama top. It looked like a cigarette burn hole but the center was the livid color of raw meat and he saw a deeper red splotch surrounding it, deeper even than the red of the silk.

The man who had slammed shut the door behind him was tall and lean, with a long scar down the right side of his jaw. In one of his gloved hands he carried a black pistol, its long barrel pointing directly at Mangan's chest. The automaker's heart started beating high in his throat, and he felt as if it were going to choke him.

"Who the hell are you? What's going on here?" Mangan snapped.

The man with the scar smiled a cruel smile.

"You can call me Remo. Sorry I had to ditch the girlfriend but she wouldn't cooperate. Kept trying to call the police."

"I don't even know you. Why are you . . . why did . . . ?"

The gunman shrugged. "It's nothing personal, Mangan. You're just a name on a list."

Slowly his finger tightened on the trigger. Mangan could not stop staring at the barrel. His mouth worked, but no sound came out.

There was a sudden screech, loud, unearthly, like a high-speed diamond drill scoring glass. It was followed by a shattering of glass that turned both the gunman's and Mangan's heads as if they were attached to a single yanking string.

Entering through a perfectly circular hole cut in the window with a long fingernail came Chiun, Master of Sinanju, a cold light in his eyes.

"It's him, Chiun," cried Drake Mangan. "The assassin. Remo Williams."

"Wrong both times," said Chiun. He looked at the gunman and said, "Lay down your weapon and you may win a painless death."

The gunman laughed, turned his pistol on the frail Oriental, and fired twice.

The bullets shattered what was left of the window behind Chiun. He had not seemed to move, yet the bullets missed him, somehow striking points that were on a direct line behind him.

The gunman took his pistol in both hands and dropped into a marksman's crouch. He sighted carefully. The little man did not even flinch. The gunman fired.

A section of the wall cracked and still the Oriental stood immobile.

Another shot and the same result. But this time, the gunman thought he saw a faint afterimage of the old Oriental, as if he had moved to one side and returned to his place in the quicksilver interval between the time the bullet left the gun barrel and the moment it buried itself in the wall.

"This is crazy," the gunman said. And then the Oriental was coming at him. It was the Big Nose Senaro hit all over again.

Drake Mangan had fallen back onto the bed to watch but now as Chiun advanced across the room, he saw his chance to make headlines: "AUTO MOGUL CAPTURES CRAZED GUNMAN; DRAKE MANGAN DISARMS ASSASSIN."

It would be great new material for the paperback edition of his autobiography when it came out.

He saw the gunman's eyes were fixed on Chiun. He got to his feet, then lunged across the floor at the man with the pistol.

"No!" Chiun shouted, but it was too late. Mangan was already in motion. The gunman wheeled toward him and squeezed the trigger, even as Chiun was trying to move between gunman and target.

The president of National Autos was hit and knocked back onto the bed by the impact. But there was no hole in his chest and Mangan groaned.

Another bulletproof vest, the gunman thought, and swiveled his pistol back on the advancing Oriental. But the old man was not advancing anymore. He was lying facedown on the floor.

The gunman saw the gleam of blood in the fringe of hair over the Oriental's ear. A ricochet. A one-in-a-million shot. The bullet had bounced off Mangan and struck the old man in the head.

The gunman laughed in relief.

On the bed, Mangan groaned atop the body of his dead mistress.

"Now for you." The gunman grabbed him by his lapel. The fabric felt stiff under his fingers.

A Kevlar suit. That explained it. The man had taken the precaution of wearing a bullet-resistant business suit. A lot of politicians were wearing them these days because they were light and reasonably comfortable, but could deflect anything short of a Teflon-coated bullet.

"What are you doing?" Mangan said when the gunman started to pull at his tie.

"They used to do it like this back in the old days.

They'd take a guy out to a secluded spot and open up his shirt before they whacked him. It used to be a tradition and I'm just bringing it back.''

The gunman ripped open Mangan's shirt buttons and tore a hole in his undershirt. Then he put the muzzle of the pistol to bare skin, held the struggling man down with an arm across his clavicle, and fired a single heart-stopping round.

Drake Mangan jerked like a man who'd touched a live wire, then his body relaxed.

The gunman stood up and told the corpse, "I would have preferred giving you a head shot.''

Then he quietly left the penthouse, waiting until he reached the stairs before holstering his pistol and stripping off his gloves. He took his time. It was a long walk to the street but he had all the time in the world.

He wondered if he would get a bonus for the old Oriental.

Probably not. He was probably just some overpriced kung-fu guy Mangan had hired to bodyguard him. Those guys were a dime a dozen.

9

"I still can't figure out what made the earpiece explode like that," the telephone repairman said.

"It's fixed now?" Smith asked.

"Yes. I've just got to clean up around here and I'm done."

"You're done now. I'll clean up," Smith said.

The repairman smiled. "No. We have to clean up. Part of the total service package offered by American Telephone and Northeast Bell Communications Nynex and Telegraph Consolidated Incorporated. That's the name of the new company."

"Very interesting," Smith said. The telephone rang. He walked the repairman to the office door and pushed him outside. "Thank you very much."

"I wanted to clean up."

"I'll do it. Good-bye."

Smith locked the door and ran back to the telephone.

"Hail, Emperor Smith," said Chiun.

"We must have a bad connection," Smith said. "Your voice sounds weak."

"It is a minor thing," said Chiun. "I will soon recover."

"Recover from what?"

"From the shame," Chiun said.

Smith gripped the receiver more tightly. The earpiece that the repairman had just installed was loose against his ear. He twisted it tight.

"I'm sure you will recover from the shame," he said, sensing another of Chiun's con games coming on.

"The shame of this indignity," said Chiun as if Smith had asked him for an explanation. "I am only happy that the Master who trained me did not live to see this. I would hang my head before him; his remonstrances would scourge my soul."

Smith sighed. "What shame is that?" he said. There would be no talking to Chiun until the old Oriental had gone through his full song and dance.

"In times past, Masters of Sinanju have been called upon to preserve the lives of certain personages. Kings, emperors, sultans. There was even a pharaoh of Egypt who came under the protection of a Master of Sinanju when that pharaoh ascended his throne. He was but six summers of age but the Master who protected him saw him rule until his ninety-sixth birthday. It is recorded as the longest reign in history and it would never have happened without Sinanju at his side. Now *that* was a trust of honor. Would that the current Master had such an illustrious charge."

Smith tensed. "Is something wrong?" he asked.

"But not Chiun," the sorrowful voice continued. "Chiun is not given kings to guard. Not even a lowly prince. Or a pretender. I could hold my head high if I were charged with guarding a pretender to a worthy throne."

"Did something happen to Drake Mangan? Is he all right?"

"Instead, I have been given a fat white merchant, a merchant whose life is not even important to his loved ones. How can one do one's best work when one is asked to work at such an unworthy task? I ask you. How?"

"Is Mangan dead?" demanded Smith.

"Pah!" spat Chiun. "He was born dead. All his life, he

lived a living death, eating and drinking poisons that increased his deadness. If he is more dead now, it is merely in degree. The only difference between a living dead white man and a dead dead white man is that the latter does not bray. Although he does still smell.''

''What happened?'' Smith asked wearily.

Chiun's voice swelled. ''A terrible creature descended upon him. Huge he was, his bigness as that of a house. A veritable giant. But the Master of Sinanju did not fear this apparition, this giant whose enormity rivaled that of a great temple. The Master of Sinanju moved forward to confront him, but it was already too late. The fat white merchant who was already dead before Sinanju ever heard of him, became still.''

''All right,'' Smith said. ''He got Mangan.''

''No,'' said Chiun. ''His weapon did. These guns are a menace, Emperor. Perhaps it is time that laws were passed.''

''We'll discuss it later,'' said Smith. ''He got Mangan. But you got him, is that correct?''

Chiun hesitated before answering.

''Not precisely correct.''

''What does that mean?'' demanded Smith, who had seen the seemingly frail Master of Sinanju rip through a squadron of armed soldiers like a hurricane through a cornfield.

''It means what it means,'' said Chiun haughtily. ''The Master of Sinanju is never vague.''

''All right, all right. He got away. Somehow he got away from you. But you saw him. It wasn't Remo?''

''Yes and no,'' Chiun said.

''I'm glad you're never vague,'' Smith said dryly. ''Either it was or it wasn't Remo. Which was it?''

Chiun's voice dropped into a conspiratorial whisper. ''He gave his name. It was most strange. Amateurs seldom appreciate the value of advertising. But this one gave his name.''

''Yes?''

"He said his name was Remo Williams. But he was not the Remo Williams we know. Why would he lie?"

Smith quickly brought the CURE computer system on line and began keying a search sequence.

"Maybe it wasn't all a lie," Smith said. He typed in the name REMO WILLIAMS and hit the control button. The search program was initiated, working with a speed that would have astonished the operators of the Pentagon's "number-crunching" supercomputers; all possible public records in America were scanned for the name of Remo Williams. When Remo had been recruited to work for CURE many years ago, all files on him had been deleted. If there were now any references to a Remo Williams, it would indicate an impostor was using his name.

"Describe the man," Smith asked Chiun, activating an auxiliary computer file on which to record the description.

"He was pale, like a white, and too tall, with big clumsy feet, like a white. And like most whites, he had coarse hairs growing from his chin."

"A beard?"

"No. Not like mine. I have a beard. This white thing had hair ends growing from his face."

Smith keyed the fact that the killer had needed a shave.

"Age?" asked Smith as he watched the search program run on the split screen. Millions of records, glowing an electronic green, scrolled past his eyes in a blur. It hurt to look at the running program and his fingers poised to record the answer to his question.

"He is no more than fifty-five winters, perhaps less," Chiun said. "Do you know him now?"

"Master of Sinaju," said Smith slowly, "think carefully. Did this man look like Remo? Our Remo?"

There was a long silence over the line before the Master of Sinanju replied.

"Who can say? All whites look alike. "Wait. He had a scar on his face, along the right side of the jaw. Our Remo has no such scar."

But Smith could tell from the tremor in Chiun's voice that the Master of Sinanju was thinking the same thing that he was, thinking that the one eventuality that the people who had originated CURE had never foreseen, finally had come about.

"Could this shooter of guns be Remo's father?" asked Chiun. "Is that what you are thinking?"

The search file stopped running before Smith could answer. The computer screen flashed: NO FILE FOUND . . . PRESS: ESCAPE KEY.

Smith hit the escape key and brought up Remo's original CURE file.

"At fifty-five, the man would be the right age. But he couldn't be. Remo is supposed to be an orphan. He has no known living relatives of any description."

"Everyone has relatives," said Chiun, thinking of his wicked brother-in-law, now dead. "Whether they want them or not."

"Remo was an infant when the nuns found him on the doorstep of St. Theresa's Orphanage," said Smith, skimming the Remo file. "It's not clear who named him. Perhaps they found a note with the baby or the nuns named him. The records that might have told us—if they ever even existed—were destroyed in a fire years before Remo joined CURE. St. Theresa's is long gone, too."

"Remo must never learn of this," Chiun said.

"Agreed," said Smith, looking away from the file. Sometimes it bothered him to read it. He had done a terrible thing to a young policeman once, and even though it was for a greater purpose, that didn't make it any less of a terrible thing.

"This man who calls himself Remo Williams is your assignment, Chiun. I expect you will carry it out."

"If this man carries the same blood as Remo, then I have as much to lose as you," Chiun said coldly. "More."

Smith nodded. He knew that Chiun saw Remo as the next Master of Sinanju, the heir of a tradition that went back to before the recording of history. It was one of the great conflicts in the arrangement between Smith and Chiun that each saw Remo as his own. Neither bothered to ask Remo what he thought.

"Good," said Smith. "I have heard from Remo, our Remo, but I have refused to tell him where you are. I will hold him off as long as I can and in the meantime, perhaps you can dispose of this matter."

"Consider it done, Emperor," Chiun said.

"The other two big car men are James Revell and Hubert Millis. They have announced that they will be at Lyle Lavallette's press conference tomorrow. If an attempt is to be made, it might be made there again."

"This killer's hours are numbered, O Emperor," said Chiun gravely. "You do not know where our Remo is?"

"He was in Utah. I expect he'll be coming here to find out where you are. I'll try to stall him until I have your assignment-completed call," Smith said.

"That will be fine," Chiun said and hung up.

Smith closed down Remo's file. Chiun would take care of this man who might or might not be Remo's father. And that would be the end of that and Remo would never know. Perhaps it was unjust but what was one more injustice on top of the others? When Remo Williams had become the Destroyer for CURE, he had lost all his rights, both natural and constitutional. Losing a father he never knew he had wouldn't really make much of a difference.

Remo Williams, the Destroyer, arrived in Detroit around midnight.

After Smith had refused to tell him where Chiun was, Remo had been at a loss until he remembered that Smith had mentioned Detroit. Mentioned it twice, in fact. Smith had thought Remo was calling from Detroit, and why would he have thought that?

There was only one good answer: Smith had jumped to

the conclusion that Remo was in Detroit because the CURE director knew that Chiun was already in Detroit.

That was simple and it annoyed Remo that Smith would not expect him to figure it out. The more he thought about it, the more annoyed he got and when he reached the Detroit airport, he went to the car-rental counter and asked for the most expensive car they had.

In his wallet, he found a credit card for Remo Cochran.

"I'm sorry, sir, but all our cars are the same rate," the clerk told him.

"Okay," Remo said. "Then I want four of them."

"Four?"

"That's right. I don't like to be seen in the same cheap car too long. It hurts my image."

"Well, is it just you?"

"Yes," Remo said. "Do I look like more than one?"

"No, sir. I was just wondering who will drive the other three cars."

"Nobody," Remo said. "I want them to sit here in the parking lot until I come back for them. Better make it a three-month rental on all four."

With discounts for long-term use and for Remo's excellent driving record, but adding in penalties for renting on a Friday which cost Remo the weekly special rate which was only good if your week started on Tuesday, and adding in the insurance which Remo insisted he wanted, the bill came to $7,461.20.

"You sure you want to do this, sir?" the clerk said.

"Yes," Remo said.

The clerk shrugged. "Well, it's your money."

"No, it's not," Remo said. Let Smith chew on that bill when he received it. "Where's your nearest phone?"

The clerk pointed to a booth three feet from Remo's left elbow.

"Didn't see it," Remo said. "Thanks."

"You want the numbers of every hotel in the city?" the information operator asked in a frightened voice.

"Just the best ones. He wouldn't stay anywhere except at the best hotels," Remo said.

"I'm sorry, sir. But making quality judgments on various hotels is not the policy of American Telephone and Greater Michigan Bell Consolidated Amalgamated Telephonic and Telegraphic Communications Incorporated."

"Gee, that's a shame," Remo said, "because now I'll just have to get the telephone numbers of every hotel in Detroit. Every hotel."

"Well, maybe you can try these," the operator said reluctantly. She gave Remo a half-dozen hotel numbers, and he started dialing.

"Hotel Prather," said the first hotel's switchboard.

"Do you have an elderly Oriental staying there? He probably arrived with a bunch of lacquered steamer trunks and gave the bellboys a hard time?"

"Under what name would he be registered?"

"I don't know. It could be anything from Mr. Park to His Most Awesome Magnificence. It depends on his mood."

"Really. You don't have his name?"

"Really," Remo said. "And exactly how many Orientals fitting that description do you think you have in the hotel?"

The switchboard operator checked. No such Oriental was staying at the Hotel Prather.

Remo asked the same questions of the next three hotels. His fifth call confirmed that an Oriental fitting that description was indeed staying at the Detroit Plaza and that the bell captain who had overseen the carrying of the gentleman's trunks up twenty-five flights of stairs, because the gentleman did not wish his luggage transported by elevators that might crash, was recovering nicely from his hernia operation. Did Remo wish to ring the old gentleman's room?

"No thanks," Remo said. "I want this to be a surprise."

Chiun's door was locked and Remo knocked on it twice. Chiun's voice filtered through the wood. "Who disturbs

me?'' he asked. "Who galoomphs down the hall like a
diseased yak and now pounds on my door interrupting my
meditation?''

Chiun knew very well who it was, Remo knew. The old
man had probably heard him when he got off the elevator a
hundred feet away and had recognized his footsteps on the
heavy commercial hallway carpet.

"You know damn well who it is," Remo said.

"Go away. I don't want any.''

"Open the damn door before I kick it in," Remo said.

Chiun unlocked the door but did not open it. When
Remo pushed it open, the old man was sitting on the floor,
his back to the door.

"Nice reception," Remo said. He looked around the
room. It was exactly what he expected, probably the
honeymoon suite. It looked perfect for starting a harem.

Chiun sniffed. That was his answer.

"Don't you want to know where I've been?" Remo
asked.

"No. It is enough that I know where you have not
been," Chiun said.

"Oh? Where have I not been?''

"You have not been seeing Nellie Wilson to arrange for
the Assassin Aid Concert. And here I have gone to all the
trouble of getting permission from that lunatic, Smith.''

"I didn't have time for Willie Nelson, Little Father,"
said Remo. "I was in a plane crash.''

"Paaah.'' Chiun waved a long-nailed hand over his
head in dismissal of such trifles.

"I realized something, Chiun.''

"There is always a first time for everything," Chiun
said.

"I finally understood what you mean when you say
feeding your village is not just a responsibility, but a
privilege too." He saw that Chiun was slowly turning
around to look at him. Remo said, "I helped save the
people on the plane. It was like they were family, my

family for a little while, and I think I know how you feel.''

"One cannot equate the survival of my very important village with saving the lives of a bunch of worthless fat white people,'' Chiun said.

"I know, I know, I know,'' Remo said. "I know all that. It was just that the idea was the same.''

"Well, perhaps you are not so hopeless as I thought,'' Chiun said and his hazel eyes softened. "Let me see your hands,'' he said suddenly.

"What for?''

Chiun clapped his hands together. The sound shook a nearby coffee table and rattled a window.

"Your hands, quickly.''

Remo extended his hands, palms up. Chiun took them and stared at them. His nose wrinkled.

"Want to check behind my ears too?'' Remo asked.

"You have fired no guns recently,'' Chiun said.

"I have fired no guns in years. You know that,'' Remo said. "What's with you?''

"You are,'' said Chiun, turning away. "But not for long. You must return to Folcroft. Emperor Smith has need of your services.''

"Why do I get the impression that you're trying to chase me away from here?'' Remo said.

"I have no interest in your impressions,'' Chiun said. "I am here on a personal matter that concerns the Master of Sinanju. Not you. Be gone. Go see Smith. Perhaps he can make use of you.''

"Not so's you'd notice,'' Remo said. "Look . . .'' he said, then stopped dead. He saw a streak of red that scored the scalp under the hair over Chiun's left ear. "Hey. You're hurt.'' He reached forward and Chiun slapped his hand away angrily.

"I cut it shaving,'' Chiun said.

"You don't shave,'' Remo said.

"Never mind. It is only a scratch."

"You couldn't be scratched by a rocket attack," Remo said. "What the hell is going on?"

"Nothing. A lunatic gunman. I will be done with him by tomorrow. Then we will speak of other matters. We will make plans for the concert."

"Somebody with a gun did that to you?" Remo said and whistled. "He must have been real good."

"Only his name is good," Chiun said. "Tomorrow he will be dog meat. You return to Folcroft."

"I'm staying," Remo said.

Chiun swept out his hands. His fingernails shredded the heavy damask drapes.

"I don't need you," Chiun said.

"I don't care. I'm staying."

"Then stay out here and leave me alone. I will have nothing to do with you," Chiun said and walked into the bedroom, slamming the door behind him.

"I'm staying anyway," Remo shouted through the door.

"Stay if you must. But stay out of my way," Chiun said.

10

Remo heard the door from the bedroom to the outside hallway open, then close. Chiun was leaving. He went to the door of the suite, listened for a moment, then heard the elevator doors in the middle of the floor open and close.

Chiun was riding downstairs.

Remo ran from the room and into the stairwell, racing down the steps in giant jumps that looked effortless, but which touched only one step between each landing. It was the way a sixty-foot-tall giant would have walked down those steps.

Remo was not moving at top speed since he knew he had plenty of time to get to the lobby before the elevator arrived. Then he would hide there and follow Chiun and see just what was so important that Chiun could not tell him about it.

In the lobby, he sank into a soft wing chair and held a newspaper up in front of his face. Over the top of the newspaper, he could see the elevator's control lights. The elevator was now passing the fourth floor on its way to the lobby.

It reached the lobby; the door opened. The elevator was empty.

Where the hell was Chiun? Remo stood up and looked around. He found Chiun sitting in a wing chair directly behind his.

"Sit down, you imbecile," Chiun said. "You are drawing attention to yourself, acting like a man looking for a lost dog."

Remo grinned in embarrassment. "I heard you leave the room," he said.

"I heard you following me," Chiun said.

"I came down the steps to get here before the elevator," Remo said.

"So did I," Chiun said.

"So now what do we do?" Remo asked. "Do we play hide-and-go-seek all over Detroit?"

"No," Chiun said. "You go back to the room. Or go see Emperor Smith in Folcroft. Or go find Nellie Wilson and convince him to sing for our concert. Any would be acceptable."

"And you?" Remo asked.

"I have business which does not concern you," Chiun said.

"Not a chance," Remo said. "You move from here and I'm going to be on your tail like burrs on a beagle."

Chiun brought his chair around and sat down next to Remo. His hazel eyes were sincere and thoughtful as he said, "Remo, there are some things you do not understand."

"That's true enough," Remo said, "but I always count on you to explain them to me. You're my teacher and I trust you."

"Then you must also trust that I have your best interests at heart when I tell you that you are not yet ready to learn something."

"I don't buy that," Remo said. "What am I not ready to learn?"

"Many things. The proper greetings for Persian emperors. The things one must not say to a pharaoh. The proper

method of negotiating a contract. Many of the legends and
their deeper meanings. Many things."

"You're not trying to dodge me because I don't know
how to say hello to a Persian emperor," Remo said. "This
is something that concerns me and I want to know what it
is."

"You are a willful stubborn child," Chiun said angrily.

"Just so that we both understand it," Remo said.

Chiun sighed. "You may follow me. But ask no questions. And stay out of my way."

In the huge parking lot of Dynacar Industries, just off
the Edsel Ford Parkway in Detroit, workmen were scram-
bling around tying a green ribbon around a package.

If it were not for the fact that the package was six feet
high, six feet wide, and fifteen feet long, it would have
looked like a wedding gift, even to the elegant silvery-
white wrapping paper it was covered with.

Two dozen reporters and cameramen had already showed
up, fifteen minutes before the scheduled press conference
of Lyle Lavallette, and they milled around the big package, trying to see what it contained.

"It's a car. What do you expect? Lavallette didn't call
us here to show us some goddamn refrigerator."

"Hey, listen. He got shot a few days ago and then
Mangan got killed last night. For all you know, there may
be a goddamn hit squad under that ribbon and they're
going to blow us all away."

"I hope they start with you," the first reporter said. "It
may be a car but it sure as hell stinks."

"I thought I was the only one who noticed that,"
another reporter said. "Maybe it's these workmen."

"What's that you said, asshole?" snarled one of the
workmen. There were four of them, lying on their stom-
achs, clutching measuring tapes and trying to arrange the
foot-wide green ribbon atop the package into a perfect
floral-style bow.

"Nothing," said the reporter nervously. "I didn't say anything."

"We can smell it too," the workman said. "And we don't like it any better than you."

"It smells like rotting garbage," another reporter said.

"Tell us about it. Hey, move that over a quarter of an inch. There." The workman picked up a walkie-talkie from atop the package and spoke into it. "How's that?" He looked upward as a helicopter swirled into view over the parking lot. A voice answered back through the helicopter loud enough to be heard by the reporters.

"Looks perfect. Now lock it down."

The workman set about taping the bow in place with transparent package tape.

"Damn Lavallette and his goddamn perfectionism," one of the workers grumbled.

"What do you expect from a maverick auto genius?" a reporter asked.

"Not packages that smell," the workman said.

"Just cars that stink," another workman said.

Watching from an upstairs window of the Dynacar plant was Lyle Lavallette. He felt good because he knew he looked good. A new girdle, developed in Europe for pregnant women, had trimmed another half-inch off his waistline.

His personal beauty consultant, who was on the Dynacar payroll as a design coordinator, had just given him a skin-tightening-cream facial and had also cleverly found a way to cement the loose hair that had bothered Lavallette three days earlier to another hair, to guarantee that it could no longer pop up and embarrass him in front of the photographers.

"Good, good, good, good, good," he said. "The press is almost all here. No sign of Revell and Millis?" he asked Miss Blaze.

His secretary was wearing a heart-stopping tight sweater

in fuchsia. She had been wearing a red sweater, but Lavallette had made her change it because he was wearing an orange tie and he thought the colors might clash. Changing at the office was no problem, however, since Lavallette had insisted that she keep a dozen different sweaters in her desk, to help entertain reporters who might come to see them.

"Mr. Revell and Mr. Millis haven't arrived yet," she said. "But I called their offices and they're on their way."

"Good. I was worried that they might cancel just because Mangan got killed last night."

"No. They're coming," Miss Blaze said.

"Okay. I want you to wait for them downstairs," Lavallette said. "And when they come, you greet them and then take them to their seats on the dais."

"Okay. Any special seats, Mr. Lavallette?"

"Yes. Seat them on the left," he said.

"Is there a reason for that?" she asked.

"Best reason of all," Lavallette said. He smiled at his secretary. "It's downwind," he said.

"Nice place you bring me to," Remo said.

"Nobody invited you to accompany me here," Chiun said.

"It smells like the town dump."

"That is because there are many white people here," Chiun said. "I have noticed that about your kind."

"Why are we at a car company anyway? Dynacar Industries. I never heard of it."

"I am here because it is my duty," Chiun said. "You are here because you are a pest."

They were stopped at the parking-lot gate of Dynacar Industries by a uniformed guard who handed them a printed list of invited guests and asked them to check off their names.

Chiun looked up and down the list, then made an X next

to a name, handed it back to the guard, and walked
through the open gate.

The guard looked at the clipboard of names, then at
Chiun, then back at the list.

He glanced up at Remo. "He sure doesn't look like Dan
Rather," he said.

"Makeup," Remo said. "He doesn't have his TV makeup
on."

The guard nodded and handed Remo the clipboard.
Remo looked up and down the list and at the bottom, he
saw neatly typed his own name: REMO WILLIAMS.

There was already a check mark next to it.

"Somebody already checked off my name," he said.

"Yeah? Let's see. Where's that?"

"Remo Williams. That's me. See? It's got an X next to
it."

The guard shrugged. "What am I supposed to do? You
know, everybody who comes in here is supposed to check
off his name. Now I can't let you in without you make a
check mark on the list. That's the way it works and we've
got to do it that way."

"Sure," Remo said. "I understand."

He took the clipboard back and made an X next to a
name and walked through the gate.

The guard read the list and called after him, "Nice to
see you, Miss Walters. I watch your shows all the time."

Remo caught up with Chiun as the small Oriental moved
through the pack of newsmen, which had now grown to
more than fifty. Chiun marched through like a general,
smacking aside with an imperious hand loosely held cameras which threatened to injure his person. Cameramen
started to yell at him, then stopped and ooohed a large sigh
as Miss Blaze stepped out on the dais, leading James
Revell, head of General Autos, and Hubert Millis, president of American Automobiles, to seats at the end of the
dais.

"Look at the tits on that," one cameraman said in an awestruck voice.

"Got to admit," another one said. "Lavallette knows how to travel."

"I hope he's doing a lot of traveling up and down on that one," someone else said.

Chiun stopped near the front of the dais and shook his head.

"I never understand the fascination of your kind with milk glands," he told Remo.

"You didn't hear me say anything, did you?" Remo asked.

He looked up and saw the two men who had just sat down take our handkerchiefs and hold them in front of their faces. The stench at this spot was overpowering and Remo said, "Couldn't we find a less potent place to stand?"

"Here," Chiun said. "Slow your breathing. That will help you. And your talking. That will help me."

Remo nodded. He leaned toward Chiun. "A funny thing just happened," he said.

"I'm sure you'll tell me about it," Chiun said.

"I have never seen you so grouchy," Remo said. "Anyway, they had my name here on the guest list. Did you tell anybody I was coming?"

"No," Chiun said. He turned to look at Remo, who said, "And somebody put an X to my name." He thought it might cheer Chiun up if he played straight man and tossed him a line that could lead to a high-quality insult, so he said, "Do you think there are two just like me in the world?"

He was surprised when Chiun did not respond in the expected way. "You saw a check mark next to your name?" he said.

Remo nodded.

"Remo, I ask you again to leave this place," said Chiun.

"No."

"As you will. But whatever happens, I do not want you to interfere. Do you understand?"

"I understand and you can count on it. I'll sit on my hands, no matter what happens," Remo said. Chiun seemed not to be listening. His eyes were scanning the crowd, and then there was a smattering of applause that brought all eyes up to the podium with its Medusa's head of microphones. Lyle Lavallette, wearing a blue blazer with the new Dynacar Industries emblem on the pocket, waved to the press and stepped toward the microphones.

"Who's that?" Remo said, as much to himself as to Chiun.

"That's Lyle Lavallette, the Maverick Genius of the Auto Industry," said a reporter next to Remo. "What are you here for if you don't know anything?"

"Basically to rip your throat out if you say another word to me," Remo said, and when his eyes locked with the reporter's the newsman gulped and turned away.

Lavallette fixed a big smile on his face and slowly turned for 180 points of the compass to make sure that every photographer had a chance to get a full-face shot of him.

"Ladies and gentlemen," he said, "I want to thank you for coming today. I apologize for the slight delay in scheduling but I was busy in a hospital being treated for gunshot wounds." He smiled again to let them know he was fully recovered and that it would take more than mere bullets to stop Lyle Lavallette. He wished now that he had joked with doctors at the hospital; that would have been good stuff for *People* magazine.

"And I also want to thank Mr. James Revell, the head of General Autos, and Mr. Hubert Millis, president of American Automobiles, for coming here today also. Their presence underscores the important fact that we are not here today to unveil or launch a commercial enterprise but to announce a world-shaking scientific discovery." He looked around at the reporters again before continuing.

"I would be remiss if I did not point out our deep sorrow at the tragedy that has befallen Mr. Drake Mangan, the president of National Autos. I know that Drake—my dear, good old friend Drake—with his keen interest in technology, would also have been here if death had not closed down production on him first."

Remo heard the two men, who had been introduced as Revell and Millis, speak to each other.

"Good old friend Drake?" Revell said. "Drake wanted to kill the bastard."

"Still seems like a good idea," Millis responded.

"But no further ado, ladies and gentlemen," Lavallette said. "I know you're all wondering what the Maverick Genius of the Auto Industry has up his sleeve this time. Well, it's simply this. The gasoline-powered automobile, as we know it, is dead."

There was silence until Remo said aloud, "Good."

Lavallette ignored the comment and went on. "The internal-combustion engine, the basis for the auto industry as we have known it before today, is now a museum piece. A dinosaur."

Remo clapped. No one else made a sound. Chiun said, "Be quiet. I want to hear this." But his eyes were scanning the crowd constantly and Remo knew that the Master of Sinanju had not shown up to listen to some kind of announcement about a new bomb-mobile.

"A dinosaur," Lavallette repeated. "It's ironic, perhaps, because the dinosaur has been for years the source of our wonderful car culture, in the form of decayed animal matter that we extract from under the sands of the world in the form of crude oil. Decayed dinosaurs, the leavings of the primeval world. But those supplies have been dwindling and our four-wheeled culture has been threatened with slow extinction." He paused for dramatic effect. "Until today."

Lavallette patted his white hair, reassured to find it all in place.

"While I was fighting my lonely battle against Communist tyranny in Nicaragua," he said, "I had a great deal of time to do new research on new means of powering autos. Ladies and gentlemen, here is the solution."

He looked up and the helicopter which had been hovering over a far corner of the lot spun forward. It stopped over the silver-wrapped package in front of the dais. Lavallette nodded and a man dropped on a rope from the helicopter, attached the rope to a hook in the top of the silvery package, then pulled on the rope and the helicopter began to rise.

"Ladies and gentlemen, welcome to the public unveiling of the marvel of our age, the supercar of tomorrow here today. The Dynacar."

The package was lifted into space by the rising helicopter. It had had no bottom and as it lifted off the ground, it revealed a sleek black automobile.

Behind the automobile, in a neat row, stood three shiny metal trashcans. They were filled to the brim and the faint breeze carried the noxious stench of their contents back into the faces of the press. Revell, at the end of the dais, started to cough; Hubert Millis choked, turned and retched.

Next to the garbage cans was a small black machine that looked like an industrial vacuum cleaner.

"Just as the cars of yesterday were fueled by the refuse of yesterday, the Dynacar—the car of today—will operate on the refuse of today. No more gasoline. No more oil. No more exhaust or pollution. Gentlemen. Please."

He nodded to the workmen, who stepped up to the row of trashcans and one by one began emptying them into the top of the small black device. Old newspapers, coffee grounds, chicken bones, underwear tumbled into the round black hole. Some spilled over and fell to the ground and maggots began climbing up the side of the black machine.

The workmen hastily brushed them back. When all three cans had been emptied into the black device, one of the workmen pushed a button.

Immediately, there was a whirling grinding noise, like a combination clothes drier and trash compactor working.

Slowly, the mound of garbage that had topped the opening of the black machine began to move. It shook and lifted, maggots and all, then slowly disappeared into the machine's gaping maw.

"You are watching the Dynacar refuse converter in operation," Lavallette announced. "This device duplicates the same action that transformed the carcasses of the dinosaurs into fuel. But this is an instant processor and refiner all in one."

The grinding stopped and Lavallette signaled one of the workmen, who closed the top of the machine, then stood off to the side, fighting the dry heaves. That was bad for the corporate image and Lavallette made a mental note to have the man fired.

Lavallette stepped down from the platform. Remo noticed that the two automakers, Revell and Millis, were leaning forward, watching. Chiun, meanwhile, was still scanning the crowd.

Lavallette went to the base of the black machine and opened a small door. He turned around, holding above his head a grayish-brown lump about the size of a pack of cigarettes.

"Here you are, ladies and gentlemen. Those three barrels of trash you just saw dumped into the machine have now been converted into this."

"What has this got to do with cars?" a reporter called out.

"Everything," Lavallette said. "Because this little block here is solid fuel and it's enough fuel to run my Dynacar for a week without refilling. Imagine it. Instead of putting out your trash every Tuesday, you simply dump it in the refuse converter, turn on the motor, and from the bottom you take out fuel for your auto. In one stroke, the problems of waste disposal and fuel for the family car are solved.''

A reporter called out another question. Lavallette recognized him; he was from an independent local station which had never liked Lavallette. The station had refused to call him a maverick genius of the auto industry and had in fact called him one of the car business's greatest frauds.

''My station wants to know what happens if you're a two-car family?'' he asked, with a smirk.

''Those people can just stay tuned to your channel all day long. You produce enough garbage for the entire country,'' Lavallette said.

There was a polite ripple of laughter in the crowd. Lavellette was surprised; he had expected a belly laugh. He checked the faces of the media people and instead of the wide-eyed amazement he had anticipated, he saw perplexity, frowns, and more than a few fingers pinching nostrils closed.

''Let's get this straight, Mr. Lavallette,'' a network reporter asked. ''This vehicle runs exclusively on garbage?''

''Refuse,'' Lavallette said. He didn't like the word ''garbage.'' He could see the *Enquirer* headline now: ''MAVERICK AUTO GENIUS UNVEILS GARBAGEMOBILE.''

''Will it run on any kind of refuse?'' another reporter demanded.

''Absolutely. Anything from fish heads to old comic books to— ''

A reporter interrupted and Lavallette saw from his nametag that he was from *Rolling Stone*.

''Will it run on shit?''

''I beg your pardon,'' Lavallette said.

''Shit. Will it run on shit?''

''We haven't tried that,'' Lavallette said.

''But it might?''

''Perhaps. Actually, no reason why not.''

He felt a little relieved when he realized that no respectable newspaper in America would coin the word "shitmobile." And who cared what *Rolling Stone* said anyway?

"We want to see the car run," the *Rolling Stone* reporter said. Apparently this had not occurred to any of the other media types there because they instantly started to shout: "Yeah, yeah. Let's see it run. Drive it, Lavallette."

Lavallette gestured for silence, then said, "This is the second prototype. The first was stolen last week . . . I suspect, by industry spies. But the laugh is on them. Both the refuse converter and the engine of the Dynacar are so revolutionary that they cannot be duplicated without infringing on my exclusive patents. And to make certain that the secret of its internal operating system remains exclusively the property of Dynacar, each model will come with a sealed hood, and only Dynacar licensed shops will be allowed to service them. Anyone who tampers with the seals on the hood will find that the engine has self-destructed into unrecognizable slag—as I'm sure the thieves who made off with the only other existing model have discovered by now.

"And now. A demonstration of the Dynacar in action."

Lavallette felt the eyes of Revell and Millis on him as he made his way through the crowd. While the cameramen crowded around, he opened a small flap in the hood of the automobile and slid in the tiny cube of compressed garbage.

"That, ladies and gentlemen, is enough fuel to run this vehicle for a week."

He sat behind the wheel of the car and as the cameras zoomed in, he held up a golden ignition key for all to see.

At first, the reporters thought Lavallette was having trouble getting the car to start. They saw him slip the key into the ignition and turn it, but there was no answering rumble from under the hood, no throb or vibration of an engine.

But suddenly, with a cheery wave through the window, Lavallette sent the Dynacar surging ahead. The perimeter of the parking lot had been kept clear of automobiles and so it served him as a test track. One reporter timed it as moving from zero to sixty-five in ten seconds flat, which was high quality for a nonracing car. Lavallette sped the car around the lot and brought it back to the starting point to a quiet stop. Throughout the entire drive, the Dynacar had made no sound but for the squeal of its tires.

When he stepped from the car, Lavallette was grinning from ear to ear. He struck a heroic pose. On the dais, Miss Blaze started to clap. Reporters clapped too, not because they thought it was proper for them to do so, but to encourage Miss Blaze so that she would continue her bosom-bouncing ovation.

Lavallette gestured to the workmen, who came forward to stand in front of the Dynacar. One spoke into his walkie-talkie and a moment later, the helicopter popped back into view, still holding, suspended from its underside, the giant silver box that had covered the car. Swiftly, as with a well-rehearsed operation, the copter flew in and lowered the container down over the Dynacar. The workmen unfastened the ropes that held it and the helicopter chopped off, as Lavallette went back to the podium and said into the microphones, "I'll take your questions now."

"You claim this car is nonpolluting?"

"You can see that for yourselves," Lavallette said. "There's no exhaust, no tailpipe. Not even a muffler, I might add."

"What about the smell?"

"What smell?" asked Lavallette.

"There's a distinct odor of garbage. We all smelled it when you drove past."

"Nonsense," said Lavallette. "That's just the aftersmell of the refuse that was sitting around before. And I apologize for that, but I wanted to get the worst, most rancid waste we could just to show how efficient the process was.''

''You should have used shit,'' yelled the reporter from *Rolling Stone*.

''You were shot earlier this week by someone claiming to represent an environmental group. Do you think that shooting would have occurred if that group had known about the Dynacar?''

''No,'' Lavallette said. ''This car is the answer to every environmentalist's prayers.''

''What do you think, Chiun?'' Remo asked.

''I think you should go home,'' the old Oriental said. His eyes still flicked around the crowd.

''We've been through that. What the hell are you looking for?''

''Peace of mind. And not getting it,'' Chiun snapped.

''Fine,'' Remo said. ''You got it. I'll see you around.''

''Remember. Do not interfere,'' Chiun said.

Remo walked off in a huff. He could not figure out what was troubling Chiun. All right. The old man was allowed to be disturbed because he'd been nicked by someone's lucky shot, but why take it out on Remo? And why come here? What made him think that the gunman might be here?

Behind him, as he walked through the clusters of media people, Remo heard Lavallette still answering questions.

''Mr. Lavallette. While everyone knows that you're the Maverick Genius of the Auto Industry, you've never been known as an inventor. How did you manage to make the technological breakthroughs necessary for the Dynacar?''

Lavallette said smoothly, ''Oddly enough, there are no technological breakthroughs in this car, except for the drive train. All the other technology is on line. In the East, some apartment buildings, even some electric plants, are powered by compressed garbage used as fuel. The trick involved adapting existing technology in a form that could be afforded by the average American family. We've done that.''

"When will you be able to go into production?"

"Immediately," Lavallette said.

"When do you think you'll be ready to compete with the Big Three automakers?"

"The question is," Lavallette said with a grin, "when will they be able to compete with me?" He turned and smiled at Revell and Millis, who sat at the end of the dais, staring at the box covering the Dynacar model.

"Actually," Lavallette said, "since the tragedy that has befallen Drake Mangan, I have been contacted by a number of people involved in the management of National Autos. There may be an opportunity there for us to pool our forces."

"You mean you'd take over National Autos?"

"No such position has been offered to me," Lavallette said, "but with Mr. Mangan's death, it may be time for that company to look in a new direction. The Dynacar is the car of today and tomorrow. Everything else is yesterday.''

"Revell. Millis.''

Reporters began to call out the names of the other two car executives at the end of the dais.

They looked up as if surprised in their bathtubs.

"Would you consider joining forces with Lavallette to produce the Dynacar?" The two men waved away the question.

Off to the side of the dais, Remo saw a group of men in three-piece suits conferring in low voices. They were supposed to look like auto executives but Remo could tell by the way they stood, their hands floating free, that they were armed. Their hands never strayed far from the places in their belts or under their armpits where handguns could be tucked. He could even see the bulges of some of the weapons. Sloppy, he thought. They might as well have been wearing neckties with the word "Bodyguard" stitched on in Day-Glo thread.

With the amplified voice of Lyle Lavallette echoing over his head, Remo noticed a cameraman moving along the fringe of the pack of newsmen. Remo realized he was watching the man because he carried the video camera awkwardly, as if he were not used to its weight. The man was tall, with dark hair, and had a scar running down the right side of his jaw. His eyes were hard and cold and Remo thought there was something familiar about them.

As he watched, the cameraman moved through the crowd and then emerged on the other side of the pack, facing the spot on the dais where James Revell and Hubert Millis, the heads of the other two car companies, were sitting.

From the corner of Remo's eyes, he saw Chiun moving up toward the dais. Perhaps Chiun had noticed something too. Was this it? Was this what Chiun had warned him to stay out of?

He should just turn and walk away. This was none of his business, but as he made up his mind to do that, he saw the cameraman fumble with his right hand into the grip of the camera which he was carrying on his left shoulder. He was rooting around for something, and then his entire body tensed in a preattack mode that meant only one thing: a gun.

"Chiun! Watch out!" Remo called. The quickest way to the cameraman was through the reporters and Remo moved through them like a one-ton bowling ball through rubber pins.

The man with the scar dropped the video camera and suddenly there was a long-barreled black pistol in his hands. He dropped into a marksman's crouch and before Remo could reach him, four shots came. One, two, three, four. Their reports blended into a short burst that was almost like the percussive burp of a machine gun.

Remo looked toward the dais and saw Chiun's body lying across those of James Revell and Hubert Millis.

None was moving. Lyle Lavallette was running down the slightly elevated stage toward the fallen men and the bodyguards were coming from the other side.

Remo swerved away from the gunman and ran toward the platform. Newsmen were moving close now and Remo vaulted over them and landed atop the pile of bodies.

"Chiun, Chiun," he called. "Are you all right?"

The squeaky voice from under him answered, "I was until some elephant crashed upon my poor body."

The gunman had stopped firing; there were probably too many newsmen in the way for him to have a shot, Remo realized. He started to his feet, even as he felt the bodies of Lavallette and the bodyguards drop on top of the pile.

"I'll get the gunman, Chiun," Remo said.

He started to slip through the pack, but could not get free. Something was holding his ankle. He reached down to free it, but the pressure was suddenly released. He tried to stand again and the pressure was on his other ankle. Through the cluster of bodies, he could see nothing.

Remo lunged backward with his body and suddenly the pressure was released and Remo went sprawling onto his back on the platform.

He stood up and looked over the heads of the reporters who were clustered milling about in front of the dais. The gunman was gone.

Remo darted into the crowd but there was no sign of the man. All around him, reporters were babbling.

"Who was it?"

"Who did the shooting?"

"Did anybody get hit?"

He heard one reporter say, "I know who did it."

Remo moved quickly behind that reporter and grasped his earlobe between right thumb and forefinger.

"Who did it, buddy?" he said.

"Owwww. Stop that."

"First, who did it?"

"A cameraman. He came when I did and I saw his name on the guest list."

"What was his name?" Remo said.

"A funny name. Owwww. All right. His name was Remo Williams."

Remo released the newsman's ear, swallowed hard, then ran back to the dais to collect Chiun so they could get out of the mob scene before they wound up as stars on the six-o'clock news.

As they left the parking lot, they could hear the whooping of approaching police sirens.

11

The Master of Sinanju was not hungry. The Master of Sinanju would not be hungry for the foreseeable future, at least so long as his ungrateful wretch of a pupil continued to intrude upon his privacy.

"Well, I'm hungry and I intend to make some rice."

"Good," said the Master of Sinanju. "Make it in Massachusetts," he added, repeating a slogan he had once heard on television.

Remo bit back an answer and went into the small kitchenette of the hotel suite. On the counter, on a room-service tray, were six packages of whole grain brown rice, and as a concession to variety, one package of white rice, which according to Chiun had less nutrient value and an inferior taste. Not to mention being improperly colored.

Remo opened the package of white rice.

"Yum, yum. White rice. My favorite."

He glanced into the living room and saw a disgusted expression wrinkle Chiun's parchment features. But the old man did not move from his lotus position in the center of the floor.

"I haven't had white rice in so long, just the thought of a steaming bowl makes my mouth water."

Chiun sniffed disdainfully.

Remo put on a pot of water and measured out a half-cup of rice grains. While he waited for the water to boil, he made pleasant conversation although he was not in a pleasant mood. Still, after a half-day of argument and pleading had failed to move Chiun, he had decided on this approach.

"Sure wish we had this rice in the desert, when my plane crashed. Do you know, Chiun? I was the leader of all the survivors. Surrounded by sand. And I found myself enjoying it."

"You would," Chiun said. "I will have Smith buy you a sandbox for Christmas."

"I enjoyed being appreciated. There we were surrounded by sand and these people I had never met before looked up to me."

"So did the sand probably," said Chiun.

The first bubbles of water surfaced in the pot and Remo looked for a wooden spoon but had to settle for a plastic one.

"I think I may have helped save some lives," Remo said. "That was the part that stays with me. I guess I can understand how important you think it is to feed the villagers of Sinanju."

The rice swirled in the boiling water.

The Master of Sinanju opened his mouth to speak, a softer light in his hazel eyes, but he caught himself before the breath became a kind word and resumed staring into infinity.

Remo saw the momentary softening and went on, as he put a lid on the pot: "I used to think those people in Sinanju were lazy ungrateful bastards. Every one of them. Living off the blood money of the Master. But I've changed now."

Chiun brushed a long-nailed finger against an eye. Was he brushing away a tear? Remo wondered.

"I can understand now how it is a Master's obligation to feed the village."

He waited five minutes then opened the pot. The rice was soft and fluffy.

"Maybe someday, I'll be the one to feed the people of Sinanju," Remo said, putting the rice into two identical bowls. "I'd like that."

Remo looked at Chiun from the corner of his eye but the aged Korean averted his face.

"Care for some rice?" Remo said casually.

Chiun came up from his sitting position as if being catapulted from the floor. He cleared the space to his bedroom like a flash of golden light, the color of his day kimono.

The door slammed behind him and through the door panel Remo could hear the sound of the Master of Sinanju noisily blowing his nose. It sounded like a goose honking.

A moment later, the door reopened and Chiun stood framed in the doorway, calm and serene, a beatific expression on his face.

"Yes, my son. I think I will have some rice," he said formally.

After they had put aside their empty bowls and eating sticks, Remo said, "I would speak with you, Little Father."

Chiun held up a hand. "The proprieties must be observed. First the food."

"Yes?" said Remo.

"I think you are finally learning to cook rice properly. That rice was correctly done, not like that insidious mortar that Japanese refer to as rice. This was done in the Korean style."

"That's the way I like it in Chinese restaurants," Remo said.

"Pah," said Chiun. "The Chinese stole the correct cooking technique from the Koreans, who are widely acknowledged to be the world's greatest chefs."

Remo nodded his head in agreement, although the only

Korean dish he had ever tasted was some kind of pickled cabbage that tasted like rancid crabgrass.

He lowered his head and waited and finally Chiun said, "And now you may speak of other things."

"I know this subject offends, you, Chiun, but I must ask. Who was that gunman this afternoon?"

"Some lunatic who likes to shoot people," Chiun said casually.

"He gave his name to one of the reporters there," Remo said.

"An alias," Chiun said. "American gangsters are always using aliases."

"He gave his name as Remo Williams," Remo said.

"He probably picked the name at random from the telephone book," Chiun said.

"There aren't a lot of Remo Williamses in the telephone book, Little Father. Why did Smith send you to Detroit?"

"Business," Chiun said.

"I figured that much. That gunman's your target?"

"You should have figured that out too," Chiun said.

"I'm trying to be respectful and hold a decent conversation with you," Remo said, and Chiun, looking as chastened as Remo had ever seen him, said nothing.

"I thought about a lot of things when I was out in that desert," Remo said. "I thought about who I am and what I was, and how I never had any family, except for you. I guess that's why I was impressed when the other passengers looked up to me. It was almost like having a family."

Chiun remained silent and Remo said, "Funny that guy would have my name."

"It is one thing to have a name," Chiun said. "It is quite another just to use a name."

"You think that man was just using my name?" Remo said.

"Yes. That man is a cruel trickster, a vicious deceitful white. Without his cruel guile, I would not now bear this scar on my aged head," Chiun said.

"The wound will heal, Little Father."

"The shame will not heal. Not until I have erased that deceiver from this existence. He cannot be allowed to live." Chiun's voice trembled with a low anger.

"I am ready to help," Remo said. What was that strange look that came into Chiun's eyes? Remo wondered. It was a flash of something. Was it fear?

"No," Chiun said, too loudly. "You must not. It is forbidden."

"The shame that you feel on your shoulders rests on my shoulders too," Remo said. "You know that."

"I know that and I know many other things. Some of which you do not know, my son."

"What things?" Remo asked.

"I know what must be done and I know what must not be done. And since I am the teacher and you the pupil, you must accept this as a fact."

"I accept it as a fact," Remo said. "But you must tell me these things or I will never learn them." Chiun was hiding something, he knew. But what?

"Wait here," Chiun said quietly. He rose smoothly to his feet and padded softly to the lacquered trunks neatly stacked in the corner of the living room.

He bent deep into one of the trunks, looked around for a while, then grunted in satisfaction and came back holding something carefully in his bony fingers.

He sat down across from Remo and handed him the object he was holding.

"This is one of the greatest treasures of Sinanju."

Remo looked at it. It was fist-sized, gray and flecked with shiny particles like bits of fused sand, and cold to his touch.

"A rock?" said Remo.

"No," Chiun said. "No ordinary rock. It is a rock taken from the moon."

Remo turned it over in his hands. "From the moon? Smith must have gotten it for you." He looked up. "How'd you get Smitty to con NASA into giving you a moon rock?"

"No," Chiun said. "This rock was given to me by my father, who received it from his father, and so on, back to the one who plucked it from the mountains on the moon, Master Shang."

Remo cocked an eyebrow. "Never heard of him. And I'd be surprised if they really heard of him on the moon either."

Chiun shook his head for emphasis. "Master Shang," he insisted. "He is known as the Master who walked to the moon."

"Oh, that explains it," Remo said. "I knew the Masters in the old days didn't have spaceships but naturally they didn't need them 'cause they just walked to the moon."

"I will ignore your insolence except to point out that absolute certainty is generally the refuge of the nincompoop."

"Nincompoop or not, the first man on the moon was Neil Armstrong and he was an American and that is an absolute certainty. And why are we talking about the moon? We were talking about things that you know and I don't and it's pretty obvious now that you know absolutely nothing about the moon," Remo said. "Less than nothing."

"I will tell you the story of Master Shang," Chiun said. "It was in the days of the Han dynasty in China. Master Shang was the ruling Master in those days but he was not a great Master, except for this one feat.

"Now Master Shang often performed services for the Emperor of China in those days. This was when the Chinese could generally be counted on to pay their bills and before they became the pack of beggars and thieves they are today. At any rate, this Chinese emperor's throne was sore beset by enemies, princelings and pretenders who coveted his gold and his women, for he had a queen and many concubines, that being the tradition among emperors of China at the time, they always being a licentious and immoral people.

"Master Shang made the arduous journey from the village of Sinanju on the West Korea Bay to this emperor's court to eliminate some foe or another but each time he obliterated an enemy of the throne, more enemies would spring up.

"One day, Master Shang said to the emperor, 'Lo, but your enemies wax like the stars in the September sky. Each year I am summoned to dispatch them and each following year their numbers increase.'

"The emperor replied, 'Is this not good, because then you have more work from my court?'

" 'No,' said Shang. 'This is bad, for soon the court of China will have more enemies than subjects.'

"The Emperor of China thought on this and said, 'What is your suggestion, Master of Sinanju?' "

Chiun paused to take the stone from Remo's hands and to set it on the floor between them.

"Then the Master Shang told the emperor, 'Take the women of your enemies into your court. Make them yours and thus, by blood, your enemies will become your relatives.'

"The emperor considered this for a day and a night. Then he answered, 'Your idea has merit, Master of Sinanju. But what shall I do with my concubines? Already they overflow the royal palace.'

" 'Set them free,' said the Master of Sinanju, who had looked with favor upon one of the emperor's concubines. 'It may be I will accept one of them in payment for my services.'

"And so the Emperor of China did this and set his concubines free and one of the women, who was called Yee, became the property of the Master of Sinanju and returned to our village with Master Shang."

"All's well that ends well," Remo said. "She must

have been a beaut if the women you have there today look anything like she did.''

"Nothing ended well," Chiun said. "Upon his return, Master Shang was reviled for daring to take a Chinese woman for his own. For everyone knew then, as now, that the Chinese are unclean people with bad teeth and worse dispositions and while it is permitted to work for them, one must never sleep with one.

"But the Master Shang was smitten and what could he do? This woman, this Yee, became demanding in her ways, having been spoiled by the richness of the emperor's palace. She could not fully appreciate the magnificent simplicity of Sinanju. Her insistence upon baubles grew vexing to Shang.

"Yee would ask for emeralds and Shang would give them. She would ask for rubies and they would be in her hand. Yee would ask for—''

"There's a word for Shang's problem," Remo said.

"What is that?" Chiun asked.

"Pussy-whipped," Remo said.

"You have the ability to be gross even in moments of ultimate pathos," Chiun said. "One day, Shang saw that the treasure house of Sinanju was growing empty and he went to Yee and told her, 'My wealth is less but I am the greater for your presence,' although in truth he found this woman was becoming a bother.

"One day, Yee said, 'I want something no emperor or Master has.' And Shang grew angry. 'I have given you diamonds and rubies and emeralds and pearls. What more could you ask?'

"Yee thought long as she looked at Shang and beyond the Master she saw something bright and shiny in the night sky and a sly smile came over her avaricious pancake-flat Chinese excuse for a face.''

"No editorial comments, please," Remo said. "The legend and nothing but the legend. I want to be out of here today.''

"You can leave now," Chiun said.

"The story," Remo said.

"Legend," Chiun corrected. "So the avaricious Yee told the Master Shang that she wanted just one more thing and if he could not provide it, would she then be free to return to her people. And Shang finally understood what had been concealed from him all along: that Yee did not love him but only the things he could give her. But he also understood that he still loved her and so he gave her his promise. 'What is it you wish, my wife?'

"And Yee pointed beyond him into the night sky.

" 'That,' she said.

" 'The moon? No one can give you the moon. It is impossible. You are trying to trick me.'

" 'I will settle for a piece of the moon. A piece no bigger than my fist. Is this so much to ask?'

"Shang was beside himself for days. He did not sleep, he did not eat, for he was in love and at length he decided that if he wished to keep Yee as his wife, he must try."

"What a dork," Remo said.

"Silence," Chiun commanded. "So one clear night with a walking stick and a pack on his back, Master Shang set out to walk to the moon. He walked north, beyond Korea, beyond the colder lands above Korea, always keeping the moon before him. He reasoned that where the moon set would be his goal. For wherever the moon went by day, he would find it.

"Master Shang walked and walked until he ran out of land on which to walk, and so he made for himself a boat and betook himself north in that boat. He ran out of food, he ran out of water to drink. There were strange animals in the water and bears who swam and were the color of snow.

"Finally, Master Shang, sick with hunger, sailed into a cold sea where the sun never set. He thought himself dead

and doomed to sail the Void through eternity. Until his
boat reached a strange land.

"Now this land was white, with mountains of snow.
Everywhere there was snow and under it rock. The days
passed and still the sun did not set but only hung low in
the tired sky. There was no moon in the sky. Shang waited
for days but it did not appear. And it was then that the
Master of Sinanju knew that he had reached his goal."

Chiun lowered his voice to a respectful hush. "And so
the legend tells us, he had walked to the moon.

"Master Shang ate the meat of the white swimming bear
and broke off a rock the size of Yee's fist from a mountain
of the moon. And with extra meat in his ration pouch, he
sailed back from the land of the moon.

"When, months later, he returned to the village of
Sinanju, he told Yee, 'I have brought you a rock of the
moon. I have kept my promise.'

"And Yee accepted the rock and his story, although she
cried because she knew she would never see her homeland
again. Her days were not long after this and in the end,
Master Shang was stricken by grief and he too died. But
not in shame, for he had done a wondrous thing. And to
remind future Masters of the lesson of Shang, the rock you
hold in your hands, Remo, has been passed from generation to generation."

Chiun smiled benignly.

"Do you understand, Remo?"

"Chiun, I hate to be the one to break this to you, but
Shang didn't walk to the moon."

Chiun looked at Remo with an unhappy glare.

"You do *not* understand," he said sadly.

"He walked to the North Pole," Remo said. "The
white swimming bears were polar bears. And at the North
Pole, the sun doesn't set for six months every year. That's
why it never got dark," Remo said.

"You disappoint me, Remo," said Chiun, taking away

the rock of Master Shang. "I will have to keep this until you have learned the lesson of Shang. It is sad."

"All right. Time out," Remo said. "Answer me this. If Shang did walk to the moon, why isn't he considered a great Master? Answer me that. After all, it's not everybody who can walk to the moon."

"Shang is not greatly honored for a simple reason," said Chiun evenly. "He married a Chinese and this is just not done. Had he not partly atoned by walking to the moon, he would have been totally stricken from the records of Sinanju."

The telephone rang and Chiun said, "It is Emperor Smith."

"How do you know?"

"It is simple. I am here. You are here. Smith is not here. Therefore, it is Smith."

"Very good," Remo said. "What else can you foresee?"

Chiun put his fingers to his temples and closed his eyes as if peering into the future.

"I can see who will answer the phone," he said.

"Yeah? Who?"

"You, Remo."

"How do you know that?"

"It is simple," said Chiun, opening his eyes. "Because I am not going to. Heh, heh. Because I am not going to."

"Very funny," said Remo and walked across the room to answer the telephone.

"All right, Smitty. It's your dime," he said pleasantly.

"Remo?" Smith's voice was sharp. "I was calling Chiun."

"So you got me. Don't sound so disappointed. Chiun's not answering phones at the moment."

"What are you doing in Detroit? Where were you at two o'clock this afternoon?"

"With Chiun, at some car exhibition. Smitty, did you know there's a guy running around calling himself by my name?"

"Let me speak with Chiun, Remo," Smith said.

Remo tossed the phone to Chiun, who snatched it from the air and announced, "Hail, Emperor Smith. Your fears are groundless for Remo is with me and all is well."

Remo listened to Chiun's side of the conversation patiently. Normally, even from across a room, he could hear both sides of a phone call, but Chiun had the earpiece so tightly pressed against his head that Remo could not hear anything but the old man's voice.

"I cannot explain," Chiun said. "Not now. Rest assured, all will be rectified in time. Yes. No more carriagemakers will die. You have the word of the Master of Sinanju and you need no other assurances," Chiun said curtly, then hung up.

"What was that all about?" Remo asked.

"Emperor's business," Chiun said.

"Are we back to that again? Come on, Chiun. Tell me what's going on."

Chiun waved for Remo to sit and Remo lowered himself reluctantly to the floor.

"My son, you trust the Master who made you whole, do you not?"

"You know I do," Remo said.

"Then I call upon you to listen to that trust. Emperor Smith wants you to return to Folcroft. Do this. I will join you in a day. Two at most. Trust me, Remo. There are some things you should not yet know. This is one of them."

Remo sighed. "I will do as you say."

"Good," said Chiun. "Now go. I have much to do."

"I hope Smith thanked you for saving those two guys' lives today when that gunman opened fire," Remo said.

"Thanks are not necessary. It is part of my mission."

"And what's the other part?"

Chiun silently rose and placed the moon rock back into one of his steamer trunks.

He would not answer, Remo knew, so he walked to the door, but in the doorway, paused.

"Chiun. That guy with my name? Is he the reason you and Smith are so upset?"

"No," said Chiun, although it hurt him to lie to his pupil. But it was as he said. There were some things that Remo was better off not knowing.

12

The President was disturbed; Smith could tell by his language.

"What the heck is going on, Smith? You assured me that Drake Mangan would be protected and he's dead. Now somebody tries to kill Revell and Millis too."

"We had protection there," said Smith. "Something's just gone wrong."

"Gone wrong? You're not supposed to have anything go wrong. How is that possible?"

"I'm not sure," Smith said.

The President's voice was cracking. "Not sure? Are you telling me that you can't control your people? I hope you're not telling me that because I'm tempted to give you a certain order. You know the one I mean."

"That is your decision, sir," said Smith, "but I think it would be a mistake at this time. And I've been assured that no more Detroit executives will be lost."

"They don't grow on trees," said the President. "We've lost Mangan and I don't want to lose any more."

"If you have no specific orders for me, Mr. President, I must return to monitoring the situation."

There was a heavy silence over the safe line to Washington and for a long moment, Smith thought that the order to disband was coming. Instead, the President said, "Well, okay, Smith. Do your best. What the heck. Nobody got killed today so I guess that's something and who knows, tomorrow might be better. It usually is."

"I hope so, Mr. President," said Smith as he hung up.

Was the President correct? Smith wondered. Would things be better? Or were they so far out of control now that nothing could mend them? Chiun had just assured him that Remo was not the Detroit assassin, but why was Remo in Detroit in the first place? How had Remo found Chiun so quickly? Was it possible that the two of them were working together, at cross-purposes to Smith?

If there were one more death, Smith knew the President would dissolve CURE. He had always been prepared for that day. There was a poison pill that he would unhesitatingly take and a coffin ready to receive his body. A simple computer command would erase all the CURE files and Smith's final order would be to Chiun: eliminate Remo and return to Sinanju. There would be no trace of CURE's existence after that.

Well, one trace, Smith thought. One large one. America still survived, but no one would suspect that a secret agency had ever been responsible for that.

A chilling thought flashed into Smith's mind. Could he trust Chiun to eliminate Remo upon command? If not, then what would happen without Smith to control the two deadliest assassins in human history?

He shuddered and brought up his computer link.

Chiun had assured him that Remo would return to Folcroft immediately. That would at least be a sign that things were still in order. Smith logged onto the main computer net that recorded all flight reservations in and out of Detroit. The names and destinations began scrolling up. Smith stopped the file when he recognized the name Remo Cochran. It was one of Remo's cover identities. And Remo Cochran had confirmed reservations on a Detroit–New York flight.

Good. Now all that had to happen was for Remo Williams to walk through the gates of Folcroft Sanitarium. Then, and only then, would Smith feel that the situation was under control.

Remo drove to Detroit City Airport, turned in the keys to his rental car, and reminded the counter clerk to keep the other three vehicles, unused, in the lot for the next three months. "Just in case," he said.

Then Remo bought a one-way ticket to New York City on Midwest-North Central-McBride-Johnson-Friendly Air, which until its most recent merger five minutes before had been Midwest-North Central-McBride-Johnson Airways. The flight was delayed an hour so that crews could quickly repaint the new name on the plane, so Remo bought three newspapers and threw away the news, sports, and business sections and began reading the comics.

It took him twenty minutes to read the comics because he didn't understand them. When he was growing up, comic strips featured funny characters doing funny things. Now they seemed to be about what people ate for breakfast and how so-and-so needed a different haircut. Maybe someone someday, Remo thought, might do a comic strip that was funny again. Would anyone read it? Or had the world grown too tired for funny comic strips?

He threw away the comics and the front-page headline of one of the papers he had thrown away caught his eye. It read: "GUNMAN ATTACKS AUTOMAKERS; COPS HINT IDENTITY IS KNOWN."

Remo picked up the news sections of the three papers and read them. Each had basically the same story: a gunman had attacked Revell and Millis earlier that day but was not successful. Police said that the gunman appeared to be the same one who had wounded Lyle Lavallette earlier in the week and said he had apparently entered the press-conference area with false press credentials. While police would not release the name the gunman used, it was apparently the same name he had used earlier when Lavallette was wounded at the Detroit Plaza.

Next to the story on the shootings was another which told how Lyle Lavallette had invented an automobile which got its power from household refuse and the Maverick Genius of the Auto Industry had proclaimed this the end of the Detroit gas-burners.

When Remo put the newspapers down, his face wore a stricken expression. The gunman who had attacked today had struck three days ago—while Remo was out in the desert—and had used the name Remo Williams at that time too. Why hadn't Chiun told him? What were Chiun and Smith trying to keep from him?

Remo ripped the articles from the paper and jammed them into his pocket.

"I thought you were leaving town," the rental agent said when Remo reappeared at the booth.

"Changed my mind," Remo said. "I'm going to take one of my three cars. Give me the keys."

"Fine, sir. Here they are. Would you like to rent a replacement car to leave in the lot?"

"No. The two I've got there should be enough. I need directions to American Automobiles."

"Just take the Parkway west. You'll see the signs," the clerk said.

Remo nodded and left the airport. He was so angry that, as he drove, his fingers dug into the warm plastic of the steering wheel as if it were taffy. Chiun had lied to him. There was something going on, something that both Chiun and Smith were hiding from him. But what could it be? Who was this gunman who was using his name? Remo could have gotten him today if it had not been for Chiun grabbing Remo's ankle and preventing him from giving chase.

He concentrated, trying to remember the man's face. There was something familiar about him, something around the eyes. Where had he seen those eyes before, dark, deep-set, and deadly?

And he remembered. He saw those eyes every time he looked into a mirror. They were his own eyes.

Remo was doing ninety on the Edsel Ford Parkway. Screw Chiun. Screw Smith. There was something going on and Remo was going to find out how it concerned him.

The newspapers had gotten one fact wrong. All three had written that the gunman had sprayed shots at both Revell and Millis, but Remo had been there. He had seen the man take his stance, had seen the angle of the shot, and he knew that James Revell had been the intended target. The gunman had shot Lyle Lavallette and killed Drake Mangan and tried to kill James Revell. Only Hubert Millis was left on the list. Remo wanted to see that gunman again. All he had to do, he was sure, was attach himself to Hubert Millis and wait.

He hoped it wouldn't be a long wait.

At Folcroft Sanitarium, Smith saw by his watch that the flight on which Remo was booked had left Detroit City Airport ten minutes before. He called a New York service and arranged for a private limousine to meet the passenger who traveled under the name of Remo Cochran and bring him directly to Rye, New York.

That done, he drew a paper cup of spring water from his office cooler and settled down to call up the news-digest file from his computer. It was a constantly running data collector that keyed off the wire services and network media computers. Smith had programmed it to collect only those reports that contained certain buzzwords that indicated CURE might be interested. Stories about corrupt politicians would automatically be downloaded into the CURE files by the word "corruption." An arson story would wind up in the same file, keyed by the word "arson."

The constantly expanding file kept Smith up-to-date on slow-breaking events that might one day mushroom into priority situations for CURE. And when they got into priority situations and all other possible solutions had failed, Remo Williams—the Destroyer—was called on. The Ravine Rapist had been just such a case. There was no question of the man's guilt, but apprehending him and trying him and convicting him was so long and so unsure a process that many other innocent people might have been killed along the way. Remo prevented such a waste.

Smith speed-read his way through the file. He took no notes, although lately he had noticed his memory was not so sharp as it once was and notes would have helped. But notes were dangerous so he forced his memory to respond.

When Smith came to the string of reports concerning the shootings in Detroit, he reached for the button that would skip over that section, but he was stopped by a sidebar cross-reference:

SEE FILE # 00334
Key: REMO WILLIAMS

Smith sipped his spring water, wondering what possible cross-reference would contain Remo's name.

When he saw what it was, his spring water went down the wrong pipe and it was a full minute before the coughing spasm subsided enough for him to read the wire-service story.

It was datelined Newark, New Jersey, four days earlier. The report read:

Police are still investigating the fatal shooting of an unidentified women whose body was found last night in Wildwood Cemetery.

The woman, whom authorities estimate was in her mid-fifties, was found sprawled over a grave. An autopsy showed she had been shot at close range by a .22-caliber pistol. Three bullets were recovered from her body.

Authorities are puzzled by the absence of identification, although the woman appeared to be well-dressed and the autopsy showed that she had been in good health prior to her death. A floral display was found beside the body and police suspect that the woman was placing flowers at a grave when her killer attacked. A preliminary investigation showed that the nearest grave belonged to Remo Williams, a former Newark police officer who was executed for the murder of a minor drug pusher more than ten years ago.

Efforts to trace the woman's identity through friends or relatives of the deceased Remo Williams have proved unavailing. According to police sources, Williams had no family.

Police speculate that robbery may have been a motive in the woman's killing.

Smith shut down the computer. It was impossible. First there was the killer in Detroit who was using Remo's name. And now, after all these years, someone had visited Remo's gravesite. In all the years since the casket had been laid in that grave, no one had ever stopped to pay respects to the memory of the dead policeman. Smith knew this because a cemetery worker, who thought he was working for a sociological-research center, filed a monthly written report listing the patterns of visitation to selected graves in Wildwood Cemetery. There was no such sociological-research center and the report went directly to CURE. And every month it noted that no one had visited Remo Williams' grave.

And now this.

Who could the woman have been? An old girlfriend, carrying a torch after all those years? Not likely, Smith thought. She was too old. Old enough to be Remo's mother, in fact.

"Remo's mother," Smith whispered hoarsely in the silence of his shabby office. "Oh, my God. It's all unraveling."

*   *   *

The black car pulled into the deserted construction site
like something propelled by air. Only the soft crush of its
tires in the bulldozer-gouged earth warned of its approach.
It was early evening and the construction crew had gone
home for the day. A crane stood off to one side of the
framework building, like a mutant monster insect.

The black car with its tinted windows circled the crane
before drawing grille to grille with the car already parked
there. The dark-eyed gunman with the scar down his right
jawline was leaning against the parked car. He flicked a
cigarette away.

"Williams." The testy voice emerged from the black
car, disguised by the sealed windows. Williams walked up
to the vehicle. Because of today's demonstration by
Lavallette, he now recognized it as a Dynacar. So his
employer had not been boasting when he said he had
stolen one of the Dynacar models.

"What do you want?" the gunman asked.

"What did you think you were doing today?" the voice
from inside the Dynacar demanded.

"Trying to fulfill my contract," the gunman said.

"I don't like it. You could have ruined everything."

"What ruins everything," the gunman said, "is when
you don't level with me and tell me what I'm up against."

"What do you mean?"

"Today, I would have had Revell except that old
Chinaman got him out of the way. It was the same Chinaman
who showed up at Mangan's apartment last night. Who the
hell is he?"

"I don't know," answered the voice from inside the
Dynacar. There was a pause, and then the voice again:
"What I do know is that I didn't tell you to hit anybody
today and you've got to do it my way, on my schedule.
Anything else is unprofessional."

"I don't like being called unprofessional," the gunman
said softly.

"These are the rules. You take them one at a time. Don't hurry. No head shots."

"Just tell me who you want done first," the gunman said.

"Try getting Millis," the voice from inside the car said. "Revell is probably spooked by now and we've already put the fear of God into Lavallette. I think Millis."

"Okay," the gunman with the scar said as the Dynacar abruptly slid into reverse, turned, and drove from the construction site.

The gunman had not realized that the car was still running. No matter what the press thought about the Dynacar, it was one spooky machine.

He got behind the wheel of his own vehicle and while he waited, lit a cigarette. It tasted stale. He had kicked the habit years ago, but this job was getting to him. Everything had been getting to him, ever since Maria had died. Half the time, it was painful to think of her and the other half of the time, he could not get her face out of his mind. Once she had been so beautiful and so loving.

Something else was also bothering him. His early hunch had been that his employer was a business rival of Lavallette's and now he was sure of it. There was only one reason why he would have been upset about the shooting spree at the Dynacar demonstration. He was one of the executives attending it.

The man had told him to go take out Hubert Millis of American Automobiles. The gunman thought that could mean only one thing: he was a contract killer for James Revell and today he had almost killed the man who hired him.

No wonder the man in the Dynacar had been upset. Served him right though for not leveling with the gunman from the start.

Who was that damned old Chinaman anyway? Who was *he* working for?

And the gunman had gotten the feeling today that there

was somebody else with the old man. But he hadn't seen his face.

It didn't matter. If either of them showed, or got in his way again, he was taking them down and he didn't care if it took head shots to do it.

13

The sun was slowly setting over the Great Lakes region and there was a cooling breeze off Lake Erie. The leaves were thinking of turning color. Children, only a few weeks back to school, had fallen out of the habit of play. Rush hour was over; life was settling down and in their homes, people were eating dinner or preparing to feed their minds with a diet of prime-time pap. The peace of the fall season had settled over every part of the town of Inkster, just outside Detroit.

Except for the American Automobile plant, which looked like a combat-ready military base.

Brand-new American Vistas, Stormers, and Spindrift Coupes ringed the electrified fence surrounding the headquarters of one of the Big Three automakers, like wagons pulled into a circle. One ring of cars was outside the twenty-foot-high fence, and another inside.

Six separate roadblocks, only thirty yards apart, controlled the single access road leading to the main gate and American Auto security guards, attired in green uniforms and toting semiautomatic weapons, prowled the grounds.

It was an impressive sight as Hubert Millis stared down from his office atop the American Auto corporate building, smack in the center of the headquarters complex. He filled with pride, watching the American Auto vehicles arrayed to protect him.

The head of the company's security said proudly, "Nothing will get through that, Mr. Millis." He was a young man in a neat brown suit who possessed a genius for security-systems analysis. He would have been prime FBI material, but American Autos paid him more than he could ever hope to earn working in Washington.

Millis nodded absently and turned his attention to the television set in the room. The station had concluded its 120-second summary of international news, national news, sports, and weather and was now starting its twenty-eight minutes of coverage of the auto industry. Millis, a sturdy man with a nervous habit of wringing his hands, turned up the sound as he saw the picture on the screen of Lyle Lavallette.

The announcer said, "Industry sources are predicting that Lyle Lavallette may be asked to head National Automobiles. This after the tragic death last night of Drake Mangan, shot and killed in the penthouse apartment of a Ms. Agatha Ballard, who was not believed to be acquainted with Mr. Mangan."

"Right, a total stranger," Millis hooted. "He'd been humping her for three years." He remembered his security guard was in the room and mumbled, "Well, at least that's what I heard. Something like that."

The announcer went on about industry sources. "They" said that Lavallette's new Dynacar might be the biggest thing to hit Detroit since Henry Ford. "They" said that National Autos was thinking of asking Lavallette to run the company so that it could control the development of the Dynacar. "They" said that General Autos and American Automobiles might even follow suit, especially if this environmental killer kept up his attacks on auto-industry officials.

"They" said a lot more but Millis did not hear it because he turned the television set off.

"Bullshit," he said. "Every one of us fired that god-damn Lavallette because he's a goofball. It's going to take more than one damned gunman to make me turn over the company to that loser." He went to the window and looked out over the cars massed in the parking lot. "You sure nobody can get through?" he asked his security chief.

"I don't think a bumblebee could get in here."

"I believe you're correct, Lemmings," Millis said. "You know, though, I think it might have been more artistic if you had used different models from our car fleet out there. Sound advertising, you know."

Lemmings looked confused. "I did, sir."

"You did?"

Millis looked through the triple-thickness window again. From this vantage point, every one of the encircled cars looked alike. He paid design engineers six-figure salaries so that American Automobiles' cars were distinctive and original and stood out from the competition and this is what he got?

"They all look alike," Millis said.

"Isn't that the idea?" asked Lemmings. "Mass produc-tion and all that?"

"But they all look exactly alike. Funny I never noticed that before. Does everybody else's cars look exactly alike?"

"Yes, sir," said Lemmings. "Much more so than ours do."

"Good," Millis said. "Then we're still the industry leader. That's what I like around here. Hey! What's that?"

"Sir?"

"Something's happening at the gate. See what it is."

Lemmings picked up the phone and got the gate. "What's going on down there, people?" he said.

"Someone trying to get past the gate, Mr. Lemmings."

"What's his business?"

"He says he has to see Mr. Millis. And he won't take no for an answer," the security guard said.

"So what's the problem? Just run him off."

"Impossible, sir. He's taken our guns."

Lemmings looked out the window and saw an assault rifle fly over the Cyclone fence, followed by a shotgun. They were, in turn, followed by assorted handguns and a truncheon. Then a telephone handset sailed after the weapons and the line in Lemmings' hand went dead.

"I think we have serious trouble at the gate, Mr. Millis."

"I can see that," Millis said. "Must be a hit team. God, do you think that gunman belongs to some terrorist gang?"

Then another object appeared in the air over the fence. One man, and at that long distance, he didn't look impressive, but he floated up the Cyclone fence as if he were being pulled by a magnet.

"No hit team," Lemmings said. "Just that skinny guy in the black T-shirt."

"How's he getting over that fence? Is he climbing or jumping?" Millis asked.

"I can't say, sir, but it doesn't matter. When he touches the electrified wire on top, he's gone."

But the skinny guy was not gone. He kept going and landed on both feet, perfectly balanced on the electric wire that ran along the top of the fence.

"Shouldn't he be dead now?" Millis asked.

"No, sir. He knows what he's doing. He timed that jump perfectly to land on the wire with both feet. The charge is fatal only if the person touching the wire is grounded."

"I don't understand that 'grounded' business. That's what the electrical department's for," Millis said. "I thought when you touched a hot wire, you died."

"If you ever saw a pigeon land on the third rail of a subway, you'd understand, Mr. Millis."

"I don't ride subways. I own six cars and they all look alike."

"That man won't be hurt by the current as long as he doesn't touch another object while he's on the wire."

"He can't stay there forever, can he? Unless these terrorists belong to a circus. Maybe they're all acrobats and wire walkers and like that," Millis said.

"There's only this one, so far," Lemmings said, and as he spoke, the man on the electrified fence jumped and seemed to float to the ground, just as he had seemed to float up to the wire in the first place.

"I'll have him stopped in his tracks," Lemmings said and dialed the main security outpost on the office phone.

Hubert Millis watched the man in the black T-shirt run across the grassy ground that separated his office building from the first defense perimeter. A tiny puff of dust kicked up near his feet. Then another. But still the man kept coming.

"What's wrong with those guards of yours? Can't they hit just one running man?"

"They're trying," said Lemmings. "What's the matter with you people?" he yelled into the telephone. "Can't you hit just one running man?"

"Wait," Millis said. "He's turning. I think he's running away."

Lemmings rushed to the window. The thin man in black had doubled back. The dust-puff marks of high-powered rifle bullets still pursued him, still missed, but now the man was running in the opposite direction.

He vaulted toward the Cyclone fence in a high-arcing leap. This time he did not land on the electric wire, but cleared the whole fence and landed on his feet, running, on the other side.

He kept on going. "We scared him off," Lemmings said happily. "My people did it."

"Maybe," said Millis. "And maybe not. I saw him before he turned back. He was looking at that building on the other side of the highway. It looked like something caught his eye and made him change his mind."

"Begging your pardon, sir, but that doesn't make sense.

Obviously, he's after you. He wouldn't turn back after coming this far."

"Yeah? Then why's he running toward that building?" asked Hubert Millis.

Remo Williams had gotten past the American Auto guards without a problem. Like all fighters who relied on weapons instead of the powers locked inside their own bodies, they were helpless once their weapons were taken away.

The fence too had been easy. The hair on the backs of Remo's arms had registered the electrical current even before he had consciously become aware of it. The few seconds he had spent balanced on the wire had given him time to scan the complex layout, and once on the ground, the ragged fire of the inner security forces—anxious not to shoot their own men—had been easy to evade.

Millis would be found, he knew, on the top floor of the tallest building in the complex but as he cleared the space toward that structure, he had caught the glint of something out of the corner of one eye.

On the roof of a building outside the complex, the dying red sunlight was reflected from something glass. Remo's eyes spotted the source of the light.

A man was crouched on the roof. He was sighting down the scope of a long-barreled weapon and even at the distance of five hundred yards, Remo had recognized the man as the scar-faced gunman he had encountered earlier in the day.

And because Remo was interested in Hubert Millis only as a lead to the gunman who called himself Remo Williams, he had doubled back and headed for a showdown with the man who had stolen his name.

The sniperscope checked perfectly. He could see Hubert Millis through it and the gunman laughed aloud because for all his effort in erecting defenses, Millis had overlooked the possibility of a sniper's nest outside his building complex.

Millis was in frantic conversation with an underling and there appeared to be some kind of disturbance at the gate, the gunman saw. No matter. It would be over in a very few minutes.

Crouched on the roof, the gunman locked the telescope sight and from an open briefcase, extracted the add-ons that transformed his Beretta Olympic into a working rifle.

He screwed the collapsible shoulder stock into the nut built into the pistol's butt, extended it, and tested the feel. Good.

Next he fitted a mounting, like a silencer, over the barrel. It received the rifle barrel smoothly. Finally he exchanged the ammunition clip for an extra-long sixteen-round version that stuck out from below the butt.

When he was done, he carefully went back over the job, making sure that everything was fitted together perfectly. Then he hefted the weapon to his shoulder and peered into the light-gathering scope.

He saw the front door of the American Auto corporate headquarters.

He raised the rifle so his scope saw the sky, then slowly lowered it until he was zeroed in on the highest floor. Millis was still there, talking to a younger man who looked like a cop on vacation. Perfect.

The gunman took a deep breath, then began the slow controlled pressure on the trigger to ensure a smooth first shot. Only one would be necessary and he sighted carefully at Hubert Millis' chest.

Then the gun barrel kicked up and knocked him backward.

He found himself sitting down, his finely crafted weapon sliding to a stop a few feet away. What had happened? He had not even fired.

The gunman got to his feet and scooped up his weapon. It appeared undamaged. No. Wait. There was a nick along the gun barrel and then he noticed a rock lying on the gravel roof. It had not been there a moment before. He was sure of it. He picked it up. It was not a rock but a shard of brick, exactly the color of the walls of the building he stood upon.

Someone had thrown it. But who? How? There was no one else on the roof and no other roof in throwing distance. Besides, he had felt the gun barrel being knocked upward. That meant the shard had come from below.

But that was impossible. He was twenty stories above the ground.

He looked over the parapet anyway.

He saw a man. An impossible man. The man was climbing the sheer face of the building, somehow holding on to the cracks between the bricks. And he wasn't just crawling, he was moving fast.

As he watched, the gunman saw the climbing man's face grow more distinct. It was looking up at him and he recognized the face of the man he'd noticed at the Dynacar demonstration, the one who had run toward the old Chinaman when the shooting started.

What was he doing here?

The gunman decided it didn't matter. He drew a bead on the white face of the climbing man and fired.

The man stopped climbing and scuttled sideways like a jumping spider. The bullet missed and the gunman fired again. This time, the man jumped the other way. It was more of a hop and the gunman actually saw him float in midair for only the length of time it took for his eye to register the phenomenon. Then the man was perched and climbing again.

The gunman took his time, lining him up in the scope.

This time the man stopped, whacked a fragment of brick from the building face with the side of his hand, and flipped it casually. The fragment hit the gunman in the shoulder. It was only a small fragment, hardly larger than a pebble, but it struck with enough force to knock him back twelve feet and tumble him onto his back.

He was getting to his feet when the man came over the edge of the roof.

"Well, well, well. If it isn't Mr. Environment," Remo said. "I've been looking all over for you. The Sierra Club wants to give you an award."

The gunman looked for his Beretta. It was too far away and he had no backup weapon. He never carried one; he had never needed one before.

Remo came at him and the gunman felt himself lifted to his feet so fast the blood rushed from his head. When his vision cleared, he was looking into familiar eyes; they were the eyes of cold death.

"Well, give me my award and let me get out of here," the gunman said. He grinned and raised his hands in a gesture of empty-handed surrender.

"Age before beauty," Remo said. "You start. What's your name? Your real name?"

"Williams. Remo Williams," the gunman said.

"I don't think that answer's truly responsive," Remo said. The gunman found himself flat on his back on the roof again, a searing pain in his right shoulder.

Remo was smiling down at him. "It only gets worse, pal. Your name?"

The gunman shook his head. "It's Remo Williams," he said. "Check my wallet. My ID."

Remo ripped open the back of the man's pocket and extracted his billfold. There was a driver's license, a Social Security card, three credit cards, and an organ-donor card.

They all said "Remo Williams." Remo ripped up the organ-donor card. "You won't need this last one, I don't think," he said. "Your organs aren't going to draw much interest in the medical market."

"I don't know why you don't believe me," the man said. "I'm Remo Williams. Why's that so hard to believe?"

"Because that's my name," Remo said.

The gunman shrugged and tried to smile past the pain in his right shoulder.

"Who knows? Maybe we're related. I'm from Newark," he said. "Not Ohio. New Jersey."

Remo suddenly felt dazed. His own voice said softly, "That's where I'm from too."

"Maybe we *are* related," the gunman said. He got to his feet; the shoulder pain had gone and he glanced toward his gun.

Remo said, "I'm an orphan. At least I thought I was an orphan."

"I had a son once," the gunman said, still eyeing his weapon. He edged a step closer to it. "But my wife and I separated and I never saw him again. You'd be about the right age."

Remo shook his head. "No. No. Not after all these years," he said. "It doesn't happen that way."

"No, sure," the gunman said. "Just a coincidence. We just happen to be two of the forty or fifty thousand guys named Remo Williams who come from Newark, New Jersey." He took two small steps sideways toward his gun. He noticed that the younger man seemed not to be seeing anything; there was a dumb uncomprehending expression in his dark troubled eyes.

"I can't believe this," Remo said. "Chiun told me to stay away from you. He must have known."

"I guess he did," the gunman said. Chiun must be the tricky Oriental who kept getting in the way. "But nothing's thicker than blood. We're together now. Son." He casually retrieved his weapon; the younger man seemed not to notice. His face was an expressionless mask.

"Smith must have known too. They both knew. They both tried to keep me from meeting you. From knowing the truth."

"I bet," the gunman said sympathetically. "They both knew, but you can't keep family apart, son. You're with me now and I have some work to do. Then we can get out of here.''

Remo's vision cleared suddenly. "You're a professional hit man," he said.

"A job's a job," the gunman said.

"It's my job too, sort of," Remo said.

"Must run in the family, son," the gunman said. "But just watch. I'll show you how the old man does it."

The gunman walked to the edge of the roof and hoisted his weapon to his shoulder. Maybe he could finish this up quickly, he thought.

"I can't let you do that," Remo said.

The gunman started to pull on the trigger. "I guess here's where we see if blood is really thicker than water," he said.

14

Sergeant Dan Kolawski did not understand.

"Twenty-three years on the job, I'm going to be fired over a freaking clerical error?"

"No," he was told by the lieutenant. "I didn't say you're *going* to be fired. I just said you *might* be fired."

"Over a freaking clerical error? Is this the way Newark's finest are being treated these days? Wait until the goddamn union hears about this."

Kolawski's voice rattled the windows of the police precinct building. Heads turned. The sergeant's face was turning crimson.

The lieutenant laid a fatherly arm about Kolawski's trembling shoulders and led him to the men's room.

"Look, Dan," the lieutenant said once they were inside and safe from eavesdroppers. "You've had the request since yesterday. Why didn't you send the file the way you were supposed to?"

"Because it was unauthorized. There was no backup requisition form for the file. See?" He pulled a wrinkled piece of paper from his pocket and shook it in the air. His voice shook too.

"See? There's nothing on here to say who authorized it."

"I know that," said the lieutenant. "You know that. But I just got chewed out by the captain, who got chewed out by the mayor. I even got the impression that the mayor himself was chewed out by somebody over this."

"Over a freaking ballistics report? Over a freaking Jane Doe killing?"

"Calm down, Dan, will you? I don't understand it and you don't understand it. Let's just get it done and get on with our lives."

"All right, I'll send it. But this smells."

"Right," the lieutenant said. "But let it smell someplace else. Send the damn thing."

Sergeant Kolawski went to the records bureau, filled out a form, and a clerk in khaki uniform gave him a preprinted form, headed "JANE DOE #1708."

Kolawski saw the form was wrinkled and swore under his breath. He knew from past experience that wrinkled sheets had a tendency to jam in the fax machine, which is what they called the device used to transmit photocopies of documents over the telephone.

Kolawski made a Xerox copy of the file, returned the original to Records, and took the copy to the fax machine.

The machine was a desktop model. It was attached to a telephone used exclusively—except for an occasional personal call by a cop to his bookie—for fax transmission between police departments all over the country. It was also hooked up to the FBI, and dealing with the FBI was a large-size headache because they wanted everything just so and they wanted it yesterday.

But this one was even more of a problem than the FBI usually was. Maybe the CIA was behind this strange ballistics requisition, Kolawski thought. But there was nothing on the form to say who was going to receive the document. Just a phone number and, by God, that was against regulations and the reason Kolawski had not sent the report in the first place.

Kolawski dialed the 800 area-code number. The line rang once and a dry voice said, "Proceed."

"I must have the wrong number," Kolawski mumbled, knowing that no government agency would answer an official phone without some kind of identification.

"Stay on the line and identify yourself," the dry voice demanded.

"Just who do you think you're talking to?" Kolawski said. "This is police business."

"And you're late," the dry voice said. "You have the report?"

"Yes."

"Transmit immediately," the voice said.

"Keep your shirt on," Kolawski said. He decided he had the right number after all. He fed the report into a revolving tube like an old-fashioned wax recording cylinder, then pressed a button. He replaced the telephone receiver in its cradle as if he were hanging up.

The cylinder revolved with the report wrapped around it. In some way that he did not understand but took for granted, the report was duplicated and the image broken down and transmitted via phone lines to a similar machine which would then generate a high-quality duplicate of the original.

When the cylinder stopped revolving, Kolawski picked up the phone and said, "Did you get it?"

"Affirmative. Good-bye."

"Hey. Wait a second."

"I don't have a second," the dry voice said and the phone went dead.

"Freaking CIA spooks," Kolawski said. "They're ruining the world, those bastards."

In Folcroft Sanitarium, Dr. Harold W. Smith took the fax copy to his desk and laid it next to three similar documents. They were also ballistics reports but they were printed on FBI stationery. They listed their subjects' names as Drake Mangan, Agatha Ballard, and Lyle Lavallette.

The reports were alike in several particulars. Mangan and his mistress had been killed and Lavallette wounded by .22-caliber bullets, an unusual caliber for murder victims. Except in mob hits. On mob hits, because they were almost always done at close range by someone friendly with the victim, the .22 with its low muzzle velocity was preferred.

Smith skimmed the text of the reports. He understood enough about ballistics to figure them out. Every gun barrel was grooved in a distinctive way to put spin on a fired bullet. This added force and stability to the projectile, which otherwise would tumble erratically when it emerged from a gun barrel. But a consequence was that, like fingerprints, each gun barrel was distinctive and every bullet it fired bore the marks of its travels.

Smith had played a hunch when he ordered the ballistics reports. There was no reason to think that there was any connection between the murder of an anonymous woman at Remo Williams' forgotten grave and the sudden wave of violence directed at Detroit's automakers, but the synchronicity of the events demanded an investigation.

He had gotten the FBI reports immediately; the Newark report had been delayed through clerical incompetence. But now Smith had them all on his desk, side by side, and he began to wish he hadn't because now his worst nightmares were coming true.

For the ballistics report told him, certainly and absolutely, that the unknown woman in Newark had been killed by the same gun that had killed Drake Mangan, his mistress, Agatha Ballard, and that had injured Lyle Lavallette.

The same gun. The same gunman. Smith shook his head. Whatever was happening in Detroit, it had all begun at the grave of Remo Williams.

But what did it all mean? Maybe Remo himself would know when he arrived.

The telephone rang and Smith, already on edge, was

startled. Then he saw it was not a CURE line but one used for Folcroft's routine business and he relaxed slightly.

"Dr. Smith?" a voice said.

"Yes."

"This is the limo company. You asked us to pick up a patient at the airport. A Remo Cochran?"

"Yes," said Smith sharply, squeezing the receiver involuntarily.

"We didn't connect with him."

"Then look harder," Smith said.

"No. He's not there. Our driver says he wasn't on the plane in the first place."

"Wasn't on the plane . . ." Smith said hollowly. Even though the dying sun flooded through the big windows of his office overlooking Long Island Sound, it seemed to Smith as if the room had suddenly darkened.

"You're certain?" he asked.

"Yes, sir. Was he delayed? Should we wait for the next flight or what?"

"Yes. Wait. Contact me if he arrives. No. Contact me if he doesn't. Call me as soon as anything happens. Or doesn't happen. Is that clear?"

"The next flight isn't for four hours. This is going to cost."

"I know," Smith said. "I know this will cost. I know more than anyone," he said as he hung up the telephone.

15

"What did you say to me?" the gunman asked coldly.

He lowered his Beretta Olympic rifle-rig carefully. He knew that if he fired, he could kill Hubert Millis in the building across the highway with one shot, but he also knew that the frightening man with the thick wrists and the dead-looking eyes could kill him just as easily.

He turned carefully. It all depended on how he handled the situation. Killing Millis was a priority but not the same priority as living. Living was Priority Number One.

"What did you say to me?" he repeated more firmly.

"I said I can't let you kill him," Remo said. His hands hung at his sides. They were his weapons, his surgical instruments, but here on this roof, in the dying sun, facing the man who shared his name, they felt old and useless.

"I heard what you said," the gunman replied. He rubbed the scar along the right side of his jaw. "That's not what I meant."

"What are you talking about?" Remo said.

"Shouldn't that have been, 'I can't let you kill him, Dad'?"

"Dad?" Remo said. "I can't call you Dad. I don't even know you."

"Maybe you'd prefer 'Pop.' I hate 'Pop' myself, but if it's what you want, son . . ."

"Son . . ." Remo repeated softly. "Dad," he mumbled. He felt bewildered and shrugged. "I never called anyone Dad before. I was raised in an orphanage. Nuns took care of me."

"Not very good care," the gunman said. "They didn't even teach you how to address your own father. Instead I get threats. You were threatening me, weren't you?"

"I didn't mean to. But I can't let you kill someone in cold blood."

"Why not? I told you it was my job. You want to deprive your old man of a living? I'm not getting any younger, you know. What is this Millis guy to you anyway?"

"I don't even know him," Remo said.

"Fine. Then you won't miss him." The gunman turned and brought the weapon to bear again.

Remo took a hesitant step forward. "No."

"Okay, kid," the gunman yelled and tossed the weapon to Remo. "You do it then."

Remo caught the rifle instinctively. It felt ugly, awkward in his hands. It had been years since he had held any kind of weapon. Sinanju had taught him that weapons were impure, unclean things that defiled the art and ruined the man who used them.

He dropped it.

"I can't. Not that way."

"I might have known. I'm not around and you grow up to be a pansy. Look at you. You dress like a bum. You talk back. I ask you to do one little thing and you deny me, your own father."

"But . . ."

"I never thought I'd say this, especially right after finding you after all these years," the gunman said, "but I'm ashamed of you, son. Ashamed."

Remo hung his head.

"I thought you said you were a killer," the other man said. "Isn't that what you told me? And I said to myself, 'Remo, your son is a man. He's following in your footsteps.' That's what I said to myself."

The man spat disdainfully.

"I didn't know you were a wimp. Now are you going to let your father do his job? Are you?"

Remo did not answer. He looked toward the man and then toward the fire door that led down from the roof.

His mouth worked and he was about to speak when there was a crash at the fire door and it popped up like a piece of steel bread ejected from a toaster. Pieces of hinge and padlock flew like grenade shrapnel.

A head appeared in the opening like a ghost rising from its grave, except this ghost wore a purple kimono instead of a shroud and spoke in a voice that crackled like a loose electrical wire.

"Remo! What are you doing with this man?"

"Little Father, it's—"

The gunman interrupted. "What did you call him?" he demanded as he reached for his Beretta, which still lay on the graveled roof.

"Well, he's not really my father," Remo said. "But he's been like a father to me."

"*I'm* your father, Remo. Don't you ever forget that," the gunman said.

"Lies," snapped Chiun, his face flushed with fury.

"No, Chiun," said Remo. "I think it's true."

"Stand aside," Chiun said. "I will deal with this most base of deceivers." He stepped up from the stairwell.

"No," Remo said.

The gunman grabbed his weapon. *Good, if the kid keeps the old gook busy, I'll be able to wrap this up.*

"You say no to me, Remo?" Chiun demanded. "Are you crazed?"

"Keep him busy, kid. I'll just be a moment," the gunman said.

"I can't let you hurt him, Chiun. I'm sorry."

"And I cannot let this amateur thug harm someone under the protection of Sinanju."

"Didn't you hear me, Chiun? He's my father. My *father*. I didn't even know he was alive."

"Not for long," Chiun said. He moved around Remo and instinctively Remo swept out a hand. The hand almost touched the person of the Master of Sinanju, when Remo's feet suddenly tangled together. He tripped and went down.

Remo bounced back to his feet as if he were on a trampoline.

"Chiun," he said and the Oriental whirled. A long-nailed finger flashed warningly at Remo, then at the gunman.

"I cannot let this man live."

"You knew he was my father all along, didn't you? Didn't you?" Remo cried.

"I am doing this for your own good," Chiun said. "Now stand back."

"This is why you didn't want me around here, isn't it? You and Smith knew about him. You knew he was my father, didn't you?"

"*I* am your Master," Chiun said. "Nothing else in the universe has a meaning in your life. Now leave us, Remo."

A kind of sick horror rode over Remo's features as he said, "You can't hurt him, Chiun."

"That man," said Chiun stonily, "has profaned the sacred personage of the Master of Sinanju." He touched the spot over his ear where the ricocheted bullet had hit him. "He has attacked someone under Sinanju's protection. He must die."

"Kick his ass, son," the gunman yelled. "I know you can do it."

Remo looked at the gunman, then at Chiun. His decision showed on his face.

"You may not raise your hand against the Master of Sinanju," Chiun intoned gravely. "Though I love you as one from my village, Sinanju comes first."

"I don't want to fight you, Chiun. You know that."

"Good. Then wait below," Chiun snapped.

Suddenly a shot sounded and Chiun's bald head whirled, the tufts of hair dancing.

"Aiiieee," he shrieked.

"Got him," the gunman grunted. "One shot and picked him off clean."

"Murderer," cried Chiun and moved toward the man, but Remo dove between the two of them.

Chiun stopped and his hazel eyes narrowed as he looked at Remo.

"So be it," he said. "You have made your choice, Remo. You are lost to Sinanju and lost to me."

He watched only for a moment, before realizing that ordinary people could get hurt just by being close, and the gunman slipped out the fire door, collapsing his Olympic pistol into his briefcase on the way down.

He walked down, shaking his head all the way. He had never seen a fight like it. It had started like a ballet. The old man's movements were slow and graceful. A sandaled toe floated out and Remo's body became a blur as he avoided it. Remo's counterthrust was a lunging handspear that seemed to go wrong only because the old man side-stepped with such exquisite speed that he seemed not to move at all.

If they were master and pupil, the gunman thought, they were the two scariest people on earth. Remo's thrusts looked faster because the human eye read them as a blur, but the old man was so blindingly quick in his movements that the eye did not register them at all.

The gunman had had enough; all he wanted to do was to get away. When he reached the ground floor of the building he told the guard at the desk that there was a fight on the roof. He had been able to hear it from his own top-floor office, he said.

The guard did not recognize him, but guards everywhere

responded to men wearing well-tailored suits and carrying leather briefcases.

The guard telephoned for a security team to go to the roof, then took out his pistol, checked the action, and rode the elevator upstairs.

When he got to the roof, he shoved his way through a crowd of uniformed guards who stood around the doorway.

"What's the matter? Why aren't you doing anything?" he demanded.

"We tried. No good."

"No good? What do you mean, no good? I see two guys at it and you say no good."

One guard held up a swollen purple hand.

"I just walked up to touch the old guy on the shoulder. I don't know what happened but my hand went numb. Now look at it."

"Does it hurt?"

"No, but I got a feeling it will when the nerves come back to life. *If* they do."

"Aaaah, I'll handle this," the security guard said. "They're not even fighting, for Chrissake. They're dancing. I'm going to break it up."

"Don't do it," the guard with the purple hand said in a quivering voice. "Don't get between them."

The security guard from the desk ignored him and stomped across the rooftop. He held his pistol in his right hand, waved it at the two men, and said, "Okay, cut the crap. You're both under arrest."

He did not know which one of them did it, but in a movement that his eyes could not register, someone wrapped the barrel of the pistol around the fingers of his shooting hand. He looked down at his fingers trapped inside a corkscrew of twisted steel and yelled to the other guards: "Call out the National Guard."

Remo was against the edge of the building when he saw, far below, the figure of the gunman walking toward a car.

He leaned over the parapet and without thinking, he cried out:

"Don't go. Dad. Wait for me."

And then Remo was over the edge, down the side of the building. Chiun waited a moment, and then, as the security guards in the doorway watched, his head seemed to slump forward and he turned and walked toward the exit door.

The guards made way for him as he walked by, and later, one of them would swear he had seen a tear in the old man's eye.

16

Dr. Harold W. Smith had not slept all night and now the sun was showing through the big one-way glass window of his office overlooking Long Island Sound.

Smith's face was haggard, his thinning hair uncombed. He still wore his striped Dartmouth tie tightly knotted at the throat but his gray jacket lay across the back of a chair, a single concession to the fatigue that stress and lack of sleep had wrought.

It was Smith's manner that he seemed smaller and slighter than he really was, and he wore naturally the look of a middle-management type who, in his declining years, had risen to a cushy but boring position as the director of a totally unimportant facility for the elderly, known as Folcroft Sanitarium.

No one knew him, but if someone had, it was most likely that Smith would have been described as a gray man, dull and unimaginative, who counted the days until retirement by the sizes of the piles of paper he shuffled endlessly.

Only one of those descriptions would have been true. Smith *was* unimaginative.

That was one of the reasons a long-dead President had picked him to head CURE. Smith had no imagination, nor was he ambitious in that power-hungry way that came naturally to politicians and reporters.

But the President had counted that as a virtue because he knew that a man with imagination could quickly be seduced by the unlimited power he would wield as the director of CURE. A man with both imagination and ambition might well attempt to take over America. And such a man could have done it too. CURE was entirely without controls. The director ran it with a free hand and without restrictions. A President could only suggest missions and the only order Smith was bound to obey from the President was the order to disband.

For two decades, Smith had been prepared to execute that order if the President gave it or to order the disbanding himself if CURE was ever compromised.

There would be no retirement for Harold Smith. Only a swift, painless death, and not even a hero's burial in Arlington National Cemetery for the man who had served his country with the OSS during World War II and who had occupied a high position in the Central Intelligence Agency until his supposed retirement in the sixties. The secrecy of CURE, the organization that didn't exist and whose initials stood for nothing and for everything, was too important to allow Smith even a small bit of posthumous recognition.

It was a lonely job, but never a boring one, and Smith would not have traded it for any work in the world because he knew its importance. Only CURE stood between constitutional government and total anarchy.

To remind himself of that, each morning Smith would come into his office, press the concealed button on his desk that raised the main CURE computer terminal, and consider that CURE was the most powerful agency on earth because it had unlimited access to unlimited information and it knew how to keep the secrets.

This morning, as he did every morning, Smith tapped out a simple code on the computer, and on the video screen appeared the first paragraph of the Constitution of the United States of America in glowing green letters.

Smith began reading, slowly, carefully, sounding out the words in his mind.

We, the People of the United States, in order to form a more perfect union, establish justice . . .

He could have recited the entire thing from memory, but to this rock-ribbed native of Vermont, the Constitution was not something one recited, as the Pledge of Allegiance was recited by unthinking schoolchildren, but a sacred document that ensured Americans the freedoms they enjoyed. To most of them, it was an ancient piece of paper kept under glass in Washington, a piece of history they took for granted. But to Harold W. Smith it was a living thing and because it lived, it could die or be killed. Smith, sitting quietly behind his desk and looking small in the Spartan immensity of his office, stood on the firing line in an unknown war to defend that half-forgotten document and what it represented to America and to the world.

Yet every time he entered his office, Smith knew he betrayed that document—by wiretapping, by threat, and so often these days, by violence and murder. It was the ultimate tribute to Smith's patriotism that he had accepted a thankless job whose very nature filled him with revulsion.

And so, in order not to lose sight of his responsibility and perhaps as a kind of penance toward the living document in which he believed implicitly, Smith read the Constitution from his video screen, reading slowly, carefully, savoring the words and not rushing through them, until in the end they were more than just words on a computer screen. They were truth.

When Smith had finished reading, he closed out the file and picked up the special telephone that connected directly to the President of the United States of America. But the telephone rang just as he touched it.

Smith snapped the receiver immediately to his ear and said, "Yes, Mr. President."

"Hubert Millis has just come out of surgery," the President said.

"Yes, Mr. President. I know. I was just about to call you regarding that matter. I assume you'll be issuing the order for us to disband."

"I should. Darn it, Smith. There's no excuse for not protecting Millis. What went wrong?"

Smith cleared his throat.

"I'm not certain, Mr. President."

"You're not certain?"

"No, sir. I've had no communication from my people. I don't know where they are and I don't know what happened."

"I'll tell you what happened. Despite everything, Millis was shot and is lucky to be alive and your people didn't do anything to stop it. If he had been killed, I want you to know that your operation would have been terminated immediately."

"I understand, sir. My recommendation precisely."

"No, you don't understand. There's a lot of talk now that the Big Three auto companies are all going to make a deal to have Lyle Lavallette come in and run their companies, because they can't compete with the Dynacar anyway. I want Lavallette protected. If he goes down, Detroit may be down the tubes. And I want your people either on the job or eliminated. Do you understand? They're too dangerous to be running loose."

"I understand, sir."

"You keep saying that, Smith, but somehow I don't find it as reassuring as I used to. I expect to be hearing from you."

"Yes, sir," Smith said. He replaced the special phone and tried, for the hundredth time in the hours since he had learned of Hubert Millis' brush with death, to call Chiun at his hotel.

As he held the telephone he wondered if he would ever

again begin a working day reading the Constitution of the United States from a computer terminal.

In the honeymoon suite of the Detroit Plaza Hotel, in the early-dawn light, Chiun, reigning Master of Sinanju, watched the sun ascend in glory.

He sat before the glass doors of the balcony which gave the clearest view of the sunrise. He rested on a straw mat, a single taper illuminating the room behind him with a smoky, angry light. As the sun rose, the light of the taper faded before it, like the glory of old empires fading before new ones.

Many Masters of Sinanju had preceded Chiun. They were all of the same blood. Chiun's blood. But there was more than a blood link connecting Chiun with his ancestors. They were all of the sun source and one with the sun source—the awesome power that enabled the Masters of Sinanju to tap the godlike power that lay within all men.

But only those could come to the sun source who had trained under a Master already possessing the sun source and only after a lifetime of training. Sinanju had been handed down to each generation of Chiun's ancestors from the time of the first great Master, Wang, who legend said had received the source from a ring of fire that descended from the stars.

It had been a proud, unbroken tradition until the day of Chiun. Chiun, whose wife bore him no heir. Chiun, who then took a white man from the outer world because there were no worthy Koreans left in Sinanju. Chiun, whose pupil was so ungrateful that when asked to choose between the gift that was the sun source and a white meat-eater who had so little use for him that he left him on a doorstep as a child, had made the wrong choice.

And now it had come to this.

Chiun hung his tired old head in sadness and seemed to hear the voices of his ancestors speaking in the stillness:

—Oh, woe, that Sinanju should come to this.

—It is the end. The greatest line of assassins in the universe will soon be no more.

—Gone, gone. All gone. Our honor besmirched and there is none to carry on our line.

—Shame. Shame to Chiun, trainer of whites, who chose a non-Korean. Shame to him who let the future of Sinanju slip through his fingers while he lived in luxury in a corrupt land.

—All we were, you are now. When you are gone, the glory of Sinanju will be no more.

—And we will be voices in the void, nothing more. Voices without hope, without one of our blood to carry on Sinanju.

—And you will be one of us, Chiun.

—A voice.

—In the void.

—Without a son.

—Without hope.

—That will be your destiny, Chiun, final Master of Sinanju.

—And your shame.

—Oh, woe, that Sinanju should come to this.

Chiun lifted his head at the sound of the ringing telephone, then turned away. But the ringing continued, insistent, and finally he rose from his lotus position and glided to the phone. He picked it up but spoke no greetings.

After a pause, Smith asked, "Chiun?"

"I am he," said the Master of Sinanju.

"I've been trying to reach you, Chiun. What happened? Millis is in a coma."

"I have no answer for you," Chiun said.

Smith noticed the old Korean's voice was empty of feeling. He said, "Remo never arrived. He wasn't on the plane."

"I know. He is lost to us, lost to Sinanju."

"Lost?" Smith demanded. "What do you mean lost?"

"He is with the one of white skin who is his father," Chiun said.

Smith said, "But he's alive, right? He's not dead."

"No," said the Master of Sinanju as he hung up the receiver quietly, pain in his hazel eyes. "He is dead."

17

If he could only take care of that lunatic gunman, things would be perfect for Lyle Lavallette. He considered that as he sat in his office, first trying, then rejecting a pair of elevator shoes that his cobbler in Italy had just sent him. They were guaranteed to make him a full inch taller than his even six feet; but when he tried them on, they wrinkled his socks and so he tossed them in the wastepaper basket. Maybe if he were only five-feet-eleven, but he was six feet tall already, and the extra inch wasn't worth wrinkled hose.

He had expected more competition from the Big Three when he unveiled the Dynacar. But with Mangan's killing, the board of directors National Autos seemed prepared to offer Lavallette the opportunity to head the company. And he had already heard from two board members at American Autos, whose president Hubert Millis lay near death in a hospital. Only Revell's company, General Autos, seemed to be holding firm, but Lavallette figured that Revell was shaky and with a good pension offer, could probably be persuaded to take early retirement. That would clear the way for Lavallette to take over General Autos too.

No one had ever done it before. He would head the entire car industry in the United States. It had been his dream since he was a little boy playing with matchstick cars and trucks. And it was coming true.

"Miss Blaze, things are looking up," he said as his secretary entered the office.

"I don't know, Mr. Lavallette. What about that awful man who tried to kill you? I won't rest easy until that man is in jail."

"I'm not afraid of him," Lavallette said, tapping his bulletproof Kevlar suit. Even his tie was bulletproof. It was not technically necessary but he had had a set made, for a thousand dollars, because he liked his ties to match his suits. At any rate, his public-relations firm told him they could probably get him a page in *People* magazine with that tie: "LYLE LAVALLETTE, THE MAVERICK AUTO GENIUS WHO WEARS METAL TIES."

Lavallette like the idea. He liked it all a lot and after this was all over, he might just keep wearing bulletproof ties.

He checked his tie knot in one of the three full-length mirrors in his office. They were strategically placed so that, no matter how Lavallette faced visitors from behind his desk, he had at least one unobstructed view of himself. That way he knew whenever his tie was crooked or his hair not precisely combed, or if any similar near-catastrophe threatened.

Lavallette smiled at his own image now in the mirror facing his desk, and thought he was showing a little too much gum. He tightened his face. Yes, that was it. Too much gum was bad. It took away from the brilliance of his shiny ceramic teeth and he wondered if there was such a thing as gum-reduction surgery. It might be easier to submit to surgery than to have to keep adjusting one's smile. He made a mental note to look into it.

"I think you're very brave," Miss Blaze said.

Lavallette popped out of his self-absorbed mood.

"What's that you say?"

"I said I think you're very brave. I know if I were in your shoes, I'd be petrified." Miss Blaze's body shook at the thought. Her breasts shook especially, and Lavallette decided that she was at her most appealing when she shuddered in fear. Maybe he would arrange for the experience to happen often.

"I survived one attempt. I'm not afraid of another," he said.

"But when I think of poor Mr. Millis, lying in a coma—"

"That moron," Lavallette snapped. "Do you know he fired me in 1975?"

"Yes. You've told me twenty times. I think it still bothers you."

"They all did. They all fired me. But I swore I'd be back on top again. And now I am. And look where they are. Mangan's dead; Millis is going to be a vegetable . . ."

"You shouldn't speak that way about him." Miss Blaze pouted. "The past is the past. You should let bygones be bygones."

"Miss Blaze, do you know what a bygone is?"

Her pouty face opened involuntarily and her brow furrowed.

"Sure. It's a . . . a . . ."

"Never mind," Lavallette said dismissively. The recollections of the black periods in his career still rattled him whenever they came to mind. "You came in here for a reason. What is it?"

"Oh, I did, didn't I? Let me think."

Lavallette rapped his fingers on the desktop impatiently. He stopped suddenly, his face freezing in horror.

"Arggggh," he groaned.

"What is it? Oh, God, have you been shot? Tell me you haven't been shot. Should I get a doctor?"

Lavallette bolted from his chair, holding his right hand at arm's length, as if the pain were beyond bearing. Miss Blaze stared and stared, looking for telltale bloodstains but she saw none.

"What is it?" she wailed, biting her knuckles to keep herself under control.

"In that cabinet, quick. The first-aid box. Hurry."

She threw open a liquor cabinet, rummaged around, and found a teak box that said FIRST AID in gold letters.

"Here it is. What should I do?"

"Just open it," Lavallette said in a tight voice.

She undid the latch of the box. Inside, instead of the usual first-aid equipment, she saw tweezers, combs, and two long plastic boxes, one marked "right" and the other "left."

Lavallette took out the small box marked "right," still holding out his right hand.

Miss Blaze saw inside five oval-shaped objects, like wood shavings, except clear. If she hadn't known better, she would have sworn they were fingernails. Not the long tapered kind that women wore, but blunt mannish versions.

She saw Lavallette go frantically to work on the tip of his right index finger with a gold tool of some kind. It almost looked like a pair of fingernail clippers.

When the tool stopped clicking, a sliver of fingernail fell onto the desk.

Lavellette lifted one of the oval shapes from the box and carefully, with tweezers and adhesive, laid it over his right index fingernail.

The anguished expression slowly left his face as he examined the nail with a magnifying glass.

"A hundred-dollar manicure ruined because of you," he said at last.

"Me? How me?" she said.

"You made me wait and I was drumming my fingers and my nail chipped. Forget it. What was it you wanted, and it better be good."

"Oh," Miss Blaze said. "The FBI is on line one. They want to know if you'll reconsider their offer to put you under round-the-clock protection."

"Tell them no. I can handle this myself. Tell them I have it covered."

"And the Army is out in the lobby. They say they have an appointment."

"The Army? I didn't ask to meet with the Army."

"Colonel Savage said you did."

"Oh. Savage. You ninny, he's not the Army. He's part of my new bodyguard team."

"I thought you weren't afraid of anyone," Miss Blaze said.

"I'm not. But if that killer comes around again, I want to be ready for him this time."

"Should I send them all in? There's at least thirty of them, all dressed up in those jungly clothes with rifles and ropes and boots and all that Rambo stuff."

"No. Just send in Savage."

"Gotcha."

"And don't say 'Gotcha,' Miss Blaze. Say, 'Yes, sir.' You're not waiting on tables in a diner anymore. You're the personal secretary to one of the most powerful executives in America. And one of the most handsome," he added as an afterthought, checking his cresting wavy white hair in a mirror.

"Don't forget brave. You're also brave."

"Right. Brave. Send in Savage."

Colonel Brock Savage had prowled through the swamps of Vietnam in pursuit of Vietcong guerrillas. He had hacked his way through two hundred miles of the jungles of Angola. In the deserts of Kuwait, he had lived for eight weeks as a bedouin in order to infiltrate a sheik's inner circle. He was a specialist in underwater demolition, night fighting, and survival tactics. His idea of a vacation was to parachute into Death Valley with only a knife and a bar of chocolate and see how long it took him to get out.

All these qualifications were described in the "Positions Wanted" advertisement Lavallette had answered in *Soldier of Fortune* magazine. Lavallette could have had the FBI at his disposal for free but he didn't want only protection. He wanted men who would accept his orders without qualm or questions, regardless of what those orders might be.

Colonel Brock Savage and his handpicked mercenary team fit Lavallette's needs perfectly. Savage was perfect—except he was not used to the boardrooms of executive America.

That fact became apparent when Savage, resplendent in jungle fatigues and battle gear, tried to enter Lavallette's office. He got through the doorway all right, but his Armalite rifle, slung low across his back, caught its muzzle and camouflaged stock against the doorjamb.

"Ooof," grunted Savage before he fell.

He landed on his rump. The cartridge-jammed bandoliers crisscrossing his chest ripped. Cartridges broke loose, scattering across the floor like marbles. A folding knife fell out of his boot. A packet of K-rations popped loose.

Under his breath, Lavallette groaned. Maybe he should have gone with the FBI after all.

Brock Savage struggled to his feet, weighed down by almost one hundred pounds of destructive equipment. Finally, he shook off his bandoliers and rifle. After that, it was easy.

"Colonel Brock Savage reporting for duty, sir!" he said, scuffing the smeared K-rations off his boots and into the expensive carpet.

"Don't shout, Savage," said Lavallette. "Pick up your gear and sit down."

"I can't, sir. Not with all this equipment."

Lavallette took a second look and realized that if Savage could sit down, his canteen, K-ration packs, and other belted hardware would chew up his imported Spanish leather chairs.

"Fine. Stand. Let me explain my position and what I want you to do."

"No need, sir. I read the papers."

"Then you know the assassin who is stalking me, this

Remo Williams environmentalist nut, is bound to come after me again.''

"My men and I are ready. We'll capture him if he shows his civilian face around here.''

"I don't want him captured. I want him dead. You understand? If I wanted captured, I'd let the FBI swarm all around here. I can't have that. My Dynacar is a high-security project. Guarding it will be part of your job too.''

"Yes, sir.''

"And stop saluting, would you please? This is not a military operation.''

"Anything else, Mr. Lavallette?''

"Yes. Throw away those stupid ration packs. Dynacar Industries has a wonderful subsidized company cafeteria. I expect you and your men to eat in it.''

"Yes, sir.''

"In the blue-collar section, of course.''

18

"Tell me about my mother."

"Kid, I've told you about your mother three times already. Give me a break, will you?"

"Tell me again," Remo Williams said. He sat on a big sofa in a Detroit hotel room, following with his eyes the man who was his father, feeling a strange mixture of distance and familiarity. His father had just gotten off the telephone and was looking for a fresh shirt.

"Okay. Last time. Your mother was a wonderful woman. She was beautiful and she was kind. She was intelligent. In the right light, she looked like twenty-three even when she was forty-three."

"How'd she die?" Remo asked.

"It was awful," the gunman said. "Sudden death. One minute she was fine; the next minute she was dead."

"Heart attack," Remo said and the gunman nodded. "It really broke me up," he said. "That's why I left Newark and came out here."

"You haven't told me why you left me at the orphanage when I was a baby," Remo said.

"Your mother and I just weren't making it. We tried but you know how those things are. We got divorced and she got custody of you. You understand?"

"Yes,''' Remo said. In the evening light, he thought he could see the family resemblance in his father's eyes. They were the same flat unreflective black as his own.

"So, anyway, in those days, it was tough for a woman to be divorced and to have a kid. Neighbors, family, nobody would talk to her and finally, she decided it would be best if you went to the nuns. I was furious when I heard about it, but if I came to get you, it would look like I was saying your mother didn't know how to take care of you. So I left you there, even though it broke my heart. I just figured . . . well, I figured there was no looking back.''

"I guess not,'' Remo said. "Do you have a picture of her? Sometimes, I used to try to imagine what my mother looked like. When I was a kid, I used to lie in bed when I couldn't sleep and make up faces.''

"Is that so?'' the gunman said as he put on his jacket. "And what'd you think she looked like, kid?''

"Gina Lollobrigida. I saw her in a movie once. I always wanted my mother to look like Gina Lollobrigida.''

"That's amazing, son. It really is. Your mother looked exactly like her, exactly. You must be psychic or something.''

Remo looked up and said, "Where are you going?''

"Out. I've got business to attend to.''

"I'll come with you.''

"Look, kid. It's good that we found each other after all these years but I can't have you following me everywhere. Now relax. I'll be back in an hour or so. Go get yourself fed or laid or something. Practice. That's it. Practice. 'Cause when I come back you've got to start telling me how you do all that stuff with walls and fighting and all.''

The hotel-room door slammed on Remo's hurt face.

The gunman took the elevator to the hotel garage and drove his car onto the dingy street of Detroit.

"Jeez,'' he said to himself aloud. "This is going to be a bitch.''

He lit a cigarette, hating the stale taste in his mouth. He had to get rid of the kid. What he didn't need now in his life was some overgrown teenager worrying about Daddy. Maybe he would wait until Remo had taught him his tricks. Sinanju, he called it, whatever that was. He didn't know what it meant, but you were never too old to learn new things, especially if they could help you in your trade. Maybe he'd wait and learn and then one night when the kid was sleeping, just put a bullet in his brain and get away.

That was one way. The other way was just not to return to the hotel and let this Remo kid try to find him. But Remo had found him before. Whatever Sinanju was, he seemed to be able to do things that normal people couldn't do. The old Oriental too, for that matter, and he had to be eighty if he was a day.

The gunman wondered why the old Oriental was hounding him. First, he showed up at the Mangan hit, and then at the Dynacar demonstration and then at the Millis shooting. All because the man who hired him had insisted on sending the stupid environmental warning to the newspapers. That part had been dumb and unprofessional, but it was part of the job. The old gook though; he wasn't part of the job.

He had tried to escape from the two of them that early evening when he had left them fighting on the rooftop. But even as he was pulling out of the parking lot, he saw the kid coming down the side of the building and running after him.

He had sped up to seventy-five, then slowed to sixty-five once he got to the interstate highway, thinking he was free. And suddenly the passenger door was pulled open.

He had stomped on the gas pedal and swerved to the right so the twin forces would slam the door shut, but the door would not close. It was being held open, and then a voice had yelled, "Hey. Keep the wheel steady."

It was the kid, Remo, running alongside the car, holding

the door open, and then he hopped into the passenger seat
and slammed the door after him.

"Don't worry, Dad," the kid had said. "I'm all right."

Just the memory of it made the gunman's mouth dry.

It was going to be hard to shake this Remo. At least for
a while. The best way to stay alive was to play along.

And what if the kid was right? What if Remo was his
son? It was possible. A guy who could run as fast as a car
could be anything he wanted to be.

Remo Williams sat in the darkness of the hotel room
which to his eyes was not darkness at all, but a kind of
twilight.

It was something he did not even think about anymore,
this power of sight, but simply allowed his eyes to adjust
to the darkness. Unlike ordinary eyes, the pupils did not
simply dilate to catch all the available light; it was something more. Chiun had once called the phenomenon "fishing for light." Somehow, in a way Remo was trained to
achieve but never to understand, his eyes fished for the
light and even in utter pitch darkness, he was able to see.

Remo wondered if it was a talent that had been in all
men back in the days before artificial light, before camp-
fires and candles, when man's earliest ancestors had to
hunt by moonlight, and sometimes, without even moonlight. Remo did not know; he only knew he had the power
to do it.

Thanks to Chiun.

His feelings toward his teacher, as he sat in the darkness
that was not darkness, were confused.

Chiun had always done what was best for Remo, except
when Sinanju came first. That was understood between
them. Sinanju was the center of Chiun's personal universe.

But this was different. Chiun—Smith, too—had hidden
from Remo the truth about his father. It was hard to take
and even harder to understand.

It was all hard. Remo had not thought of his parents for

years. They had been no part of his childhood, much less his adult life. They were simply an abstract concept because everyone had parents at one time and Remo just assumed that his were dead.

Once, well into his Sinanju training, Remo discovered he could tap into his early-life memories, calling them up the way Smith called up information on his computers. So he sat down one day to call up the faces of the parents he must have seen when he was an uncomprehending infant.

Chiun had found him seated in a lotus position, eyes closed in concentration.

"What new way have you found to waste time?" Chiun had asked.

"I'm not wasting time. I'm calling up memories."

"He who lives in the past has no future," Chiun had said.

"That's not real convincing from somebody who can recite what every Master of Sinanju liked to eat for breakfast. All the way back to the pharaohs."

"That is not the past. That is history," Chiun had sniffed.

"Says you. Now would you mind? I'm trying to summon up the faces of my parents."

"You do not wish to see them."

"Why do you say that?" Remo asked.

"Because I know," Chiun had said.

"No, you don't. You can't possibly know. You knew your parents, your grandparents, all your forebears. I know nothing about mine."

"That is because they are not worth knowing," Chiun had said.

"Why is that?"

"They are not worth knowing because they were white," said Chiun.

"Hah!" Remo shot back. "I've got you there. All the time you're trying to convince me I'm part Korean, just to justify your giving Sinanju to a white. Now you're changing your tune."

"I am not changing my tune. You are changing your hearing. You are not white, but your parents were. Somewhere in your past, overwhelmed by generations of diluting mating with non-Koreans, there is a drop of proud Korean blood. Perhaps two drops. Those are the drops that I train. It is my misfortune that the white baggage has to come along with them."

"Even if my parents were white," Remo had said, "that doesn't make them not worth knowing."

Chiun said loudly, "They are not worth knowing because they thought so little of you that they left you on a doorstep."

Chiun had stalked off and Remo closed his eyes again but he was not able to recall his parent's faces. A moment before, he had been all the way back into his early days at St. Theresa's Orphanage, and was sure that in another minute, he would have his parents in his mind. But not now. Chiun had ruined it with his remark and he wondered if Chiun had been right. After that failure, Remo never tried to summon up those infant's memories again.

And now that he had found his father, alive and not dead, Remo wondered if it would have been better to have left the past alone, as Chiun had said. Because now Remo could trust neither Smith nor Chiun. Both had betrayed him and while he could have expected it from Smith, he felt bewildered about Chiun's reaction.

Remo knew he had now lost a father who was not really his father, and he had gained one who was, but who didn't seem like it.

Maybe when we get to know each other. Maybe then it will feel right, he told himself. *Maybe it will feel like it did between me and Chiun*. But even as he thought that, he knew it would never be. Between Remo and Chiun, there had been more than a relationship of human beings; there had also been Sinanju. And now it was no more.

Remo did not know what Chiun would do next. But he knew Smith's next move. Smith would order Chiun to find

Remo and return him to Folcroft and if Remo refused, Smith would order his death. Smith would not hesitate. It was his job never to hesitate when CURE's security was concerned.

But what would Chiun do when he was given such an order? And what would Remo do if Chiun came to kill him?

Others who had seen their fight on the roof might have been fooled, but Remo was not. Both he and Chiun had pulled their blows, making sure not to try to hurt the other. The result had been a long stylized kung-fu match, the kind seen in Chinatown movies. But Sinanju wasn't like that. Sinanju was economy. Never use two blows where one would do. Never fight for two minutes when the job could be accomplished in two seconds.

Neither of the men had tried to hurt the other. But that might not be the case the next time they met. And Remo did not know what he would do.

So he waited alone in the darkness. A dream had come true in his life, but he knew a greater nightmare was about to begin.

19

The Dynacar was waiting for him at the landfill on the Detroit River.

As the gunman got out of his car, he thought that it was appropriate that the car that ran on garbage should be here, surrounded by building-high mounds of garbage.

"I'm here," he said to the opaque windows of the Dynacar.

"I can see you," the unseen man behind the wheel said. "Millis didn't die."

"He's in a coma. He may not be dead but he sure ain't moving, either," the gunman said.

"I wanted him dead."

"And he would have been if I was allowed to pop him in the head."

"I told you before—"

"I know," the gunman said. "No head shots."

"I still want him dead."

"Hey. They've got guards on him around the clock. Let's let things cool down and then I'll finish him."

"Finish him now," said the voice from inside the car.

"Why not Lavallette? I can get him next, then finish Millis."

"There's time enough to get Lavallette. He's making a

million public appearances with his new car and he'll be easy. But I want Millis dead now."

"Suit yourself, but hitting a guy surrounded by cops isn't as easy as it might sound."

"Millis next. Then Lavallette."

"What about Revell?" the gunman asked.

"I don't think we'll have to bother with him."

"There's another problem," the gunman said.

"There's always another problem with you. When I hired you, I thought I was getting the best."

"I am the best," the gunman said coldly.

"So what's the problem?"

"The old Oriental. The one at the Dynacar demonstration. He showed up at the Millis hit."

"So what?"

"I think he works for the government," the gunman said.

"Doesn't matter to me. If he gets in the way, get him out of the way. Permanently. Anything else?"

"No. I guess not."

"All right," said the voice from inside the car. "I'll pay for the Millis hit when it's done."

And the Dynacar silently moved out of the dumping ground like a black ghost on wheels.

The gunman got back into his car. It was too chancy for him to go after Millis. The automaker would be surrounded by guards. But there was another way perhaps.

He lit another cigarette as he thought it over.

And he also thought that it would be very interesting when it came time for him to go after Lyle Lavallette again. Very interesting indeed.

20

There was no longer any doubt in Smith's mind. The unidentified woman who had been killed at the grave of Remo
Williams was Remo's mother. And her killer—the same
man who was running amok in Detroit—was Remo's father.

There was no other explanation. As Smith had reasoned
it out, it must have been a family argument and probably
the only close relative the dead woman had was the husband, her killer. That explained why no one had reported
her missing to police.

Smith still did not understand how, after so many years,
the parents had found Remo's grave. They had never
attempted to contact Remo in all the years he was a ward
at St. Theresa's Orphanage. They had kept their distance
during Remo's tour of duty in Vietnam and during his
years as a Newark beat patrolman.

But somehow, later, they had accomplished what Smith
had long assumed was impossible. They had found their
son, or, more precisely, they had found the grave that they
believed contained their son's body.

But now Remo was really dead. And his father was
slaughtering the heads of Detroit's automotive industry.

Even with all the pieces in place, it still made no
real sense to Smith. And there were still loose ends.

An exhaustive records search had turned up no Remo Williams Senior living anywhere in the United States. Smith still did not have a name for the woman who must have been Remo's mother. The woman's morgue shot, circulated nationwide after Smith pulled some behind-the-scenes strings, had yet to bring forth anyone who knew the woman.

Where had the couple been living all these years? Smith wondered. In another country? Under assumed names? On the moon?

Whatever the truth was, Smith had made a mistake many years ago. The mistake was in selecting Remo Williams to be the man who did not exist. Smith had done it, supposing Remo to be a man without a past, but he had had a past and now that past had caught up with him. It had caught up with all of them.

Even with most of the answers in front of him, Smith wondered about the loose ends. He would look into them.

But that would have to wait. First, there was still the Detroit matter.

Drake Mangan was dead and Hubert Millis was near death in a hospital. Confidential reports said that James Revell had gone out of the country. That left Lyle Lavallette and the more Smith thought of it, the more sure he was that the gunman would be back to finish the job on Lavallette.

Perhaps not, if Smith could help it.

Remo was gone, but there was still Chiun. Smith picked up the telephone.

The Master of Sinanju was packing his steamer trunks when the phone rang and he answered it in the middle of its first ring.

Smith's voice crackled over the line.

"Chiun?"

"Hail, Emperor Smith," Chiun said. It was his customary greeting but its delivery was anything but customary because the voice sounded barren and tired and Smith realized he should proceed cautiously.

"Master of Sinanju, I know how you must be feeling at a time like this," he said.

"Hah! No man can know. No man who is not the blood of my blood."

"All right, then. I don't know. But just because Remo is gone, it doesn't mean that the world stops. We still have a mission."

"*You* have a mission," said Chiun, folding the last of his sleeping robes and gently packing it in the final open trunk.

"Let me remind you, Chiun," Smith said sternly, "that we have sacred contracts. One stipulation of our contract is that in the event of injury, incapacitation, or the death of your pupil, you, as his trainer, are obligated to render whatever service is necessary to dispose of unfinished business. This Detroit matter comes under that obligation."

"Do not speak to me of obligations," Chiun hissed. "All whites are ungrateful. I gave Remo what no white has ever before achieved, and I gave you the use of Remo. And what have I to show for all my sacrifices? Obligations!"

"You have been well paid. In gold. You are a rich man. Your village is rich."

"I am a poor man," snapped Chiun, "for I have no son, no heirs. My village eats, yes. But will their children eat, or their grandchildren, after I am gone and there is none to take my place?"

Smith resisted the urge to remind Chiun that the United States government had shipped enough gold to the village of Sinanju to feed its entire population well, for the next millennium. Instead, he said, "I've always understood that a Sinanju contract is unbreakable. And that the word of Sinanju is inviolate."

Smith felt strange throwing back Chiun's own arguments at him, but it worked. Chiun was silent for a moment. In his hotel room, Chiun felt something hard under the sleeping robe he had just packed away and reached for it. It was a silken pouch containing the shard of speckled gray rock; the rock of the Master Shang, the rock which Sinanju tradition said Master Shang had taken from the mountains of the moon.

Hefting the rock in his hand, Chiun remembered the lesson of Shang and, his voice clear again, he said to Smith, "What would you have me do?"

"I knew I could count on you, Chiun," said Smith, who knew no such thing.

"This killer who goes by Remo's name," Smith said. "My belief is that he will next attack Lyle Lavallette of Dynacar Industries."

"I will go to this carriagemaker. I will protect him. This time there will be no excuses from Sinanju."

"Don't just protect him, Chiun. Stay with him. Ask him questions. We still don't know why those auto men are targets for assassination and I don't believe it has anything to do with environmental protests. Maybe there is some common link between them all, other than their business, that you can find out. Anything would be helpful. And if the killer shows up again, take him alive if possible. We've got to know if he's doing this for personal reasons or if he's in someone's employ."

"I understand. I will protect the carriagemaker. And I will find out what he knows. Which, of course, is very little because he is a white and an American besides."

Smith ignored the remark. He paused a moment, then said, "Would you tell me how Remo died? Do you mind talking about it?"

"He fell into bad company," Chiun said.

Smith waited but the old man spoke no more. Finally, the CURE director cleared his throat and said, "Well, okay, Chiun. Communicate with me as soon as you have something."

"I have something now," said Chiun. "I have the ingratitude of whites. It is a larger thing than any Master of Sinanju has ever had before."

He hung up and at Folcroft, Smith thought that the
bitterness Chiun felt toward Remo was strange. He would
have thought Chiun would be racked by sorrow, but there
was no sign of it. Still, you could never tell about Chiun
and Smith forced it out of his mind and turned his attention
back to the loose ends surrounding the murder at the grave
of Remo Williams. Even at this critical time, in the last
few hours that CURE might continue to exist, those loose
ends ate away at him.

21

"So what have you been doing all your life, kid?" the gunman asked after the cocktail waitress had brought them drinks. They were in a quiet corner of the best restaurant in Detroit. The lighting was dim and there was a view of the downtown area through the spacious windows. By night, the dirt was forgotten and Detroit looked like a city carved from ebony and set with jewels of light.

"I've been working for the government," Remo answered after a pause. He felt uncomfortable talking about his work.

"Come on. You've got to level with your old man. Before, you told me you were in the same line as me," the gunman said.

"I am. For the government, sort of."

"I get it. Secret stuff, huh?"

"Right," Remo said. "Secret stuff."

"Well, tell me about it. And drink up. That's good bourbon."

"I can't," Remo said.

"You can't tell your own father what you've been doing for a living all these years?" the gunman said.

"I can't tell you that either," Remo said. He pushed the tumbler of brownish fluid away from him. Even the smell bothered him. "What I meant was, I can't drink this stuff."

"That's the way it goes. Name your own poison," the gunman said. He looked around for a cocktail waitress.

"I can't drink anything."

"Jeez, my son, the teetotaler. Is that what you're telling me, Remo?"

"My system won't handle alcohol," Remo said.

"You got something wrong with you?"

Remo stifled a laugh. It wasn't that there was anything wrong with his system. It was just the opposite. He was such a finely tuned human machine, thanks to Sinanju, that like a racing-car engine, the wrong mixture in the fuel tank would throw his performance off. In some cases, as with alcohol, it could have serious or fatal effects.

"What are you smiling about?" the gunman asked.

"Just thinking of Chiun," Remo said. "He said we're funny people because we eat the meat of dead cows and we drink the juice of rancid grass."

"Forget Chiun," the gunman said.

"What I mean was I can't drink stuff like this. It screws me up."

The gunman took a healthy sip of his own drink. "If you ask me, a man who doesn't drink is already screwed up."

Remo was silent. The man across the table from him was a stranger. He kept looking into the older man's face, looking for something, a flash of recognition, a long dormant memory, a hint of a shared experience, but there was nothing. Remo was confused and sad and more than a little uneasy. In another time and place, he and this man could have been enemies, and over the years for CURE, Remo had killed hundreds of professional hit men. But for circumstances, he might have killed the man who sat across from him without hesitation, never dreaming that the target might be his own father.

The waitress came back and asked for their order.

"Prime rib. Bloody rare. Mashed potatoes. Any green vegetable's okay."

Remo said, "I'll have rice. Steamed."

When Remo did not add anything else to his order, the waitress said, "And?"

"No 'and.' That's it. Just the rice. And a glass of bottled water, please."

"Yes, sir," the waitress said dubiously, taking away their menus.

"Rice?" the gunman said, "Just rice?"

"I'm on a special diet."

"Skip it for just one night. How often is it you find your father? Isn't that reason to celebrate? Have a steak."

"I can't," Remo said

"Those nuns really did a job on you," the older man sighed. "Or maybe it was hanging around with that old Chinese character?"

He quickly changed the tone of his voice when he saw the look that came into Remo's eyes. It scared him and he reminded himself to go light on that subject in the future. Or there might not be any future.

"Okay, suit yourself," the gunman said. "I want to talk to you about something."

"You never told me where I was born," Remo said suddenly.

"You never asked. Jersey City."

"I grew up in Newark," Remo said.

"That's where I worked. We moved there."

"What other relatives do I have?" Remo said.

The gunman shook his head. "Just me. I was an only child and so was your mother. Both our parents are dead. You've got nobody else but me. Listen to me, now. This is important."

"I'm listening," Remo said, but he was thinking of Chiun. The old Korean had, through the legends and history of Sinanju, given Remo more family than this man, his own father, had. He wondered what Chiun was doing right at that moment.

The gunman said, "Before, up on that roof, you told me you were a professional. Okay. I'm not going to ask you who you worked for or anything like that. I just want to know if you were straight with me when you said that."

"I was straight," Remo said.

"Okay. I believe you. Now listen to your old man. That guy I clipped. Millis. He didn't die."

"No?"

"No. And that means I don't get paid."

"Right," Remo said.

"That means I gotta finish him."

"Why don't we just forget him and leave town?" Remo said. "We can try some other place. Maybe some other country. Get to know each other."

"Look. I gotta finish him. And the way I see it, if you hadn't been screwing around on the roof, I would have gotten a clear shot and he would have been history."

Remo shrugged. "Sorry," he said.

"That doesn't cut it. I've got a reputation to maintain and this is going to hurt it. I'm not a rich guy. I need to work from time to time."

"I said I was sorry."

"I accept that," the gunman said. "But what are you going to do about it, son?"

"Do about what?" Remo said, who was getting an idea of what the older man was hinting at. The thoughts of Chiun fled from his mind.

"I mean that you owe me, Remo. You owe your old man for screwing up his hit and I want you to take care of Millis for me."

"I can't do that," Remo said.

"Can't? Everything I'm hearing from you tonight is can't. I can't drink, Dad. I can't eat, Dad. That one word is seriously going to jeopardize our relationship, son."

Remo looked down at the table and the gunman said,

"Millis is in a coma. It should be easy. I'll even loan you my best piece."

Remo's answer was a growl. "I don't need a weapon to take somebody out."

"No, I guess you don't," the older man said and lit a cigarette. "Then it's settled?"

"This isn't right," Remo said.

"I know you've killed for the government. You told me that. I'm just asking for my due. If you can work for them, you can work for me. Do it or take your 'can'ts' and get out of my life." The gunman set himself. If the kid was going to turn on him, it would be now.

"It isn't right," Remo said hollowly, as if he had not heard the other man speak. "I killed for my country in Vietnam. I killed for Chiun and for Smith . . . for the government. And now you. It isn't right that we meet and you tell me to go kill somebody for you. That's not what a father's supposed to be."

The older man relaxed and his tone grew sympathetic.

"It's the breaks, kid. You've got to go with the flow. For you, the choice is buy or fly. What's it going to be?"

"I don't know," Remo said. "We'll see." He looked up as the waitress brought their food.

"Sure we will, son," said the gunman. "Sure we will. You sure you don't want some of my prime rib?"

22

He had never been to Wildwood Cemetery.

More than a decade before, Smith had arranged for a man to be buried in the grave that bore the name of Remo Williams. He had made the funeral arrangements, ordered the headstone, and bought the cemetery plot. He had even arranged for the body that went into the grave. It was not Remo's body but that of some homeless derelict whom no one would ever miss. Smith had known the derelict's name once but he had long since forgotten it. That man had had no family, either. And there was no CURE record of the person.

And during all that he had never visited the cemetery and now, as he stood over the grave marked "Remo Williams," Smith felt the rush of emotion that he had ignored for more than ten years.

Smith did not cry, not outwardly. But what he felt was a wave of strangling feelings. He had picked a policeman, a cop with a clean but undistinguished record, and arranged for his ruin. Overnight, Remo Williams had gone from being a respected policeman to a man on trial for his life. Smith had rigged it all—the drug pusher who had been found beaten to death in an alley, Remo's badge conveniently next to the body. And he had set it up so it took place at a time when Remo would have no alibi.

He had not had to bribe the judge who sentenced Remo to the electric chair in the New Jersey state prison, although he would have done that if necessary.

And finally he had made the necessary arrangements so that the electric chair was rigged and Remo Williams survived it and came into the employ of CURE and into the care of Chiun, the latest Master of Sinanju.

Not once in all the years had Smith allowed himself a moment of remorse over what he had done, but now that Remo was dead, it all flooded into his mind.

Still, no tears came. It was too late for tears just as it was too late for Remo. It was probably too late for CURE too.

Remo's grave stood in the shade of a dying oak tree, half its limbs gray and bare and without leaves. It was the most utilitarian grave Smith had ever seen, a square of granite marked with a cross and Remo's name and no more. Smith had ordered the headstone from a catalog and, to save costs as much as a security measure, had ordered the stonecutter to leave off the dates of birth and death.

Grass grew uncut around the grave. Groundskeeping was not a high priority at Wildwood, which was one of the reasons Smith had chosen it. Wildwood was a small burying ground, tucked away in a seldom-visited area outside Newark, hidden in woods and surrounded on all sides by a wrought-iron fence which was in the final stages of collapse.

Wildwood got few visitors.

Remo's grave was not alone. There was one on either side, spaced closely together. On one side, an older stone bore the name D. Colt. On the other, there was a larger stone bearing the family name DeFuria, and the names of several generations of DeFurias who had been interred in the ground around it.

Smith tried to reconstruct the murder of the anonymous

woman in his mind. He stood where he knew she must
have stood. He imagined the direction from which the
bullets had come and tried to calculate the impact. He saw
where the flowers she held in her hands had fallen.

It all seemed reasonable enough, but still something did
not make sense. Why hadn't she visited the grave before
all this? And how had she found Remo after all these
years, even in death?

Those bothersome questions, more than anything else,
had brought Smith to Wildwood and, standing over Remo's
grave, they bothered him even more.

Smith took out a spiral notepad and jotted down the
names on the stones on either side of Remo's grave and
made a note to ask Chiun where Remo's real body was.
Perhaps he could arrange for Remo's burial here at Wildwood. This time for real. He owed Remo that much, at
least.

And then he walked out of the cemetery.

He did not look back. It was too late for looking back.

23

When the gunman told him that the hospital might be a tough place to penetrate, Remo considered telling him what he knew: that a hospital is not a fortress, not designed to keep people either in or out. It is just a hospital, a place where sick people go to become well, and one could put a thousand guards around a hospital and its security would still leak like a sieve.

But he decided to say nothing; the older man would not understand.

He slipped out of the car as the gunman slowed down along the John C. Lodge Freeway in the center of Detroit. As the door closed behind him, Remo heard the gunman say, "Give 'em hell for your old man, kid."

The car sped off and Remo vaulted the retaining wall along the edge of the freeway and made for the hospital grounds. Remo wore black and in the darkness of the night, he was a silent thing that moved from tree to bush, from bush to car as he worked toward the hospital's parking lot.

The hospital itself was a large complex and in the artificial light of the ground floods, the main building appeared bone white and cold.

Remo slipped past idly patrolling security guards. He

had not expected any trouble from them. If there was trouble, it would come on the floor where Hubert Millis, president of American Autos, lay in a coma.

Once he got to the big entrance doors, Remo rose from his crouching walk and sauntered into the lobby as if he were delivering coffee and Danish.

A brassy-looking nurse stood behind a reception desk, making marks on a clipboard.

"Yes, sir," she asked Remo.

"What floor is Mr. Millis on, please?"

"Visiting hours are from three to five P.M.," she said

"That isn't what I asked," Remo said pleasantly.

"And visiting is restricted to immediate family."

"I didn't ask that either," Remo said.

"Are you a relative?" the nurse asked.

"Just part of the family of man," Remo said. He noticed the clipboard and reached across the desk to snatch it up.

"Give that back," the nurse snapped.

Remo found Millis' name and the room number 12-D. That meant the twelfth floor. Or did it mean D ward?

"Where's the D ward?" Remo asked.

"There is no D ward," the nurse said huffily.

Remo handed her the clipboard back. "Much obliged," he said. Good. It would be a lot easier to get to the twelfth floor than to spend his night hunting everywhere for some frigging D ward.

"Guard!" the nurse yelled.

"Now you've done it," Remo said when a uniformed security guard came around the corner.

"What is it?" the guard demanded, a hand hovering near the butt of his holstered revolver.

"This man is asking questions about the patient in 12-D," she said.

"What's your problem, buddy?" the guard asked.

"No problem," Remo said breezily. "I was just leaving."

"I'll walk you out," the guard said.

"Fine. I love company," Remo said.

His hand on his weapon, the guard followed Remo into the cool evening. He was torn between calling for help on his walkie-talkie and cuffing the intruder on general principles, but the man had not really done anything wrong. He had simply asked some questions about the patient in room 12-D, which the guard knew was under twenty-four-hour watch by a team of FBI agents.

The FBI agents had snubbed the guard when he offered to help them.

"Just stick to your post, old-timer," the FBI team leader had said. They had given him no specific instructions so now he was not sure what to do with the skinny guy in black.

And then the question became academic because suddenly Remo was no longer there.

He had been standing alongside the guard and now he was not there and the guard did a 360-degree turn, saw nothing, and then moved over toward the bushes alongside the front door. All he saw were shadows but they were funny shadows, darker than most, and they seemed to be moving, and then he was sure, they were moving, but it was too late then because slowly he slipped into unconsciousness.

Remo caught the guard after he released his oxygen-blocking hold on the man's neck. He carried him as easily as if he were a child to a nearby parked car, popped the lock with a finger, and put the man behind the wheel, where he would awaken, hours later, not exactly sure what had happened to him.

By that time, Remo expected to be gone.

The face of the hospital building was sheer, without handholds, but there were windows, and Remo hopped lightly up onto a ground-floor window ledge. From there, he reached the second-floor window, and in that fashion, using the windows as rungs in a ladder that was the hospital itself, Remo started upward. To anyone watching

it would have seemed easy and for Remo it was. Several
of the windows he reached were open or spilling light and
because his approach depended on stealth, Remo worked
sideways a window or two before he could resume climbing again. It was like playing checkers against the hospital
wall, with the windows as the squares and Remo as the
only moving piece.

He passed the twelfth floor and on the level above, he
scored the glass of a darkened window with his fingernail
and pushed hard on the circle he had made.

The circle turned and Remo grabbed an edge that swung
outward and pulled. Soundlessly, the ring of glass hung
free in his hand and Remo flipped it off to the side like a
Frisbee. It zipped across the parking lot and embedded
itself in the side of a tree, the way a single straw can be
driven into wood by a tornado's wind.

Remo reached an arm through the hole and silently
unlocked the window. His eyes automatically adjusted to
the darkness of the room as he slipped inside. It was a
sickroom, not in use. There were two beds and the room
reeked of the hospital smell that was ninety percent chemical disinfectant and ten percent the scent of sickness and
despair.

Remo pulled a sheet from one of the beds and ripped it
several times. When he was done, he pulled it over his
head. It looked sort of like a hospital patient's gown, if
one did not look too hard. Remo kicked off his shoes.
Being barefoot might help him pass as a patient.

No one gave him a second glance in the hospital corridor and at the nearest exit, Remo found a stairwell down
to the twelfth floor.

He started down, still not sure what he was going to do
when he got there.

FBI Field Agent Lester Tringle never forgot the advice
he had given in the FBI training academy: "Always expect
trouble. Then, if it comes, you're prepared."

So even now, on this piece-of-cake detail guarding a man in a coma, Tringle was ready for trouble. He stood outside Room 12-D, cradling in his hands a short-snouted machine pistol with a complicated telescope and box arrangement on top.

Personally, Tringle had no little regard for the laser-sighted armament. He was a crack shot and felt he did not need any fancy gadgetry, but his area supervisor had insisted. The White House considered Hubert Millis' survival a high national priority—not so much because of who he was as because so many auto manufacturers had been attacked lately. It looked bad for America if one crazed gunman could pick off the heads of the country's auto industry with impunity.

Crazy stuff, thought Lester Tringle, and even crazier that the gunman had written that letter to the paper and then signed his name, Remo Williams, at a guest register at one of the shooting sites.

He did not expect him to try to storm the hospital, but if he did come, Tringle would be ready and so he had relinquished his sidearm for a machine pistol that could fire over one thousand rounds a minute along a beam of red laser light.

There was one big benefit to laser-sighted weapons when a man worked in a team as Tringle was doing tonight. It made it a lot less likely that you'd be shot by your own teammate, because the lasers made a marksman nearly infallible. You just touched the trigger lightly and the beam shot out. A red dot, no bigger than a dime and visible under day or night conditions, appeared on the target. If the red dot appeared over a man's heart, you could bet a year's salary that when you pulled the trigger all the way, the bullets went where the dot was. That meant a lot fewer innocent bystanders and other agents shot, and for Lester Tringle, who planned to live long enough to collect his pension and open a tavern in Key West, Florida, that was important. And he always con-

ceded that the laser was especially useful with a machine
gun because the wild spray of bullets from a machine
weapon could do enormous damage if it went where it
wasn't supposed to go.

Tringle pushed away from the wall where he was leaning when he heard a sound from down the corridor that
sounded like the burp of automatic-weapon fire.

The sound died almost as soon as it started, which was
strange, for even the shortest pull on the trigger of one of
these machine pistols meant a full-second burst of about
fifteen rounds.

"Hey, Sam," Tringle called out. "What's going on?"

There was no sound from the East Wing hall. There
were no elevators at that end of the building and Agent
Sam Bindlestein was guarding a stairway exit. But now he
wasn't answering.

Tringle pulled his walkie-talkie from under his armored
vest.

"Harper, do you copy?"

"What is it?" Agent Kelly Harper's voice crackled
back.

"Something's up, I think. I don't want to leave here.
Everything quiet at your end?"

"That's a roger."

"Then come running and watch your back."

Three heavily armed agents were all the local FBI office
had thought were needed for the job. But now, with one
agent unresponsive and a second leaving his post, Agent
Lester Tringle wondered if that might not have been a
serious miscalculation.

He called Bindlestein's name into his walkie-talkie a
half-dozen times but got no response, then saw a patient, a
thin man with high cheekbones, walking toward him wearing a ragged-looking hospital robe.

"You there," Tringle called, turning toward the man
and bringing his weapon almost up to chest height. "You
don't belong here."

"I'm lost," Remo said. "I can't find my room. Can you help me out?"

"You're on the wrong floor. This is a restricted floor. There are no other patients here."

"I'm a patient and I'm here," the patient said reasonably.

"Well, you don't belong here. There's an elevator down the hall. Take it to the lobby and someone down there will help you."

But the patient kept coming. Then Tringle noticed that although the man's arms were bare, his legs, under the robe, were not. He was wearing black pants, and hospital patients never wore anything under their robes.

Tringle brought his machine pistol perfectly level with the man's stomach and touched the trigger lightly. A red dot appeared over the man's navel.

"I am ordering you to halt," Tringle shouted.

"I stopped taking orders when I left the Marines," Remo said.

"I'm *asking* you to halt then. Don't make me shoot."

The red dot wavered as the patient kept coming. There was no weapon in his hands, Tringle saw, but there was a confident expression in his dark eyes.

"One last time. Stop where you are."

"I told you, I don't know where I am. How can I stop where I am if I don't even know where that is?"

Tringle let the intruder get to within ten yards, then tapped the trigger.

The burst was short, only a dozen rounds or so, and a wall behind the patient erupted into a cloud of plaster and paint chips.

The man kept coming. The red laser dot still floated over his navel. Tringle blinked furiously. Was this a ghost? Had the bullets gone right through him?

He fired again, a longer burst this time.

And this time, Tringle saw the blurry motion of the patient as he slid away from the bullet track. Tringle

corrected right. The red dot found the patient's chest and
he fired again.

The patient floated left. The sound of the weapon, in
this narrow hallway, was not loud, since the weapons had
been silenced.

Tringle swore to himself. The silencer must be throwing
off his aim. But almost as soon as that thought flashed
through his mind, he rejected it. The laser was supposed to
make up for the silencer's bias.

Tringle clamped down on the trigger and a long volley
of bullets spewed forth. The man in the hospital robe
seemed to ignore them and just kept coming.

"Why are you shooting at that patient?" Agent Kelly
Harper asked, as he trotted up, holding his gun at his side.

"Because he's unauthorized," Tringle said hotly.

"He's also unhurt. Are you firing blanks?"

"Look at the walls behind him and see if you believe
that," Tringle said hotly. The walls behind and on either
side of the patient in the ragged robe were riddled and in
places hunks of plaster hung loose like peeling skin.

"Isn't your laser working?" Harper asked.

"You try yours," Tringle said.

"This is the FBI. I'm asking you to stop where you
are," Harper called out.

"Make me," Remo called back.

"Okay. That's excuse enough," said Harper as he lined
up on the approaching figure's unprotected chest. By that
time, Remo was almost on top of the pair. Harper pulled
the trigger, intending to fire a brief burst, but for some
reason, his machine-gun muzzle pointed at the ceiling all
by itself. He tried to take his finger off the trigger but it
seemed to be attached and would not move.

Then Harper noticed that the patient was standing next
to him, a finger massaging Harper's elbow lightly, a cruel
smile on his lips, and somehow he knew that the touch of
the man's hand on his elbow was responsible for his arm
pointing upward, trigger finger frozen.

Remo lowered the agent to the floor while Tringle backed up to get into better firing range.

"You just killed an FBI agent," Tringle said coldly.

"He's not dead. He's just out of it. Like you will be in a second."

"Like hell," Tringle snapped, and fired. He didn't bother to check where the laser dot was pointed. At this range it would not matter.

But it did matter. Bullet holes peppered the walls, but the patient was not even touched. He was laughing aloud.

"You can't laugh at the FBI that way," Tringle cried, tears of frustration welling in his eyes.

"No? What way can I laugh at the FBI?"

Tringle did not answer. He was busy trying to yank the empty clip from his gun so he could ram home a fresh one. In training, he had consistently performed that operation in less than 2.5 seconds and had received a commendation for that speed.

He found, though, that it meant very little in actual practice because before he got the old clip out, the gun began falling apart and he was left holding a finely machined piece of junk. The laser targeting system still worked however. Tringle knew this because he could see the red dot dancing on the unconcerned face of the patient, who was holding portions of Tringle's gun in his right hand and who was raising his left hand slowly to the FBI agent's weeping face.

Then there was nothing more to see because Tringle was on the floor, unconscious.

Remo put the two agents in a closet and covered them with blankets because it was cold in the closet. In a few hours, they would be clear-headed enough to receive official reprimands for dereliction of duty and only Remo would know that they were not at fault. There had been only three of them and three was not enough.

Remo entered the unlocked door of Room 12-D.

Hubert Millis lay wide-eyed on the bed, tubes plugged

into his mouth, his nose, and his arms. His breathing was barely noticeable amid the beeping and blipping of electronic monitoring devices.

Remo passed a hand over the man's eyes. There was no reaction, not even a dilation of the pupils to interception of the light. Remo could sense that the man was very close to death. A quick thrust to the temple might be more mercy than murder.

He reached his right hand toward the man's head, then withdrew it. He had killed many times but this was different. This man was not a criminal, not someone who deserved death, but just a businessman who happened to wind up on somebody's hit list.

But Remo's own father had asked him to kill the man. His own father.

Slowly he raised his right hand again.

The EKG machine suddenly stopped beeping. Another machine kicked into life; the sound it made was a long, drawn-out, tinny "screeeeee."

Alarm horns rang out in the corridor. Somewhere, someone was yelling. "Code blue. Room 12-D."

A team of doctors burst into the room. They ignored the bullet-shattered corridor walls and pushed past Remo as if he were not there.

A nurse stripped the nightshirt from the scrawny chest of Hubert Millis. A doctor touched a stethoscope to the man's chest and shook his head.

Someone passed him a pair of disks, attached by cable to a wheeled machine.

"Clear," the doctor yelled.

Everyone stepped back. When the disks touched Millis' chest, his body jumped off the bed from the shock. Then it lay still.

Three times the doctor reapplied the shock procedure, one eye cocked at the EKG machine, whose steady line of light indicated no heart action.

Finally, the doctor dropped the disks and stepped back.

"That's it. He's gone. Nurse, prep him for removal."

And still without noticing Remo, the doctors left the room.

The nurse still stood by the bedside and Remo took her arm.

"What happened?" he asked urgently.

"He flatlined."

"That means he's dead, right?"

"That's right. Heart failure. You were in the room with him. Who are you?"

"Never mind that. What killed him? I have to know."

"His heart just gave out. We half-expected it."

"It wasn't the excitement, was it?" Remo asked. "Excitement didn't kill him?"

"Excitement? He was in a coma. He wouldn't have got excited in a car bombing."

"Thanks," Remo said.

"Don't mention it. What were you doing here anyway?"

"Wrestling with my conscience," Remo called back.

"Who won?"

"It was a draw."

24

When Remo returned from the hospital, he found the older man slouched in a chair, watching an episode of *The Honeymooners*.

"How'd it go?" the gunman asked, without taking his eyes from the screen.

"Millis is dead," Remo said.

"Good. You do good work, kid. Sit down and watch some TV."

"I think I'll go to sleep," Remo said.

"Sure, son. Whatever you want, you do it."

"We going to be leaving town soon?" Remo asked.

"Hold your horses. I got some things to do yet," the gunman said.

"Like what?" Remo said.

"Business. I got business. You gonna pester me? I want to watch this. Ed Norton just knocks me out."

"I thought Millis was your business."

"He was," the gunman said.

"Well, Millis is dead."

"What do you want? A freaking medal? You owed me that hit 'cause you screwed it up on me before. Now we're even and get off my case. I got other things to do."

Remo had gone into the bedroom and lain down, but he

had been unable to sleep. His entire adult life had been spent yearning for a family, but maybe having a family was not all it was supposed to be.

He meant nothing to his father, out in the other room, laughing uproariously at the rerun he had probably seen a dozen times. And that was family.

Chiun, on the other hand, for all his carping and complaining, cared about Remo. And Chiun wasn't family, not real blood family anyway.

Was "family" just a label, meaningless unless there was sharing and trust and love involved? Remo didn't know. He lay on the bed groping for something to say to his father. But all the important questions—who Remo was, where he was born, all the rest—had been answered and now there were no more questions to ask and Remo felt empty.

He heard the telephone ring in the other room and focused his hearing on the gunman's voice when he heard him say hello. Most people could not hear properly because untrained ears were not able to filter out all the background noise and concentrate on what a person wanted to hear Most people lived in a world of static, but Remo could direct his hearing in a narrow range so he was able, without real effort, to hear both sides of a telephone conversation.

He heard his father say, "When are you going to pay for the Millis hit?"

"As soon as you get Lavallette," a voice answered.

"Wait a minute. This is supposed to be pay as you go, remember?"

"Millis isn't even cold yet and this is an emergency. I can't explain it now. I want Lavallette hit and I want him hit right away."

"That's not our agreement," the gunman said.

"I'll pay double for Lavallette," the voice responded.

"Double? You really do want Lavallette hit, don't you?"

"Was there any doubt?"

"I guess not. Okay, I'll do it."

"He'll be at his office at eight o'clock this morning. One last thing. No head shots. You get him in the face or head and you don't get paid."

"I remember."

"But this time it's especially important. I have my reasons."

The gunman hung up the telephone and in the empty room, Remo heard him say, "I guess you do. Damned if I can figure out what they are, though."

At his apartment, Lyle Lavallette hung up the telephone and laughed nervously.

The game was almost over. This was the last risk and when he got through this one, he was the big winner.

Who would have thought it over the last twenty years? Who would have thought it when all three of those ungrateful bastards had fired him from their auto companies?

Well, now, it was payback time and the Dynacar was the way to do it. Within a month, Lavallette expected that he would be the head of all three of America's major car manufacturers. He would control the industry as no man before him, not even Henry Ford, had ever done.

And who knew what was next?

Maybe Washington.

Maybe the White House itself.

Why not? Everything else had worked perfectly so far.

It was a master stroke to have hired a killer and then to have named himself, Lyle Lavallette, as the first target. That way, when the other car moguls were removed, no one would think of pointing a finger at Lavallette.

And it had worked. He had panicked the other car companies and they were all coming around.

The only loose end left was the killer. He didn't want that man around, maybe to be arrested, maybe to talk. Even though he didn't know who had hired him, it was possible that some smart investigator might be able to get him singing and put two and two together.

The assassin had to go, so Lavallette had called him and told him when the target would be vulnerable.

The killer would come in the morning.

And be met by Colonel Brock Savage and his mercenaries. End of the gunman. End of the problem.

It was perfect.

Lavallette put a hairnet over his sprayed hair and got carefully into bed. He wanted a few hours' sleep. He wanted to look good when he went before the TV cameras tomorrow and told the world that the crazed Detroit assassin had been killed.

25

"So that's the Dynacar. When do you go into production?"

Lyle Lavallette looked at the new public-relations counsel he had hired and said, "Don't worry about that now. More important things take precedence."

They were standing inside the large garage of the Dynacar Industries building. The public-relations man was confused because he had gotten the impression from watching the news broadcasts that Lavallette was ready to begin construction of the revolutionary car immediately. But the inside of the Dynacar plant was as barren as a baseball stadium in December. There were no workers, there was no assembly line, there were no parts or equipment. It was just a big empty warehouse.

"I'm not sure I follow you, Mr. Lavallette," the public-relations man said. He had been a newspaperman for fifteen years before getting into public relations "to make some real money," but his newspaper background gave him the uneasy feeling that he was involved in some kind of scam.

Even looking at the sleek black Dynacar which stood in solitude in the middle of the plant's floor did not dispel that feeling.

"Listen and I'll make it simple for you," Lavallette

said. "I've been planning to go into production, but now with that crazy killer running around loose, things have changed."

"How?" the public-relations man said.

"First of all, when Mangan got shot, the directors of his company started reaching out for me to take over their company and consolidate it with the Dynacar production. Right?"

"Right."

"And that story you planted yesterday about American Autos reaching out for me to do the same thing is going to work. They'll be on the telephone before the morning's over."

"How does that explain why you're not building Dynacars?" the P.R. man said.

"Wait. I'm not done. Now we all know that Revell from General Autos has gone on vacation because he's scared for his life. What we want to do is to plant some stories; get General Autos to ask for me too."

"To run their company?" the P.R. man asked.

"Exactly."

"You mean, you want to run all three big auto companies as well as Dynacar?"

"Now you've got it," Lavallette said.

"Nobody's ever done that before."

"There's never·been a Lyle Lavallette before. And that explains why we're not doing production here. If I'm going to merge my company with the Big Three, I'll use their production facilities to build Dynacars. That way, in a year, I'll be able to do what it'd take me a century to do here by myself. I'll have a Dynacar in every garage. You understand now?"

"Perfectly," the P.R. man said. What he understood was that Lyle Lavallette, the Maverick Genius of the Auto Industry, was as loose as ashes. Who would believe that the Big Three of the auto business, who lived to compete among each other, would all turn to the same man to head their companies? It sounded like something that might be considered in Russia, but not in the United States.

"Good," Lavallette said. "So keep planting stories about mergers. How with the new Dynacar, only I can save the Big Three. Maybe you can call me the Maverick Savior. That might be good."

"Okay," the P.R. man said. Why not? The money was good.

"And one important thing." Lavallette said.

"Yes, sir."

"Try always to photograph my left side. That's my best side."

"You got it, Mr. Lavallette. Does this car really run on garbage?"

Lavallette shook his head. "Refuse. Not garbage. We always say 'refuse' around here. If we get this thing tagged as the garbagemobile, we could run into a lot of public resistance. Refuse." He smoothed a hand over his hair. Good. Everything was in place. "And to answer your question, it runs like a charm and it's the greatest discovery in automobiles, maybe since the wheel. Try to get that printed somewhere. The greatest thing since the wheel."

"You got it, Mr. Lavallette," the P.R. man said.

In the White House, the President of the United States was sipping coffee in his bedroom when an aide came in holding a scroll of paper that contained a brief report on the overnight news events.

The top item reported that Hubert Millis, president of American Automobiles, had succumbed at 1:32 A.M. in Detroit.

The President excused his aide, opened the drawer of the nightstand, and picked up the receiver of a dialless phone that was hidden beneath two hot-water bottles and a copy of *Playboy*.

He waited for the voice of Harold Smith to come on the line. The President had decided, and it was time—time to order the dismantling of America's ultimate shield against chaos.

He was going to tell Smith that CURE must disband. The agency had failed and it was time to go back to more traditional law-enforcement agencies, like the FBI. He had always liked the FBI, especially since he had once played an FBI man in a movie.

But no one answered the phone.

The President remained on the line. From past experience, he knew that Smith was seldom away from his headquarters and when he was, he carried a portable radiophone in his briefcase, hooked up to the private line in his office.

He waited five minutes but there was still no answer. The President hung up. He decided he could give the order after lunch as easily as before lunch. A few hours' difference wouldn't matter.

It wouldn't matter at all.

26

Chiun, Master of Sinanju, allowed the doorman of the Detroit Plaza Hotel to summon his conveyance.

When the taxi pulled up, the doorman, wearing a uniform that reminded Chiun of those worn by the courtiers to the throne of France's Sun King, opened the door for him, then closed it gently after Chiun was seated in the rear.

Then the doorman leaned into the cab window with an expectant smile.

"You have done well," Chiun said. "Now remove yourself from my field of vision."

"You must be new to our country, sir," the doorman replied, still smiling. "In America, good service is usually rewarded with a tip."

"Very well," said Chiun. "Here is a tip. Do not have children. Their ingratitude will only cause you sorrow in your declining years."

"That wasn't the kind of tip I had in mind," the doorman said.

"Then here is another," Chiun said. "People who delay other people who must be off on important business often have their windpipes ripped from their throats. Onward, driver."

The cabby pulled into traffic and said, "Where are you going, buddy?"

"To the place of the carriagemaker. Lavallette."

"Oh. The Dynacar guy. Sure. Hang on."

"In what direction is his place?" Chiun demanded.

"Direction? Oh, I'd say west."

"Then why are you driving north?"

"Because I have to drive north to catch the interstate that goes west," the cabby replied good-naturedly.

"I am familiar with the tricks of your trade," Chiun said. "Do not drive north. Drive west."

"I can't do that."

"You can. Simply point your wheels west and proceed."

"In a straight line?"

"I am paying only for the miles driven to our destination. The west miles," Chiun said. I will not pay for unnecessary deviations from our route."

"I can't drive in a straight line. There are little things in the way like skyscrapers and trees."

"You have my permission to drive around such obstacles. But west, always west. I will keep track of the west miles for you," said Chiun, resting his eyes on the clicking digital meter.

The driver shrugged and said, "You're the boss, buddy."

"No," said Chiun. "I am the Master."

"Just as long as I'm still the driver."

As they drove, Chiun kept his eyes on the meter but his mind was on Remo.

He had not lied when he had told Smith that Remo was lost to Sinanju. The appearance of the older Remo Williams—Remo's natural father—had torn Chiun's pupil in another direction, away from Sinanju. Chiun had hoped to prevent this difficulty by killing the gunman before Remo had ever known of his existence. But it did not work that way.

However, Chiun *had* lied when he told Smith that Remo was dead. In a sense, it was true. Without Chiun to guide

him, without someone to keep him on the path of proper
breathing and correctness, Remo's powers would atrophy
and perhaps fade entirely. It had happened to Remo before
without Chiun and it would probably happen again. Remo
would cease to be Sinanju.

But what Chiun had feared more was that if Smith knew
that Remo was still alive, no longer under Chiun's control,
Smith would order Remo's death and Chiun would be
bound by contracts to obey that order.

It was not time for that. There was still a chance to
bring Remo back into the care of Sinanju.

Which was why Chiun journeyed through the cool dawn
to the place of the carriagemaker. Not for the carriagemaker
and not for Smith and not for a moment to benefit this
stupid land of white people who were all ingrates.

Chiun traveled in the hope that if there were another
attempt on the life of Lyle Lavallette, his would-be assassin would not come alone. He would bring Remo.

Then, Chiun knew, this matter would be resolved.
Forever.

The taxi arrived at the Dynacar Industries plant forty
minutes later.

"That'll be $49.25," said the driver. The fare was three
times what it would have been if he had been permitted to
drive on the interstate.

"That is a reasonable fare," said Chiun. He reached
into the folds of his kimono and brought forth one of the
new United States gold pieces in the fifty-dollar denomina-
tion.

The driver looked at it and said, "What's this?"

"What it appears to be. Coin of the realm. Fifty dollars
gold. American."

"Where's my tip and don't give me any of that 'don't-
have-children' routine. I already got nine of them. That's
why I need a tip."

"Yesterday's gold fixing on the London market was

$446.25," Chiun said. "Surely, $397 is enough of a tip for following directions."

"How do I know this is real?" said the driver.

"Because when you die in five seconds because of your insolent tongue, I am going to take another just like it and place them over your eyelids to smooth your journey into the other world. I would not use counterfeit coins to do this."

"You mean, it's real?"

"Isn't that what I've been saying?"

"And it's really worth $440?"

Chiun corrected him. "$446.25."

"Want me to wait to bring you back to the hotel?" the driver asked.

"No," said Chiun.

The guard at the gate to the large empty Dynacar parking lot wanted to know what Chiun's business was.

"It is my business and not yours. Let me pass."

"You're not an employee, not dressed like that. I can't let you in without a visitor's pass. You got a visitor's pass, old-timer?"

"Yes," said Chiun, raising his open palm for the guard to see. "Here it is."

The guard looked, expecting to find an ID card in the old man's hand, but he saw nothing. He saw nothing twice. First he saw nothing because the Oriental's hand was empty. Then he saw nothing again when Chiun took his nose between thumb and forefinger and squeezed until the man's sight clouded and he fell back on the seat inside his small guardhouse.

As he slipped from consciousness, the guard had a half-second realization of what was happening. He had heard of nerves in the human body that were so sensitive, they triggered unconsciousness when pressed in a certain way. But he had never heard of any such nerve in the tip of the nose.

When he woke up three hours later, he was still thinking that thought.

Lyle Lavallette was sitting behind the wheel of the Dynacar in the big empty plant, making "vroom, vroom" noises with his mouth. The first inkling he had that he was not alone was the slight tipping of the vehicle on the passenger side.

He looked over to see an elderly man with Asian features, dressed in a flower-emblazoned red brocade robe, sitting beside him.

"I am Chiun," the Oriental said. "I am here to guard your worthless life."

Lavallette recognized the man. It was the same Oriental who had used his own body to shield James Revell from the gunman's bullets at the Dynacar demonstration the previous day.

"What are you doing here?" Lavallette said.

"I have just told you. Have you wax in your ears? I am here to guard your worthless life."

"I'm worth over ten million dollars. I don't call that worthless."

"Ten million dollars. Ten million rocks. It is the same thing. Worthless."

"Savage!" Lavallette yelled through the open car window.

Colonel Brock Savage, sitting with his men in a small room off the main garage floor, heard the shout. He slipped the safety off his Armalite rifle and gave his men the hand signal to follow him as he trotted up to the driver's side of the Dynacar.

Lavallette, a panicked expression on his face, mouthed the word "him" and pointed toward Chiun.

"Surround the car," Savage ordered his men. "You! Out," he barked at Chiun, pointing his Armalite through the window so that, if he had to fire, he would riddle the unarmed Oriental.

Lavallette realized Savage would riddle him too because

he was directly in the line of fire and shouted, "Get over the other side, you maniac. Don't shoot me."

Savage ran around the car and Chiun pointed a finger at him. "Do not point that weapon at me," he said.

"Get out, gook."

"And do not give me orders. I do not take orders from whites who dress like trees," Chiun said.

"I'm a private merc, idiot. The highest-paid merc in the world. And I'm trained to kill."

"No," said Chiun. "You have been trained to die."

To Lavallette's eyes, it looked as if the old man had simply walked through the closed car door, but in fact Chiun had opened the door so quickly that Lavallette's slow eyes still held the afterimage of the closed door simultaneously with registering the Oriental's leap from the car.

Brock Savage squeezed the Armalite's trigger. Chiun squeezed Savage's trigger finger and the weapon dropped from the big man's hands. Chiun picked it up and snapped the barrel in half.

Savage reached for his combat knife, a ninja butterfly knife that opened like a folding rule. He flashed his hands around and the blade snapped from concealment. Then it too was on the floor next to the gun barrel.

Savage looked at the broken blade and dove for Chiun's throat, hands extended in front of him.

"Ki-ai," he shouted, but he quieted as he hit the floor with Chiun pressing a finger against an artery in his temple. Then he was unconscious.

Chiun turned to the other mercenaries.

"He is not seriously hurt," he said. "I do not wish to hurt any of you. Please take him and leave."

Two mercenaries ran forward, grabbed Brock Savage's unconscious form, and pulled him away.

Chiun led Lavallette through a door that led to the office wing of the Dynacar plant and told the automaker to take him to his office.

Inside the office, Chiun said, "You are fortunate to have me here. You were not safe surrounded by those private jerks."

"Mercs," corrected Lavallette.

"Only one of us is correct," Chiun sniffed. "And I do not think it is you."

27

The gunman had fallen asleep on the sofa, watching television, and when he awoke, he glanced at his watch, picked up his briefcase, and walked quietly from the hotel room.

Let Remo sleep. The kid, with his eternal questions, would just be a drag if he came along. He was already a large-size headache with his rice-eating, no drinking, "I can't-explain-to-you-how-I-do-what-I-do" routine.

When this hit was over, the gunman was leaving, and to hell with Remo Williams. Who needed that grief? Let him go back to his Chinaman friend.

The guard outside the parking lot at the Dynacar plant appeared to be asleep in his booth. The gunman had planned to park nearby and sneak into the property, but he had learned early on never to look a gift horse in the mouth. A sleeping guard was a gift from heaven, so he drove into the lot and parked his car near the main building.

He took his Beretta Olympic from his briefcase and slipped it into his spring-clip shoulder holster. He left the rifle add-ons in the briefcase. They would not be necessary. This, he thought, was a television hit: "up close and personal."

He walked through a large warehouse-type building where the Dynacar was sitting alone in the middle of the otherwise empty floor. His body was tensed, all his senses focused on what was in front of him. Were there guards? Could this be a trap?

But he saw nothing and he never realized that behind him, Remo had slipped out of the backseat of the car where he had been hidden and was now following him into the plant.

The gunman, if asked, would have admitted to some confusion. Until this minute, he had been certain that he had been hired by one of the company presidents who had been on his target list. But he had killed Mangan and he would have killed Revell if it hadn't been for that crazy old Oriental. That left Millis and Lavallette as his possible employer. Now, with Millis dead, there was only Lavallette. It would have been simple except his employer had called and told him to kill Lavallette today.

So who was he working for?

He decided that when he collected his last payment, he was going to pull open the door of that Dynacar and find out who was sitting behind the wheel.

But that was later. For now, he had to be wary of a trap.

He saw no one in the warehouse, and in the tall office structure attached to the rear of the work area, there was no one in the lobby.

The gunman paused to light a cigarette and for some reason, Maria's face floated into his mind. He had not thought of her since that Remo had started to pester him.

He took a puff off the cigarette, stubbed it out in an ashtray on an empty desk, and got into the elevator to ride upstairs. Maybe it was a trap, but if it was, he was prepared.

Chiun was prepared too. He sat on a small rug outside Lavallette's office. He had told the automaker to stay inside and Lavallette had disobeyed only once, when he came out to say that he had received an anonymous tip that the killer was on his way to murder Lavallette.

"Is he coming alone?" Chiun asked.

"I wouldn't know. My informant didn't say," Lavallette replied.

"Go back into your office."

"He'll get me," Lavallette said. "Colonel Savage and his people are gone. I'm dead meat."

"To get to you, he will have to pass me," Chiun said. "Get back inside."

He had pushed Lavallette inside, closed the door, and then taken up his station on the rug outside the man's office, watching the elevator door, waiting.

The moment of reckoning was coming.

Remo did not know why he had stowed away in the back of his father's car, to follow the gunman. When he saw the man with the scar start to ride up on the elevator, he slipped into a stairwell and started to walk upstairs, driven by some urge he did not understand.

When the elevator doors slid open, the gunman had dropped into a marksman's crouch, his Beretta pointed ahead in a double-handed grip. He felt prepared for anything, but he was not prepared to see the old Oriental sitting calmly on a carpet in the middle of the floor.

"You again," he said.

Chiun's face was stern. "Where is my son?"

The gunman laughed. "Don't you mean my son? He's sure of it, you know."

"And what are you sure of?" Chiun asked.

"I'm sure that he's a chump."

Chiun rose from his position without any apparent shifting of limbs under his kimono. He seemed to grow like a sunflower from the floor.

"Whatever Remo is, he is Sinanju. You have insulted Sinanju too many times already. Prepare to die."

The gunman fired two shots coming out of the elevator. One of them buried itself in the door directly behind

Chiun, but Chiun was no longer there. He was three feet to
the left somehow. And was it the gunman's imagination,
or was he standing closer now?

The gunman fired again.

And again, Chiun was suddenly in another place. He
had not seemed to move. It was like magic; the old
Oriental popped up in another place, grim and purposeful.

Now only twelve feet separated them and the gunman
fired four shots in a fanning arc. He had gotten the old
Oriental before with a ricochet; why was it so difficult this
time?

In the brief microsecond in which the gunman reacted to
the noise and flash of the pistol shots, he blinked, and in
that same blink of a second, the Master of Sinanju moved
again. The gunman's eyes opened and he seemed to be
alone in the spacious reception area.

From behind the door marked "LYLE LAVALLETTE, PRESI-
DENT," a muffled voice called out.

"Hello? Is anyone dead out there? Is it all right to come
out now? Hello?"

It was too much for the gunman. There was no possible
place where the old Oriental could be hiding. Maybe he
had the powers of invisibility or something. He started to
back into the still-open elevator, and stopped.

His gun hand seemed to catch fire. He screamed. His
pistol clattered to the floor. Something was wrong with his
arm, something terrible.

He dropped to his knees, clutching his arm. From the
corner of one tearing eye, he saw the Master of Sinanju
step out of the elevator.

"How?" he groaned.

"You may spend eternity pondering it," Chiun said
coldly. His eyes were wrathful. "Now you will answer my
questions."

Chiun knelt beside the squirming man and gently touched
his inner left wrist.

"Arrrgh," the man screamed.

"That is just a touch," Chiun said. "I can make the pain much worse. Or I can make it disappear. Have you a preference?"

"Make it go away."

"Where is Remo?" Chiun said.

"I left him back at the hotel."

"Good. You answered truthfully."

"Make it stop. Make the pain go away. Please."

"Who hired you?" Chiun said implacably.

"I don't know. I never saw his face."

"That is not a good answer."

"It's the only answer. I thought it was Lavallette but now I don't know. It might be anyone. Help me. I'm dying here."

"That will come later. Why would the carriagemaker hire you to kill himself?"

"Ask him, ask him. Just give me a break."

Chiun touched the man's arm and the gunman's contorted joints loosened and relaxed. He lay on the floor, still as death.

Chiun was at Lavallette's office door when the door to the stairwell opened. He did not have to turn to know it was Remo stepping out. The first soft footfall told him that, for no other human stepped with such feline ease. Except for Chiun himself.

"Little Father," Remo said. And then he saw the gunman's still body.

"No!" he screamed.

"He is not dead, Remo," Chiun said softly.

"Oh."

"I was going to come for you when I was finished here," Chiun said stiffly.

"Smith's orders?"

"No. I already told the emperor that you were dead. A necessary untruth."

"You both knew about him all along, didn't you?" Remo said, gesturing to the man on the floor.

Chiun shook his aged head, making the wisps of hair over his ears flutter in the still air.

"No, Remo. No one knows the truth. Least of all, you."

"This man is my natural father. You kept that from me. You tried to kill him."

"I kept that from you to spare you grief," Chiun said.

"What kind of line is that? What grief?"

"The grief you would have felt had Smith ordered you to eliminate this wretch. This is my assignment which I took upon my frail shoulders to spare you the burden."

"Oh, Chiun, what do I do?" Remo said.

"Whatever it is, you may have to do it quickly," said Chiun, pointing a long-nailed finger at the gunman, who was rising to his feet now, his pistol in hand.

"Out of the way, kid," he rasped. "I'm going to kill that yellow bastard."

"No," Remo said.

"Get out of my way, kid. You hear me?"

Remo glanced at Chiun, who quietly folded his arms and closed his eyes.

"Don't just stand there, Chiun," Remo called.

"Without a pupil, Sinanju has no future. Without a future, I have no past. I will be remembered as my ancestors have told me I would be remembered: as the last Master of Sinanju, who gave Sinanju to an ungrateful white. So be it."

"No, Chiun," Remo said. He turned to the gunman. "Put it down. Please. We can settle this some other way."

"There is no other way," Chiun said.

"For once the gook is right," the gunman said. "Get out of the way. Who the hell's side are you on anyway?"

"Yes, Remo," said Chiun. "Whose side are you on?"

The gunman lined up the shot. Chiun stood immobile, eyes closed. The gunman slowly depressed his finger on the trigger.

Remo yelled something inarticulate, then surrendering

to reflexes built into him by Chiun over the years, he moved toward the gunman.

The man with the scar whirled and fired at Remo.

The bullet missed.

"You asked for this, kid," the gunman said. His finger lowered again.

"Me, too?" Remo cried but it was too late. The killing stroke of his hand was already in motion.

It struck the man called Remo Williams squarely on the breastbone, shattering that bone and turning the connective cartilage to mucus. That was just the beginning. The force of the stroke vibrated through the gunman's body, initiating a chain reaction of breaking bones and jellifying muscles and organs.

The gunman with the scar stood poised for an infinite second, his contorted face seeming to soften as the hardness of his skull dissolved, and then he slipped to the floor like a pile of potatoes tumbling out of a ripped sack.

His last sight was of Remo's empty hand coming at him and his final thought was not his own. He could hear Maria's last words and finally he understood:

"A man will come to you. Dead, yet beyond death, he will carry death in his empty hands. He will know your name and you will know his. And that will be your death warrant."

He did not feel himself slip from his body. Instead, he felt his mind contract, tighter and tighter, until it was as small as a pea, then as small as the head of a pin, then smaller still until his entire consciousness was reduced to a point as infinitesimally tiny as an atom. When it seemed that it could compress no tighter, it kept shrinking and shrinking.

But the gunman did not care because he no longer cared about anything. His very essence became part of a darkness greater and blacker than he could ever comprehend, and not knowing where he was and what was happening to him was much, much better than knowing.

*   *   *

"I killed him," Remo said in a strangled voice. "I killed my own father. Because of you."

"I am sorry, Remo. Truly sorry for your pain," Chiun said.

But Remo did not seem to hear him. He just kept mumbling the same words over and over again in a lost little boy's voice:

"I killed him."

28

Remo sat down heavily and touched the limp body of the man he called his father. It felt as formless as a jellyfish. All that was now left of the man was a casing that surrounded broken bone and tissues.

Lavallette's door opened slowly and he peered outside. He saw the dead man and then Chiun.

"What happened to him?" he asked.

"Sinanju happened to him," Chiun said.

"Did he say who hired him?" Lavallette asked.

"No. He did not have to," Chiun said.

"Why not?"

"Because I know that you hired him," Chiun said.

"To kill myself? Are you crazy?"

"Only one stands to gain by the killings of the carriage-makers. That one is you," said Chiun.

"What motive would I have?" Lavallette said. He looked away as his secretary, Miss Blaze, walked into the reception area. She saw him, then quickly looked down at a piece of paper in her hand.

"Your public-relations man called, Mr. Lavallette," she said. "He said he's planted a story that all three auto companies are going to ask you to head them." She smiled and looked up, then saw Chiun standing by Lavallette, and Remo sitting next to the dead body.

"Oh, I'm sorry," she said. "I didn't know you had company."

"Idiot," Lavallette snarled. He ran to the open elevator, pressed the button, and the doors closed behind him.

"Well, what got into him?" Miss Blaze said. "Can I help?"

"You may leave, bovine one," Chiun said. He walked to where Remo still sat next to the body.

"Remo," he said softly. "The man who is truly responsible for this death has just left."

"What?" Remo said, looking up at Chiun's hazel eyes.

"All the pain you feel, all the hurt, is the fault of the carriagemaker Lavallette. It was he who caused all this trouble."

Remo looked again at the dead body, then got to his feet.

"I don't know," Remo said. "I don't think I really care."

"Remo, you are still young. Know this. There are so many times in a man's life when he must do things that later he may think are wrong. All a man can do is act with a spirit of rightness and then he need fear no one, not even himself."

"Rightness? I killed my father."

"As he would have killed you," Chiun said "That is not a father's love, Remo. A father would not do that."

And Remo thought back to the battle the previous evening atop the building near American Autos, thought back to how Chiun had done nothing but parry Remo's blows, had done nothing to hurt Remo, and in a brilliant flash, he understood the nature of fatherhood and family. He was *not* an orphan; he had not been since the first day he had met Chiun, because the old Korean was his true father, a fatherhood based on love.

And Sinanju, the long line of Masters stretching back

through the ages, was Remo's family. Thousands strong, all reaching their hands across the centuries to him.

His family.

"You say Lavallette's skipped?" Remo said.

Chiun nodded and Remo said, "Let's go get the bastard, Little Father."

"As you will, my son."

Lavallette sped from the auto plant in the prototype Dynacar.

Let the cops sort it out, he said to himself. *I'll deny everything. Who's to know different?*

As he turned onto the roadway, he looked into the rearview mirror to see if any cars were following him.

All he saw were two joggers. Good. He pressed down on the accelerator and the Dynacar sped ahead. But the two joggers in the mirror did not fall behind in the distance. They were getting closer.

How could that be?

Then Lavallette saw who they were. It was the Oriental and the young man with the dead eyes. They were running after him and they were gaining.

Lavallette checked his speedometer. He was going seventy miles an hour. He pressed the pedal down to the floor, but it did no good. The two men were getting bigger in the rearview mirror, and then they were abreast of the speeding Dynacar.

Lavallette glanced through his open driver's window at Remo, who was now alongside him, "You can't stop me," he snarled. "I don't care how fast you can run."

"Yes, we can," Remo said.

To prove he was wrong, Lavallette pulled the wheel hard left, turning the car into Remo, but the young man, without breaking his stride, dodged away. Lavallette laughed but then Remo's hand floated out and the fender on the driver's side of the car flew away from the tire. The passenger-side door came next. It opened with a screaming wrench and bounced down the street. Lavallette glanced over to see the old man jogging lightly alongside.

"Still think we can't stop you?" Remo said.

Lavallette hunched over the wheel. He was going eighty-five now. It wasn't possible for them to be running alongside him, but even if they were, they would soon tire.

The roof came off next after the pair of runners broke the support posts. Then the trunk lid was ripped off and then the rest of the fenders flew.

The two men grabbed one of the support posts of the car, and Lavallette could feel it slowing down, and in only a few hundred yards it came to a stop, stripped to its chassis.

Lavallette stepped out, still holding the steering wheel, which was no longer attached to anything.

"Don't kill me," he pleaded.

"Give me a reason not to," Remo said coldly.

"Why did you hire the killer?" Chiun asked.

"I wanted to get rid of the competition. With them dead and me with the Dynacar, I would have run all of Detroit."

Remo walked toward the back of the car. "If this damned thing was any good, you wouldn't have had to do that."

He looked inside the open trunk. "There's batteries back here. What are they for?"

Lavallette was pleading now for his life. He said, "The car's a scam. It doesn't run on refuse. It runs on electrical batteries, nonrechargeable."

"What does that mean?" Remo said.

"It means the car runs for a month or two and then goes dead and you have to buy a new car."

"I had a Studebaker like that once," Remo said.

"It does not turn garbage into energy?" Chiun said.

"No," Lavallette said. "That was just for show."

"The Dynacar doesn't run on garbage," Remo said. "It *is* garbage."

"You might say that," Lavallette said.

"You know what else you might say?" Remo said.

"What's that?" asked Lavallette.

"You might say good-bye," Remo said. He took the man's elegantly coiffed head between his hands and shook. Contact lenses flew out of his eyes. False teeth popped from his mouth. His corset snapped and ripped through his shirt in an explosion of elastic.

For only a moment it hurt and then Lyle Lavallette felt nothing else. Remo dropped the unmoving body beside the stripped prototype of the Dynacar and walked away.

"It is done. You have avenged yourself and Sinanju," Chiun called after him.

Remo said nothing. The set of his shoulders told the Master of Sinanju that his pupil was hurting very much inside.

Chiun walked in the other direction. Remo needed to be alone now and his teacher respected that need.

Before either man had gotten a hundred feet from the car, a gang of teenagers came out of the weeds along the roadside and began stripping the car's seatcovers and mirrors and chrome.

An hour later, there would be nothing left but Lavallette's body.

One thing had led to another and the President had not been able to call Smith and now, while waiting to greet this week's ambassador from Zimbabwe, the President was handed a note by an aide.

He looked at it, bolted from the room, and ran to his bedroom, where he picked up the special phone.

"Yes, Mr. President," the dry unflappable voice of Harold Smith answered.

"Now Lavallette is dead," the President said.

"I know, sir. My people did it."

"Your people are out of control. I'm ordering you to—"

"No, sir," Smith interrupted. "I just spoke to my

people, the older one. He informed me that Lavallette himself was behind all the shootings. The actual killer is dead too. And the Dynacar is a fake.''

"The garbage-powered car is a fake?'' the President said.

"It's a complicated story, Mr. President, but that's the bottom line. It was a fake through and through. I'll be getting you a full report. Just a few loose ends left.''

"Smith, I have just one question for you.''

"Yes, sir?''

"Are you in full control of your people?''

"Yes, Mr. President. CURE is fully operational.''

"That's all I need to know. You came very close this time, Smith. I want you to know that.''

"I know it, Mr. President. Will there be anything else?''

"Not from me. I think I need a nap. Let Zimbabwe wait.''

"Very good, sir,'' Smith said as the President hung up.

Smith returned to his computer terminal. There were only a few loose ends, but for CURE to be back to normal, they had to be resolved. It was almost dark before the answers came.

29

Smith and Chiun waited in darkness for Remo to arrive.

A brisk wind scattered the red and gold leaves in the graveyard like tiny dead things come to elfin life. Somewhere, an owl made a lonely sound. Remo came up the cemetery walk with a padding silence that made him seem more at home in these surroundings than anywhere else, Smith thought grimly.

"You're late," said Smith.

"So what?" Remo said.

"He is still hurting," whispered Chiun to Smith. "Do not heed his rudeness, Emperor. All will be set right when you give Remo the good news."

"What good news?" asked Remo.

Smith extracted a folder from his briefcase.

"I asked you to meet me here because this is where the whole thing began, Remo. At your grave."

For the first time, Remo noticed the gravestone with his name on it.

"So this is what it looks like. It's not much, Smitty. You could have sprung for an angel on the top."

"It served its purpose," Smith said. "A woman was murdered on this spot a few days ago when she was laying flowers on a grave. The flowers fell on *your* grave, Remo."

''My grave? Who was she?''

''My research has finally pieced the puzzle together. I was thrown off by the fact that the flowers fell on your grave and that the man who killed the woman, according to ballistics reports, was the same man who was doing the killing in Detroit.''

''Who was she?'' Remo asked again.

Smith pulled out a sheet of paper and a photograph.

''Her name was Maria DeFuria. She was the former wife of a Mafia hit man named Gesualdo DeFuria, a professional well-known for his use of a Beretta Olympic target pistol.''

''What does this have to do with me?''

''The emperor is explaining,'' Chiun said.

''Gesualdo DeFuria was the man you thought was your father, Remo. He was not your father.''

''Prove it.''

''Here is a copy of a note found at Maria DeFuria's house. You may read it but let me summarize. The note explains that the woman had discovered that her ex-husband had trained their son, Angelo, to follow in the father's profession. But during a team hit, the son was caught and convicted of a murder. In fact, the father was the real murderer and the son only an accomplice in training. Because of the Mafia's code of silence, the son kept quiet and was executed for the crime.''

He pointed behind Remo. ''They buried him here, in the family plot, next to your own grave.''

Remo read the name DeFuria on the stone next to his own.

''You mean the guy buried next to me was executed for a crime he didn't commit, just like I was?'' Remo asked.

''A strange coincidence but Wildwood isn't exactly Arlington National Cemetery,'' Smith said. ''This is near Newark after all. Let me finish the story. DeFuria attempted to reconcile with his wife and the truth slipped out about the son's innocence. Maria decided to go to the police with her information. We can only assume the rest. On her way, she stopped to put flowers on her son's grave. DeFuria followed her here. They argued and he shot her and the flowers fell onto your grave.''

"But he called himself Remo Williams,'' Remo protested.

"He had killed his ex-wife and had to leave town. Even the Mafia doesn't like that kind of killing. He knew he was going to need a new name so he picked the one off the headstone where his wife fell. *Your* name, Remo. If the flowers had fallen on the grave on the other side of yours, he probably would have called himself D. Colt.''

"He had all kinds of ID,'' Remo said.

"Nowadays, if you have a few dollars, you can buy any kind of identification,'' Smith said.

"But there was a family resemblance,'' Remo said. "Around the eyes.''

"A resemblance,'' Smith admitted, "but not a family one. You were both in essentially the same business. Too many deaths mark a person. I think you could call it a professional resemblance, not a family one.'' He paused. "Don't let your feelings cloud your judgment, Remo,'' he said.

"It is the lesson of the Master Shang,'' Chiun said.

"What are you talking about?''

"Don't tell me you have forgotten, Remo,'' said Chiun. "Master Shang, he of the moon rock. I told you that legend.''

"Yeah, I remember. What about it?''

"The lesson of the Master Shang lies in this stone which Shang believed he took from the mountains of the moon.'' Chiun produced the grayish stone from the folds of his kimono. "See?''

"I thought you believed that story,'' Remo said suspiciously.

"Do you take me for an idiot?'' Chiun said. "Any fool knows you cannot walk to the moon. Master Shang should have known that too. But he so desired the Chinese tart that he deluded himself into thinking he could walk to the moon to hold her love. That is the real lesson of the Master Shang. Do not desire something too much, for wishful thinking impairs the sight and not all things are as they appear. You, Remo, deluded yourself into believing that wretch was your father, because you wanted a father so badly. It did not matter to you if he was real."

"Are you trying to tell me that you knew all along that he wasn't my father?" Remo demanded.

"I am not *trying* to tell you anything. I have told you."

"Bulldookey," Remo said.

"It is nevertheless true," Chiun said. "When first I saw him, I saw that he moved like a baboon. He used weapons. He had no finesse. He bore no resemblance to you at all."

"I think you're paying me a compliment," Remo said.

"Then I withdraw my remarks," Chiun said.

"How did you dig all this up, Smitty?" Remo asked.

"My computers. They couldn't find a record of another Remo Williams having lived in the U.S. That made me suspicious of the name. It was too pat. And then the business of the woman being shot. Ballistics then said she was shot with the same gun being used in Detroit so I came here to run a check on these graves."

Smith referred to a notepad. "There was a D. Colt, but he died in 1940 and has no living relatives. That left the DeFuria family plot and once I learned that DeFuria was connected with organized crime, it all sort of came together."

Remo said nothing for a long time.

"They're going to bury him here? In this grave?"

"That's right," Smith said. "But that shouldn't concern you. He's not family."

"You know, Smitty, somewhere I've got family," Remo said.

"I researched your background thoroughly before bringing you into CURE," Smith said. "If you have parents, they would be impossible to trace."

"I want to know for sure," Remo said. "Smitty. Put your computers to work. You find out for me."

"And then what, Remo? You don't exist. You're standing on your own grave as far as the world is concerned. You can't have a family."

"I just want to know," Remo said. "I want to know if I belong to someone."

"You belong to Sinanju," Chiun said.

"I know, Little Father. And I know that I belong to you also. But this is different. It's just a loose end that I want to track down."

"Remo—" Smith started.

"Just find them, Smitty. Find them or I walk."

"I won't be blackmailed, Remo. I can always have Chiun train another person."

"I would not soil my hands with another," Chiun said. "Especially a white. Especially if I don't get Disneyland."

Smith locked his briefcase. A stony expression clouded his face.

"All right, Remo. I'll look into it. I'll be in touch."

As he walked away, Remo called, "Smitty?"

"Yes?"

"Thanks for clearing this one up for me."

"You're welcome, Remo."

After Smith left, Remo said, "Well, Chiun. Another day, another dollar."

"There will not be many more dollars if you do not return to training," Chiun said. "You are getting fat around the middle and your stroke when you dispatched that Mafia person was an abomination to see."

"We'll train tomorrow," Remo said. "I want to thank you too, Chiun."

"For what?"

"For caring."

"Who else would care for you? You are hopeless. And don't think I have forgotten your promise to get Nellie

Wilson to sing a concert for me. And don't think that I
have forgotten . . ."

Chiun recited a litany of complaints as he walked from
the grave, but when he looked back, Remo still stood
there, and Chiun was silent and walked away, leaving
Remo standing over his own grave with the dead dry
autumn leaves swirling around him, alone with his thoughts
and his longings.